I0763567

Only a Marquess Will Do

TO MARRY A ROGUE, BOOK 4

COPYRIGHT

Only a Marquess Will Do
To Marry a Rogue, Book 4

HARDBACK EDITION
Cover Art by Wicked Smart Designs
Editor: Grace Bradley Editing, LLC

ISBN: 978-0-6452047-3-5

ONLY A MARQUESS WILL DO

TO MARRY A ROGUE, BOOK 4

It's a game of instruction and seduction. But who's teaching who?

The London Season is not for Lady Victoria Worthingham. After a disastrous marriage that lasted no more than six weeks, she's sworn off men forever. But that doesn't mean she can't help her brother's best friend find his perfect match. It should be simple...unless she falls in love with him first, of course...

Marquess Albert Kester is everything ladies aren't looking for in a husband—socially awkward and bumbling as a debutante at her first ball. Writing adventures instead of living them seems to be his lot in life. Unless he can convince Victoria to stop seeing him as a project and start seeing him as a man, that is...

She's determined to see him happily settled. All he wants is her. Only one outcome is certain in this game.

Rules will be broken...and if they aren't careful, so will their hearts...

CHAPTER 1

London, 1809

Victoria stood in the modiste on Bond street, the heat on her cheeks as warm as the day outdoors. She glanced about the room, the women of the ton, those who had the power to make or ruin a lady's chances during her Season, stared at her with pity—some with amusement and glee.

Her mother's mouth had not stopped gaping when her sister, Alice, now the Viscountess Arndel, had read the latest on dit in *The Times* that morning. That Victoria's husband, the very man she had married six weeks before, had run off with a maid at the estate.

Victoria stared down at the blue silk gown the modiste had halted pinning the hem for, her face too one of shock, but at least not glee. The modiste would know better than to find pleasure in such news with the daughter of a duke.

"I do not understand," her mama said, taking the newspaper from Alice and reading the article herself.

Victoria felt her cheeks heat with embarrassment. How could Paul do such a thing to her? She had thought they were happy, settled, and ready to start the next chapter of their lives. Only last week she had farewelled him when he went to check on his country estate. That this gossip rag all of London was devouring knew more about the state of her marriage than she did was mortifying. How could she have been so wrong about a person she cared for? She was never wrong.

"Pass me the paper, Mama." Her mother handed it over to her with haste, seemingly only too happy to have the offending article out of her hand. Victoria read the printed black letters, and with each word, her world crumbled about her.

It read: ***"Mr. Paul Armstrong, the very one recently married to Lady Victoria Worthingham was seen sequestered at a local inn in Dover, the woman hanging off his every word most certainly not the Duke of Penworth's sister and new wife. That both Mr. Armstrong and his unnamed companion were soused, and too boisterous for the townsfolk was also mentioned. We can only look on Lady Victoria with pity over her most unhappy union that she so newly stepped into."***

She clamped her jaw shut, an expletive on the tip of her tongue. Paul was a wealthy landholder from Kent. A suitable gentleman for a woman such as herself. Her brother Josh, the Duke of Penworth assured her he was a good match, both financially and regarding the gentleman's reputation. When her brother returned from abroad, she would certainly have words with him regarding his character evaluations.

Not that their marriage was a love match, unlike her sisters who had found love with their spouses. But Victoria had never been one to think such a thing would happen to her. She was too opinionated, a little rough about the edges, blunt, and loved dogs and horses too much to be a diamond of the first water.

Where her sisters were refined and ladylike, she was, well, a little notched. A laugh caught her attention, and she looked over to find Miss Fanny Christi pointing and giggling over *The*

Times. Victoria glared at the social-climbing ninny and thrust the paper aside, the modiste taking it without a word.

"I apologize for wasting your time with this gown, Mrs. DeRose, but it would seem that I'm no longer in the mood for a dress fitting." Victoria held out her arms. "Please help me to remove the gown. I shall return another day to complete the alterations."

"But dear, do you not want to write and demand Mr. Armstrong returns? The article could be incorrect. Why even now he could be on his way back from the country to explain this slanderous piece."

Victoria wiggled out of the gown, leaving her only in her shift as she stepped off the fitting stool in the store and went to change back into her morning dress. "It is not, Mama. Mr. Armstrong has made his choice." *And now he would have to live with it.* "I will not be one of those pitiful wives who allow such insults to stand. While I cannot change the fact that I am married, that does not mean I'll allow him to ruin my life. If it is freedom he wishes so soon after our nuptials, then I too shall live how I like and bedamn Paul to Hades."

Stupid fool to have ruined their future in such a way. Victoria walked into the change room, pulling the small curtain closed to hide her from those in the store who watched them and their reaction to the news like a kettle of vultures over a corpse.

Only then did she allow herself a deep breath, the reaction to the news that she had been hiding from all those prying eyes. She slumped onto the soft, padded chair in the stall. While she knew their marriage would have been a practical and good match, she had liked Paul, even if it were not a love match. He made her laugh and was handsome. She had thought they would muddle along well enough. His estate was large. He had a good stable of horses and was fond of dogs, had stated she could bring her two wolfhounds with her when they married, which she had.

She pulled her morning gown from the hook where it hung. She would not have minded had he wished to break the engagement, but to marry her and then run off? What had he been thinking! The stupid man could have been honest with her. Why did he not tell her the truth, that he loved another and did not wish to marry? That's if he loved the maid at all. For all she knew, perhaps this was the way the man truly was. A gentleman without honor.

Victoria stood and slipped the dress over her head, stepping back out into the store to gain assistance with the buttons on her back. Her mama handed her her bonnet and gloves, and within a few minutes, they were ready to leave.

"I'm so very sorry about your unsuccessful marriage, Lady Victoria," Miss Christi said, the smirk on her face telling Victoria that she was not sorry at all. "And so soon into the union. How you must be suffering."

Victoria looked down her nose at her, feeling the weight and support of both her mother and sister behind her. A duchess and viscountess who would never abide such rudeness for long, and neither would she.

Victoria patted Miss Christi's shoulder, hoping the condescension was thick and clear in her touch. "Do not be sorry for me, Miss Christi. It is not my loss, but my husband's." She smiled, glad to see Miss Christi's face had paled at her words. "I hope we see you at the ball this evening. It's always lovely to see off the Season with a bang."

Miss Christi curtsied to Victoria's mama while mumbling, "Of course. Good day, Your Grace, Lady Arndel."

Victoria turned up her nose and left the store. Their coachman opened the door and helped them inside. Victoria heard her mama tell the driver they were for home, and it wasn't long before the carriage wheels were rumbling over the gravel and cobblestone roads through Mayfair.

No one spoke, all of them too disturbed by what had just transpired, no matter how it may have looked to those who viewed them in the store.

"Well, I hope Mr. Armstrong is pleased with his actions. I shall endeavor never to allow him to step foot in any of our entertainments in the future or those of my children. He is cut off from our family. Dead to us all I swear."

Alice nodded, her lips thinning in displeasure. "You should not allow him to get away with such treatment, Victoria. We ought to pay him back in some way. I could always shoot him. My aim is second to none as you know."

Victoria glanced at her sister, unsure how much help Alice would be since she was in the early stages of pregnancy. "I think Callum may take issue with me having you hie about England searching for a man who does not want to be found and shooting him. Not yet, at least." Victoria stared out onto the street, not really seeing anything other than a city she would be happy to leave. Next week, in fact, she was due to return to Paul's country estate where they were to remain until next Season. That would not be happening now.

What a waste of effort these past months had been. The courtship, the marriage, the expense. Victoria supposed she should feel more upset than she did, but she couldn't bring forth the emotions to do so. That in itself told her that to lose her husband, while humiliating, was not life-ending.

She would clasp the opportunity his foolishness had gifted her and return to Dunsleigh.

"You may do whatever you think is best, Mama. I, for one, will hold my head high at tonight's ball, and next week we shall return home and go on with things as if nothing has happened." Victoria leaned forward, taking her mama's hands. "Do not think that I am so very upset, for I am not. In fact," she said, leaning against the squabs, "I'm certain since he's decided to run off with a maid, society will punish him enough without me adding to his woes. But as for our marriage, it is over and nothing, no persuasion from him in the future will change my mind. As far as I am concerned, I will view myself as a widow from this day forward."

"I think you may be right," Alice said, rubbing her small baby bump. "You are destined for better things, my dearest. Who is attending this evening, Mama? We need to show society that we have rallied around Victoria and will not abide her being slighted."

"Well, as for that," her mama said, rattling off several families, all of whom Victoria knew and classed as friends. They would not offend or slight her in her time of need. They would be home soon. Safe from London and the gossiping ton.

While she did not know what her future held, where she would live, or what name to use, one thing she was at least grateful for... Her dowry was still her own, and no matter where Paul traveled with his lover, he could not swindle her money away. She supposed she could purchase a townhouse in London or a small country estate near Dunsleigh. All ideas would need considerable thought and once they were home, she would be able to set her mind to figuring out her future.

One thing was certain however, her future would not involve her husband. Not ever again.

Hampshire, 1811

Albert Kester, Marquess Melvin wrote the final words in his latest gothic romance novel. His quill scrawled *The End*—a little salute to himself he always signed when he'd completed a manuscript.

He leaned back in his chair, staring out at the inky-black

night. Secluded away in Hampshire near Surrey's border, he ought to feel alone, vulnerable perhaps, and yet, he did not.

He loved living in the country. The hunting lodge he now used as his writing oasis was the perfect setting for a man such as himself, a man who did not enjoy crowds or socializing. He'd never been one to have the abilities to speak pretty to females or act as one of the rogues, gambling and carousing about the town without a care.

But he would have to soon. In a week or so, his closest neighbor and influential family were returning to Surrey, and he would have to ride the ten miles between their estates and endure the weekend house party and ball the Duke of Penworth held.

And he would see her again...

Lady Victoria Worthingham, now widow to the late Mr. Paul Armstrong after the fool dabbled with the wrong married lady abroad and received a bullet through his skull for his troubles. The only woman he was certain of in England and perhaps the world to make him question his life. His way of living. So private and alone.

The invitation had arrived today, and he'd sent off an acceptance without delay before he could change his mind and remain at Rosedale.

Albert slipped the manuscript into the leather binder he used and locked the book away in a cabinet before securing the lodge and returning to the main house.

He had not brought his horse this afternoon, knowing he would be several hours here, but it did not matter. He knew his way back home, even in the night.

At least he could attend the ball at the duke's estate without the nagging guilt he always suffered when he had a book due. With it finished, he could at least attempt to enjoy the ball more.

The lights to the main house flickered through the trees and then rose high before him as he cleared the copse of forest that surrounded his estate. Tomorrow he would send his book off to his publisher and, should they like the next installment of his series, his book would be available within the next twelve months or so.

It may not be the usual occupation that a marquess would do, but he enjoyed writing stories, becoming lost in his characters' worlds. What started as a hobby was now another source of income to his estate, and it pleased him. He could control that world. He could not control the one he lived in.

His mother, who resided on an estate just outside of Bath with her new husband, was forever writing to him, asking when he would return to London for another Season. Find a bride to marry and have an heir. A grandchild she longed for.

He knew his mama had a lot of love to give. His father had been a cruel man, a bullying bastard, and all the love she had for the man withered and died only years into the marriage. Now she was happy. They both were, he supposed, in their small, different ways, but she wanted to share the love she had bottled up for so many years.

Albert, too, would like to love. He would like to court Lady Victoria, but since the scandal of her husband's affair, his running off with a maid followed by several other indiscretions all written about in the London gossip rags, Victoria looked less than interested in entering such a union for a second time.

Who could blame her for such thoughts.

While he liked the idea of marriage, he certainly had no idea what to do with a wife once the union was officiated. A problem he'd been trying to solve with extensive research. He'd purchased a collection of books on the art of lovemaking, sketches of how it was that women and men came together—drawings depicting the act of lovemaking, some of which had taken his breath away.

Albert let himself into the house, his staff well used to the strange times he came and went. He walked into the library and went directly to the latest book he had received from London about the life story of Moll Flanders, having left it on his desk before he'd set off to write this afternoon. An amusing and interesting account, with some bawdy tales that entertained him.

With his books featuring scenes similar to those he found in Daniel Defoe's book, he hoped he at least sounded as true and accurate as this author. His career would be over should the public know the truth. That one of their favorite gothic romance authors who pens tales of intrigue, horror, and passionate encounters was as virginal as a debutante newly arrived in London. A marquess, too, even more humiliating. Lords ought to know how to romance a lady or rake about town.

He was living a lie, at least portraying one. But then, he supposed his books were a work of fiction, and his characters had nothing to prove. But soon, he would need to search for a wife in earnest. Court her, as awkward and clumsy as he was when in verbal conversation with females. The thought made him frown. Next week he would see Lady Victoria, and his ineptitude would be even more noticeable. Her vivaciousness for life, her confidence shamed his introverted self. For years he had wanted the gumption to implement some of the things he'd found in the sketches with her, seduce her into marriage with him.

A dream that was unlikely to come true. He required a wife who at least wished for a husband. Lady Victoria Worthingham, as much as he longed for the position to be filled by her, was the one woman in England sworn off ever marrying again. Everyone knew it, and so did he. Someone else would have to do.

CHAPTER 2

Dunsleigh, 1811

The guests to their country ball and short house party arrived a week after the 1811 Season had come to an end. After their return, Victoria had the following day walked up to the family mausoleum and paid her respects to her papa, a man she missed more with each passing year, especially when she saw all that he missed by being gone. The many grandchildren being born, the happy marriages, the balls, and parties that she knew he loved so very much.

Tonight was the formal dinner the night before the ball, where the guests could relax and enjoy a more intimate get together after their journeys to Surrey. There would be music and games, cards for the gentlemen, and of course, the guests could stroll the extensive grounds, or enjoy the billiards room or conservatory if they chose.

It seemed all of London had descended on Dunsleigh for the ball, including a lot of the local gentry, some of whom rarely went up to London at all.

Lord Melvin one of them. After dinner, Victoria stood

beside Alice, discussing those who were in attendance. Her sister was positively glowing with a second pregnancy in as many years, and Callum, her adoring husband, kept vigil from across the room, speaking to her two brothers-in-law, the Earl of Muir and the Duke of Moore.

"What do you think of Lord Melvin? He does seem most uncomfortable with Miss Fletcher, do you not think? Why," Victoria said, sipping her ratafia with amusement, "I do believe he is sweating. Look." She shook Alice's arm a little.

Her sister cast a cursory glance, not wanting to be too obvious in their appraisal of him. "Oh dear, he's pulling at his cravat. What do you think Miss Fletcher has said to him to make him so uncomfortable?

Something about the gentleman had always drawn Victoria. She supposed as a lover of animals, of dogs especially and horses, to see a man who looked as downtrodden and as uncomfortable as a puppy surrounded by wolves would make one feel bad for the man.

Feel sorry for the unfortunate.

As one of her brother's closest friends since school, they knew him well, and for many years. In the two years since she'd seen him last, his lordship appeared even more uneasy around company. As if society made him physically ill.

She cringed when he fumbled for his handkerchief and dabbed at his brow. "He's nervous. Maybe he likes Miss Fletcher."

Victoria narrowed her eyes at the idea of Lord Melvin seeking to court the young heiress. From the way Miss Fletcher controlled the narrative of their conversation, she couldn't help but think the poor man would never get a word in.

But then he probably wouldn't get a word in with her either, so there was that. Even so, as she studied him, she couldn't help but think he'd like to bolt like one of her mares when let out of the stables after a few days. "Do you think I should save him and pull Miss Fletcher away for a turn about the room?"

Alice cast her a cursory glance. "Why the interest in Lord Melvin?" She tipped her head to the side, regarding the gentleman. "I suppose he is quite sweet-looking. A little bookish perhaps, but that is nothing if he has other skills."

Victoria snorted and covered her inappropriate lapse of ladylike manners by covering her mouth with her hand. She took several moments to stop chuckling. "I'm not even going to ask what you mean by that, Alice. But let me enlighten you, dear sister. I have seen you and your husband when you think you're alone, and so I can assume very well what 'skills' you mean."

Alice did not bat an eyelash, nor did she blush. She simply grinned, sipping her wine. "I suppose what one does not know can be taught. Myself included. I was quite enlightened after marrying Callum."

"And what are we to do should both the couples be clueless?" Not that she was or that she thought Lord Melvin would be so very naïve when it came to seduction and women. He was a man, after all. A marquess. He could not have been so secluded and innocent, no matter if he spent all of his time in the country. He probably had a gaggle of women willing and able to warm his bed in Hampshire.

She narrowed her eyes at the thought. At that very moment, his lordship glanced away from Miss Fletcher, his attention colliding with hers. The fear, the uncomfortable mess he was just an instant before vanished, and a determined light entered his eyes that she'd never seen before. What did that mean?

Alice cleared her throat, grinning over the top of her crystal glass. "Well, well, well, he certainly looks a lot more dashing when he sees you. I wonder...".

Victoria moved her attention on to the dancers, feigning interest in them instead. "Do not be asinine, Alice. I'm not the least interested in Lord Melvin and nor is he in me."

"I believe the same may not be said for his lordship."

"What about a certain lordship?" their older sister Elizabeth, Countess Muir, asked, joining them and kissing them both in turn on their cheeks.

Victoria clasped her sister's arm, having not seen her for several months since they resided most of the time at Muirdeen, their Scottish estate.

Alice nodded in Lord Melvin's direction. "Victoria has sparked the interest of a certain marquess. Although instead of a rogue, which I'm sure you would agree with me make the best husbands, he seems more righteous."

Elizabeth grinned at Victoria. "There is nothing wrong with righteousness. Henry wasn't a rogue, far from it, and he's simply delightful to be married to."

"That is true, and really, I suppose Callum wasn't either. Not a rascal one in any case. So there may be hope for our Lord Melvin after all."

Victoria stepped away from her sisters, pinning them with disapproving glares. "You forget my husband was the worst of men. Whoring his way around England and the continent. There is no 'our Lord Melvin,' and you must stop saying such things. I noticed his unease and merely commented on it. You're reading too much into my observations."

Elizabeth tossed Alice a knowing smile. "Of course, dearest, but that does not mean all men are the same," she said, her voice cajoling.

"I'm going to find Isolde. You two are impossible." Victoria strode off, locating Isolde beside her mama. Her sister's husband—who doted on his wife to the point of nauseating regularity—winked at Victoria when she came up to them. She bussed his cheek and then her sister's. "We need to disown our other two sisters, they're impossible."

Their mother raised her brow, looking over to where Alice and Elizabeth talked and laughed amongst themselves. "What have they done to you, dearest? Do you wish for me to speak to them?"

Victoria shook her head, knowing her grievances with her siblings weren't so very bad. That they teased her over a man she herself was curious about did not help. She didn't like everyone knowing her secrets. She had not thought mentioning Lord Melvin's unease would cause such curiosity. Or the fact of seeing him with a woman would disarm her so very much. After the death of her husband, she had promised herself a life of doing whatever she wished. No more husbands to make fools of their wives. The desire to travel and a life of adventure awaited her. Having children and a spouse did not.

"It is nothing, Mama. Do not trouble yourself."

Her mama studied her a moment before one of her friends waved her over to join them and she excused herself.

"Tell me you're staying at Dunsleigh for several weeks. I do not think I can stand being here with only Alice as a neighbor to keep me company."

The disappointment on Isolde's face told Victoria that she was not staying long. "We are for home next week, my love. But you may come with us if you like. We should love to have you if you wished for a little diversion. Wiltshire is very lovely this time of year."

"I best stay with mama. She'll be alone here should I go anywhere, and with Josh abroad, I had better not go too far away. But thank you, maybe Mama and I can both come and see you for a week or two before Christmas."

"That would be lovely," Isolde said.

Happy with this plan, Victoria spoke to guests as they socialized about the room. The evening was a success and in full swing by the time supper was served. Victoria stood at the threshold of the supper room doors, content to watch those who were hungry eating. She reached up and massaged her nape when a prickling of awareness skittered across her skin.

She turned and found Lord Melvin several paces behind her. His unease at the crowded supper room visible on his pinched features. Victoria took pity on the man, going into the room and picking several favorite dishes of hers before quitting the space.

"Lord Melvin, how good to see you tonight. I have some supper for you if you would like a repast."

He gazed down at the plate of food, and it seemed to break the spell of inactivity that plagued him. "Oh, Lady Victoria, I thank you. You did not have to do such a service for me."

"I'm a hostess here this evening with my mama, my lord. It is only right that each of our guests is cared for."

He took the plate, his fingers grazing hers at the interchange, and Victoria started at the feel of his gloved fingers against hers. He was warm, with strong hands that made her feel a little odd. A little too curious for her liking.

"It's crab cakes and lobster in jelly. They're my first choice at any ball. I hope you like them."

His lips tilted into a half smile. Victoria sensed that when relaxed, this man would open up like a flower. Not that she viewed most men as plants, but with her at least, right now, the fear that lurked in his dark-blue orbs had dissipated.

"I do thank you," he said again.

She stayed with him with nowhere else to be for a time, content to wait for supper to end and the dancing to begin again. "I have not seen you tread the ballroom floor this evening. Do you not like to dance, my lord?" she asked him.

He chewed and swallowed one of his crab cakes before answering, "I do enjoy dancing, and if you are not otherwise engaged, would you dance the next set with me?"

"The next set is to open with a waltz. Do you waltz too, my lord?"

"I have been known to on occasion," he drawled, his voice dropping to a deep, husky purr that she did not think him capable of. Not with his nervousness that plagued him. The man was so very curious. A sense of anticipation thrummed down her spine, and she liked the idea of being in his arms. "Then the dance is yours, my lord. Come find me when you have finished your supper." Would he falter or endure? Something told Victoria she was about to find out.

CHAPTER 3

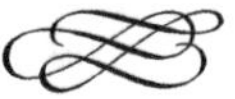

By the time supper had ended and the musicians set up for the commencement of the next set, Albert had all but lost his nerve. It was one thing to invite a woman out to dance, but it was quite another to follow through with the act.

What if he stumbled and fell, pulled Lady Victoria down with him? What if he grew more nervous than he already was and sweated profusely? The idea of stepping on her toes, hurting her delicate feet was beyond reprehensible and unforgivable.

She would never dance with him again, and he wanted her to dance with him, especially now. Now that she was out of mourning for her husband. The fool Armstrong had lost a prize when he tossed Lady Victoria over for a maid not long after their marriage. Whatever was the man thinking! Albert certainly did not know or understand such motives.

He would never throw her over for anyone else. How could he, she was perfection personified.

Like an angel, she materialized before him, holding out her

hand, a mischievous light in her eyes. "Our dance, I believe, Lord Melvin."

He led her out onto the floor, hoping his nervousness did not shine through. Women in general made him fumble like a fool, but Victoria more so than any. He didn't want her to view him as some simpleton. He wanted her to view him as so much more.

Like a gentleman. A man.

Albert pulled her into his arms as the music commenced. She was tall for a woman. Her eyes level with his chin. Her body was soft, womanly, and his, for a little time at least.

She smelled divine, like jasmine and soap. Never had he ever smelled something so sweet before. Her fingers flexed on his shoulder, and she looked up to meet his gaze. "I do believe this is our first dance, my lord."

How he wished it were more than that pitiful number. Albert had longed to ask her during the seasons he traveled to town to step out with him. He had wanted to have her in his arms more times than he could count, but his nerves never allowed him to speak the words necessary.

He wasn't sure why he was the way he was, and as much as he tried to hide his anxieties from the ton, they were always there, beneath his skin and threatening to make him miss out on life.

He supposed maybe his father's mistreatment of his family had something to do with it.

"We missed you this Season in town, my lord. Do say you're to attend next year."

He glanced down and met Lady Victoria's eyes. She was always so genuine and kind. Was it wishful thinking on his behalf that she would look at him more than a friend? If she gave him a chance to prove himself, he would not let her down.

Not an easy conquest when she was determined never to marry again, or so the gossips tittered behind their fans.

"I may attend. Will you be there, my lady, or has a gentleman now won your heart, and you're to be married?" Albert wasn't sure where the words came from, inappropriate and rude. He frowned, wishing he had a filter on his mouth at times. If he could have smacked himself about the head, he would have, knowing she wasn't long out of mourning.

Victoria laughed, easing a little of his tension. "No, I'm not engaged as I'm certain you already know. I'm home at Dunsleigh for the foreseeable future, until my brother returns home and helps me with my travels abroad. My sister is in a delicate state yet again you see, and I wish to be close to her. Josh will return from abroad before Christmas so it will be a jolly good time here. One that is sorely needed after the past two years we have endured."

Albert understood her words but did not pry any further. The scandal her husband caused, the pain and embarrassment she must have withstood would have been enough to cripple him in society permanently. And yet, here she was, rising from the ashes like the strong, capable woman he knew her to be. How fortunate she was to have a supportive family. Other than his mama, there was no one else he could turn to, but a distant cousin he hardly knew. His father had passed, and he had no siblings.

It was no wonder people concerned him so much. He wasn't used to them.

"I shall like to see Penworth again. It has been almost a year."

"Yes, by the time Josh returns home, he would have been away that long. We're all so very excited to see him again." She looked up at him, her eyes wide and clear and direct. Always with the ability to pin someone to the ground with one look. "I forget you are friends with Josh. He has so many, but you were very close once. Still are, I hope."

They were still close. He received a monthly letter from the duke, one person other than Victoria he was calm around. Not that he was so very calm around Victoria right at this moment. Having her in his arms made him want things he'd never imagined before.

His gaze dipped to her lips, and he watched as she spoke of this and that, the ball and the guests, the food, and how late the night would be. All the while, all he could think about was if the pink, pouty flesh of her lips was as soft as it looked.

With some alarm, he realized she had stopped speaking and was staring at his mouth as well. Her tongue flicked out, licking her lips, and his body grew taut.

He read the question in hers, surprise even. Albert cleared his throat, breaking the spell between them. "With you home and Penworth due to return, may I invite you all over for dinner one evening at Rosedale? I admit my staff and their exemplary cooking abilities are poorly underutilized."

She smiled, and the action made her appear more beautiful than she already was. Albert had always thought Victoria the prettiest of the Worthingham sisters, tall and bold, but also caring even though he suspected very few other than her family knew how kind she was.

She certainly always took pity on him, made him feel welcome. A marquess or not, that wasn't something every one of his acquaintances fulfilled.

"I do not believe I've ever been to your estate, my lord. I understand Rosedale is very beautiful."

Not as beautiful as you, he wanted to say. If he were a rogue, had the ability for pretty words and dark, hungry looks, he would tell Victoria all those things. Instead, he masked his feelings and said, "One of the finest in Hampshire. Although I'm very close to Surrey and it is often contested which county I live."

"We would love to attend and be your guests, but I must say, and please forgive my forwardness, but may we stay a night? I know it is some miles from Dunsleigh and may be too great a distance to travel in one day."

"Oh, of course. You are more than welcome to stay." The idea of Victoria being in his home, asleep under the same roof, where he would be even more at ease, able to speak to her without the worry of prying eyes was just the thing. If he studied up on his books regarding the opposite sex and what was expected of him as a man, maybe he could prove to Victoria that he was worth more than friendship.

That he was worth her giving up her widowhood to marry him instead.

"Then we shall come as soon as Josh has returned, and you write and invite us." The strains to the waltz started to come to a regretful end. Albert did not want to let her go, but then he had two other dancers with her yet, but both would not allow him such close intercourse.

The evening passed pleasantly after his dances with Victoria, and he was content to stand by and watch the play of guests. Some hours later, he left the ball, asking permission for the use of the library. Thankfully the duchess did not ask as to why he wanted to use the room. A little while later, he was scribbling away his words on a new book, the heroine, as all of his were, remarkably similar to Victoria in both appearance and temperament.

He wrote for hours, the sounds of the music drifting to a close, just as the ball did as well. The first signs of the new day broke across the land, and the house started to wake with the whispered words of maids and footmen. Albert wet his forefinger and snuffed his candle. He leaned back in the chair, stretching. He wrote a good amount of the book last evening, a scene where the hero required saving. His heroine coming to the hero's rescue. He did not like weak characters and rarely wrote them. He supposed because he was that very thing in a lot of ways. Awkward, sheltered, and not the least fashionable. A weak marquess just as his father had always called him.

He collected his papers, placing them in his leather folder, and left the library. The guests wouldn't be up for some hours, and so he would rest and then say his goodbyes this afternoon before heading back to Rosedale, living in the hope that Victoria would do as she said and come to stay. The time would allow him to become worldly, a gentleman worthy of her hand, the hand of a daughter and sister to a duke.

CHAPTER 4

Victoria stumbled into the library just as the day after the ball was almost at an end. The previous night had been amusing and enjoyable, but she would be happy when the Season would be officially over, and Dunsleigh would be just for her family and herself to enjoy.

Some of the guests had departed early, one of them Lord Melvin, whom she had seen off just after lunch. She walked to the desk, needing some parchment to write to her brother, when she spotted a piece of paper, the scribbly, messy writing bold and rushed as if someone had to get the words down quickly before they forgot them.

She picked up the paper, reading the words, and couldn't quite grasp what she was holding. A marvelous story, similar in tone and ability to others she had read by one of her favorite authors, Elbert Retsek. His aptitude to throw the reader into his gothic romances was something of a dream. She had often fantasized about meeting the gentleman, having him sign the many books she had of his. In fact, she was eagerly awaiting his next release, which was rumored to be coming out next year.

She read through the words quickly, unable to comprehend

how it was that these words were here. Was Elbert a guest at their home? She sat on the chair, reaching for the list of guests her mama had been checking and double-checking this past week.

She followed each guest's name, scrolling with her finger, and could not see anyone of that name on the list. Victoria frowned, slumping back in the chair. Was Elbert Retsek an alias, a pseudonym? How astonishing if he was a guest. Had she danced with him? Had she unknowingly been in the hands of one of England's up-and-coming writers, in the league of Horace Walpose or even Ann Radcliffe? Excitement thrummed through her veins at the idea of a real-life author being in their presence.

Alice strolled into the room and, spotting her, shut the door. "Ah, there you are. I wanted to come and see you before we returned home."

Victoria waved her sister over, and she quickened her steps. "Look and read this. I think it may be some pages from Elbert Retsek."

Alice frowned, taking the sample and reading it quickly. She pursed her lips. "Well, it certainly reads like him, but what is it doing here?"

"I came in here this morning," Victoria said, standing and smoothing her dress as she paced back and forth to the window, "and found it. I think he may have been a guest at the ball last evening and left this here by mistake." *Oh dear, which means he is missing an important piece of his story, for it looked like the hero was in great danger, not that she seemed too worried about the fact.* A point for why Victoria loved Elbert's stories so much. She hated weak characters in any story being outsmarted or, worse, killed.

"He'll be wanting it back then," Alice said, sitting at the desk. "What shall we do?"

Victoria made a point of looking at Alice's baby belly. "We will do nothing, but I shall. I will have to do some investigating."

"Hmm," Alice said, staring at her. "Oh, I know what you can do. Check the acceptances for the ball. Maybe your mystery guest replied himself, and the handwriting may be similar."

Hope rushed through Victoria. "Alice, that is brilliant. I shall do that straightaway." Not that she was an expert at comparing handwriting, but it was at least one way forward. What would she do when she found the gentleman who had attended? She wasn't sure. How does one approach a famous, if not closeted, author and tell them you knew who they were and that they had left part of their manuscript in one's library? He may be unsettled knowing that one of his own class knew of his profession. Not that she would ever tell a soul, not if that is what he wished. To remain anonymous would be his choice, and she would respect that.

Victoria strode over to the sideboard and opened the drawer. It was where her mama kept her invitations and responses for the current entertainments. She found the acceptances and picked them up, not willing to let them out of her sight. "I shall take these to my room and go through them. I should think it will take me several hours."

"Do come and see me when you think you've found a match. I would like to help you if I can. You know how much I love a good intrigue."

Victoria chuckled, remembering the many intrigues her sister landed herself in while being courted by Lord Arndel. Many of which Victoria was dragged into and made an accessory.

"I will, I promise." Victoria helped her sister stand and walked her to the door, bussing her cheeks before seeing her off with her husband.

Her mama came to stand beside her, waving off her daughter, and Victoria linked arms with her parent. "Only a few more guests to go, and we shall have our house to ourselves again."

Her mother led her back inside, a small smile playing about

her mouth. Her mama was still a beautiful woman for her middle age, and since their father had died, had become a lot less strict with rules and etiquette. She was more carefree, let her children live the lives they wished, within reason, and be happy. Victoria wasn't sure why their mama had mellowed. Perhaps it simply came with age.

"Did you enjoy yourself last night, my dear? From what Lucy told me this morning, you were up all night dancing."

That was true. She had stayed at the ball longer than she normally would, but then, it was a send-off to the Season, and now she could enjoy riding about the estate, looking after her dogs. Some, she knew, spoke about her behind her back, snarled that she did not mourn her husband respectfully enough, but she had. She had spent a year mourning a man who had not shown an ounce of honor during their six-week marriage. That society would judge her for his actions irked. It was one of the reasons she wanted to throw their ideals in their faces and remain a contented widow for the rest of her life.

"It was very enjoyable. Several gentlemen asked me to dance, which was nice of them, " she lied to keep her mama happy. “I was able to catch up with several friends, some of whom I shall not see again until next year.”

Her mother chuckled, her eyes bright with amusement. "I shall live in the hope that the right gentleman is out there for you, my dear. You cannot allow what Mr. Armstrong put you through to tarnish your opinion on marriage.”

Too late for that...

"Just so," Victoria said. "In fact, I wanted to let you know that I have borrowed the acceptances from the ball. I want to match up some writing samples if I can."

They walked up the stairs and into her mama's private parlor, where they would not be interrupted by other guests still staying at the house. "Really, why would you need to do that?" Her mother pulled the bell for tea. "Did a gentleman leave you an inappropriate note to rendevous with him? As a widow, you must protect yourself against such rakes."

Heat kissed Victoria's cheeks, although the idea of a wicked rendevous with a willing gentleman may not be so bad. One thing she would give Paul credit for was his bedroom abilities, and she had enjoyed the short time they had been together. Even if the idea of him with other women now soured that memory. "Of course not. You should know very well that is quite inappropriate. I would not think anyone would dare to try such things with Josh watching my every step. I do believe he still thinks me an unmarried maid."

Her mother raised one disbelieving brow. "Josh darling is not here to keep vigil. I would think many gentlemen would try such tricks. You're a beautiful woman, an heiress, and a widow."

"Well, that is not why I'm researching penmanship, Mama. I found a written page on the desk in the library and merely wanted to return it to its owner. After reading it, I should imagine it's quite important."

Having sat and picked up her sewing, her mother looked up at Victoria at her last words. "A note, you say? Left on the desk in the library overnight?"

"Yes," Victoria stated, her stomach a little in knots seeing her mother mull over the issue.

"You do not need to search the acceptances, my dear. I know who worked in the library last evening, as he sought my approval before doing so."

Victoria tried to school her features. Her mama had never been too accepting of her reading gothic romances or horror, and to find out that one of her guests could be England's latest on dit and had used the desk would never do. She would be scandalized.

"Who was it?" she asked in the most bored tone she could muster.

Her mama threaded a needle, her mouth pinched in concentration. "Lord Melvin requested use of the room late in the evening. He said he has some correspondence to finish."

Lord Melvin!

"Do close your mouth, dear. You're gaping."

Victoria shut her mouth with a snap. Lord Melvin? How could it be him!? He was so quiet, and some would say a little droll, but handsome, so handsome that every time she saw him, a little devil sat on her shoulder, and she wanted to tease him, not that she ever did. Last evening he had invited her family and herself to his estate. Could she wait until then to confront him with this idea of hers?

His written words, folded and safe in the pocket of her dress, weighed heavily on her conscience. No, she could not wait. He may need this part of his story. If she did not return it to him, he would wonder what happened to it. He would have to rewrite it.

The horror!

She was not a writer, but to think of losing any part of a manuscript would surely send fear to shiver down one's spine.

"That reminds me, Mama. Lord Melvin invited us to stay at Rosedale when Josh has returned from abroad."

"Oh, did I not tell you, my dear? Josh darling will be home next week. I received a letter from him this morning. He's in Paris right now but will start his movement back to England within a day or two."

What wonderful news. Her trip to Hampshire could be sooner than she thought. "Do you think Josh would agree to travel and stay at Lord Melvin's so soon after returning from abroad?"

Her mother set down her sewing, meeting her gaze. "I do not see why not. The Season is over, and we're now rusticating in the country for several months. I'm sure he will agree."

Victoria flopped herself down on a nearby settee. And if she were to hint to Josh that Lord Melvin may be a possible suiter, she was certain he'd have them bundled up in the carriage within the hour. Not that she was looking at his lordship as a possible match, but she was certainly curious about this story she had in her pocket. Had he written it? Was he the mysterious Elbert Retsek the whole of England was talking about? Victoria crossed her legs, grinning. Something told her he was, and what a find that shall be. What would he have to say for himself about his double life in society?

Only time would tell.

CHAPTER 5

As expected, her brother rumbled up the drive in the duke's carriage several days later. Victoria and her mama went out the front of the house to greet him. The carriage was sprayed with mud, and the two drivers and footmen accompanying Josh looked tired and worn.

Victoria turned to the housekeeper standing behind her and requested a light repast and drinks for the travel-weary duke and servants.

Josh jumped down from the carriage, and Victoria hardly recognized him. Gone was the boy they had always teased growing up. The only boy in the family, it was only right that he suffered a little bit. Not that they were ever cruel, but he had been the future duke, and it was always fun to remind him that although he would care for them all one day, he was still the youngest.

Victoria ran up to him, wrapping her arms around his waist, hugging him. "You're home. Finally."

He kissed the top of her head, pulling their mama into his arms as she joined them. They walked inside, arms linked. They were a close family, and she knew that Alice would be around later today when she received word he was home. Isolde and Elizabeth had returned to their estates, but Josh would undoubtedly visit with them soon enough.

"Ah, Dunsleigh. How I have missed our home and everyone in it. Tell me all that has happened while I was away." Josh turned and looked down at her, and Victoria marveled at how much of a man he appeared. He was taller, broader across the shoulders, his hair lightened by travel and a little too long for what was fashionable. His eyes were bright and merry, and he required a shave, his whiskers a little too long.

Had the ladies in London seen him this past Season, Victoria knew he would have been swamped. How fun next year would be when he returned to town.

"I see that you are not yet married," he teased, bussing the top of her head again as they stepped into the foyer. "Remind me to put another bullet in Armstrong, even though another husband has already beaten me to it."

"Never mind Paul is nothing but a figment of my past. And do I need to remind you that unlike you, I have married and did my duty, even if it did turn out so very poorly. I hoped you might bring back a Russian princess or an Italian heiress to be our duchess. How boring your stories will be to endure, now that we know that is not the case," she teased, electing a chuckle from her brother.

He winked. "There were many beauties, but none that I can tell you about, Lady Victoria Worthingham. The lady you are, it would not be appropriate."

"Come, my dears. We shall have tea in my parlor upstairs," their mama said.

They headed upstairs, her brother taking in the house, seemingly remembering its beauty. It was the same for all of them when they traveled, even if just to town for several months. Dunsleigh was their home, the seat for the Dukes of Penworth, and they adored the house and estate. It was home, no matter where their lives took them.

Victoria allowed their mama to sit beside Josh. She sat across from them, excited to hear everything he had to say. They spoke of his trip, the people he met, and those he caught up with from England while traveling. The places, sights, and countries sounded amazing, and Victoria craved to make a similar trip. Supposing she could convince Josh to help her, that was. With her mother determined to see her wed again, she did not think traveling was in her future unless it was with her husband.

The thought of Lord Melvin floated through her mind as Josh recounted his amusing and very wet details of falling off a gondola in Venice. She smiled but only half-listened as she thought of a way to bring up the invitation to Lord Melvin's home. If she were to raise it, her mama would be curious indeed and start to gain ideas she had no right to.

"We've been invited to several house parties. The first is closest, just over the border with Hampshire. Lord Melvin has invited us to stay."

Josh raised his brow, a look of confusion crossing his features. "I did not know Albert liked to host guests. Are you sure it's a house party?"

Their mama looked to Victoria, and she shrugged. "He invited us three to stay with him when you returned from abroad. That is all he said. I do not know if there will be others in attendance."

"Hmm," Josh said, a mischievous light entering his eye. "Mayhap my old friend has set his sights on my sister. A trip to Hampshire would be welcome, and I haven't seen Melvin for some time."

Victoria did not want to come across as desperate, but she also was eager to travel to his estate. If he was indeed the famous author, one whom she loved to read, well, she wanted to know for certain. To discuss his works and those that were yet to be written.

"I shall write to him this week and seek a date that is suitable for him."

Victoria couldn't help but smile at the idea. What would his lordship say when she confronted him with the page of writing? Would he deny it? The idea that it wasn't a work of his hand dampened the idea of traveling to his estate, and yet, he wasn't so very bad. Certainly not to look at. If only he wasn't so awkward and standoffish.

"Is there a reason as to why Melvin has invited us? Does he have his sights set on Victoria?" Josh asked their mama in all seriousness, his gaze slipping to Victoria in question.

She groaned, rolling her eyes. "I danced with him at our ball last week. He invited us while we waltzed. I'm sure it was merely a means of conversation, so we did not dance in silence."

Her mama studied her a moment before sitting closer to her son, taking his hand. "Oh, I am so happy all my children are back on English soil. We have missed you, Josh dear. Tell us, did you meet anyone suitable for my boy?"

A light blush stole over his cheeks before he shook his head. "No, Mama. No one to report as yet, but next year I promise to search for a duchess. Only a lady will do for the Penworth name."

"You, dear brother, are a snob, but we have missed you." The door to the room burst open, and Alice raced inside. Josh stood, pulling his sister into his arms and kissing her cheeks.

"How did you know Josh was back, my dear?" their mama queried. "I have not sent a missive yet."

Alice sat on the opposite side of Josh, squashing all three of them on the lounge. "My gardener, returning from Petworth, told me he had seen the ducal carriage travel through the town. I came as soon as I could get our carriage hitched."

Lord Arndel and their two daughters followed soon after,

saying a fond welcome to Josh. The pleasant afternoon turned into a dinner and night before the fire, enjoying one another's company. Victoria reveled in the comfort of having family around, of being so fortunate to have all that she did. The idea of Lord Melvin at Rosedale, alone, without family and very few friends, left her uneasy. She did not want to feel sorry for the man, but it was so very hard not to when he was so remote, so isolated, both personally and physically.

Maybe she could entice him to be more open, more available to people. If he were the famous author Elbert Retsek, then it would only help his career if he had a more public persona.

He would benefit from her skills, she was sure of it. Now, they just had to travel there so she could begin.

CHAPTER 6

Albert paced the front foyer of Rosedale, waiting to hear the sound of the Duke of Penworth's carriage. The very equipage that would bring Victoria to his estate. They had agreed to stay several days, not quite a week, and he was unabashedly excited about seeing her again.

That he would forget how to speak, how to act around her, he had decided to worry about another time. However, he looked forward to their safe arrival and seeing not only Victoria but also her brother, his good friend the duke.

"The rooms are ready for the guests, my lord," his housekeeper said, pulling his attention away from the window where he was trying to spot any carriage on the drive.

"Excellent, thank you, Mrs. Wigg." His housekeeper, pleased, nodded and started toward the back of the house.

He had planned everything for Victoria's stay, the dinners, all of which would be at least five courses. Nothing was too much for a duke's daughter. Horse rides about the estate, and boating, if she liked. His lake was one of the largest in the county, not to mention the Roman ruins that sat on an island within its center were always a location guests liked to explore.

Or would enjoy, should he ever invite any.

The sound of a carriage rumbling along the gravel pulled him back to the window, and he looked outside to see the black, highly polished carriage with the Penworth coat of arms on the door roll to a halt.

Albert looked down at his clothing, checking his attire was in order before heading outdoors. He met them at the carriage just as a footman was helping the duchess alight before the one person he seemed to be holding his breath to see once again came into view. Victoria placed her slippered foot on the carriage step, holding the footman's hand as she stepped onto the gravel drive. Her attention snapped to the house, and she looked up at it with what he hoped was pleasure before her direct, sweet gaze descended on him.

His breath caught at seeing her again and heat bloomed on his cheeks. He swallowed the unease, the fear of her rejection, and pushed past that gut-churning concern, stepping toward them all and bowing. "Your Graces, Lady Victoria, may I welcome you to Rosedale."

Victoria's mother gave him her hand, smiling. "Lord Melvin, it is lovely that you would allow us to stay here as we travel through Hampshire. We look forward to our stay, and please, call me Sarah."

Albert cleared his throat, unsure if he should follow such disregard to etiquette and forms of address that should be adhered to with a duchess. His friend, Penworth, stepped forward, shaking his hand. "Melvin, it is good to see you again. It has been too long."

Albert nodded in agreement. They had been friends since school, Eton to be exact, and as much as Penworth had tried to get him to be more outgoing, exuberant, and a charmer of anything in a silk skirt, Albert had never been able to be part of the boys' club. His nerves simply couldn't allow him to be at ease, and so eventually, he had watched his friends go off on their jaunts, and he had stayed behind. Had learned to be content with his own company.

He no longer wanted such a way of existence. He wanted a wife. He wanted Victoria if she would have him.

The woman herself materialized before him, her wide smile and bright eyes leaving him a little speechless.

"Lord Melvin, thank you for your hospitality."

"It is my pleasure," he said, turning and gesturing to the house. "Come, I have your rooms ready if you would like to freshen up. Luncheon will be served within the hour."

They made their way into the house, and he quickly took them upstairs, pointing out the rooms visible from the staircase, which were many, the library, his office that he liked to keep separate just in case of guests such as he was hosting now. The dining room, downstairs parlor, game room, and ballroom.

They made the first-floor landing, and he led them to the guest wing where two maids waited to help the duchess and Lady Victoria. Albert then led Penworth toward his room. "I hope you will be comfortable here."

Penworth glanced into his room, one of the largest and most opulent in the house, and nodded, seemingly pleased. "Of course. I'm always happy to stay with one of my oldest friends, but there is something that I do wish to discuss with you if you have a moment before lunch."

"Of course," Albert said, unable to think of what that could be, while also curious. "I shall meet you in the library whenever you're ready."

Albert did not have long to wait. Within twenty minutes, dressed in a fresh shirt and cravat, buckskin breeches, and knee-high polished boots, the duke strode into the library, his jacket idly folded over one arm.

"Rosedale is looking wonderful." Penworth walked over to the decanter of whiskey before Albert had a chance to offer him a drink, picking up the crystal decanter. "Drink?" he asked.

"It is I who should be offering you a glass, but yes, thank you."

"Do not concern yourself. I have been traveling the last year, and let me tell you, I have learned to be quite self-sufficient, which is never a bad thing, I would say."

Albert took the glass, taking a sip. "I couldn't agree more." The duke walked about the library for a few minutes before seating himself across from Albert, pinning him with his stare.

"I wanted to speak to you about the invitation that you forwarded to my family. I cannot help but ponder that there is a purpose for you doing so. Are you wanting to court my sister?"

Albert, having been taking a sip, sucked in the whiskey and choked. He coughed for several moments as he gained his equilibrium. Should he tell Penworth the truth? That he would like nothing more than to court Victoria and see if her affection for him ran deeper than mere benign fondness.

He supposed he would have to get Penworth's approval if he wished to marry his sister, so honesty was always best.

"While I have no illusions to marry Lady Victoria, I do welcome the opportunity to get to know her better. I have always liked your sister and would like to wait and see if we suit, if you agree."

Albert's stomach twisted into knots. If Penworth disagreed and did not wish him to court his sister, he was unsure what he would do. Would he go against one of the highest-placed peers in England? Would he court Victoria anyway? A rod of steel threaded up his spine, and Albert knew the answer to his own question. Yes, he would.

"We have been friends for many years, and I would welcome your suit toward her. Victoria, however," Penworth grimaced, "is of a mind never to marry again. After Armstrong, I'm sure I do not need to explain that he injured her most severely, both her heart and in society. She has grown more outspoken since the scandal, is lively, and with many hobbies. She has dogs, did you know that?"

Albert knew she had a dog, but he had assumed that it wasn't plural. "I was under the impression she had one."

Penworth chuckled, leaving his chair to pour himself another glass. He offered to Albert, and he shook his head, still drinking his first.

"She has two wolfhounds and seems to think it appropriate that both of them sleep indoors. Not to mention her horses. She has six of those. Are your stables even large enough to house her animals along with yours?"

Six horses. Two dogs. Albert felt his mouth open and close several times before a vision of her entered his mind's eye, and the numbers no longer became a concern for him. "I can always build larger stables, and as for her dogs, I can allocate a room should she wish for them to sleep indoors."

Penworth raised his brow, a wide grin lifting his lips. "Let me assure you the dogs are housetrained. Even so, what of Victoria? I would not like her to be tucked away in the country, away from town every season simply because you prefer your own company. I know we are friends, and I understand that you are not always comfortable in large crowds, but she is. You would not try to keep her here, isolated with only you for company."

"I will tolerate town if that is what she hopes for, but your assumptions are traveling a little too far ahead. I have not declared any intentions toward Victoria, and she hasn't in any way shown an interest in me in a romantic sense. I will breach the conversation with her, but not until I'm certain that there may be some hope for me."

"What will you do if she isn't looking at you with a romantic bent? Armstrong duped her before all society. Married her and fled within weeks of saying 'I do'. I fear such treatment may make others courting her difficult," the duke stated, finishing his second glass of whiskey.

"I shall be content to be her friend, as I have been, if not a very absent one." Not that Albert wanted to be such a benign gentleman to Victoria, but she was so vivacious, so different to his character, that the thought of them together even made his head spin at times.

Would they suit? That he did not know and could not say, but with her here a few days, he could gauge if there was a possibility for them. He certainly hoped that was the case.

Penworth stood, coming over to the desk and reaching out his hand. Albert shook it in turn. "Then I wish you well, my friend, and I'd be very happy should you secure my sister's affection. Victoria is a wonderful sister and will make a superb wife. You could not have picked better for yourself. Armstrong was a fool to have let her go."

Albert smiled, hope filling him at Penworth's words. Now he just needed to push down the little voice that told him he was imagining such a match and learn how to court a lady. And not just any lady, but the one for him.

Lady Victoria.

CHAPTER 7

The following day Victoria walked out onto the grounds of Rosedale, heading toward the lake where Lord Melvin was preparing two boats to go out on the water. The day was warm, the air fragrant, no doubt from the beautiful garden that grew off the terrace. She looked back at the house and saw that her mama was comfortably positioned on a small wrought iron chair in the shade of the wisteria, drinking tea and reading the morning's paper.

"Lord Melvin," she called out, waving to him.

He stood, waving back, and for a moment, she studied him. He was dressed in tan buckskin breeches and highly polished hessian boots. His shirt and cravat were highly starched, but the jacket seemed to make him appear casual due to his lack of a waistcoat.

Victoria had long thought him attractive, but seeing him outside of London, outside of everyone's grand home, there was something different about him. His casual appearance, his welcoming smile made her question keeping him as merely a friend. She had known him for several years, her brother's friendship with him had enabled that, but she'd never looked at him with anything but banality.

She hoped to find out if he were the famous writer Elbert Retsek. She wasn't here to try to win a husband, Paul had put paid to such absurd notions, but that did not mean there were not other things she could do. Other options open to her as a widow...

"Lady Victoria, I hope you slept well and enjoyed your breakfast."

Victoria had slept in late and had decided to break her fast in her room and had not seen anyone in the morning. "I did, thank you. The guest beds are very comfortable. I almost forgot where I was sleeping."

He smiled at her, placing two oars in the boat. "I thought we could go boating today if you wish. I have already asked your mama, and she said I might escort you over to the island."

Victoria glanced at the island, thankful it was not too far away, having never been too fond of deep water. Certainly not when attired in the dress and stays she currently wore. “You needn’t ask my mama for permission. I’m a widow, my lord. Have you forgotten?”

Lord Melvin cleared his throat, a blush rising on his cheeks. “No, of course not. I was merely being polite.”

She smiled, amused. “I forgive you. Now, what would you like me to do?”

“Ah,” he stammered, “I shall help you into the boat if you like.”

She strode over to the craft, pushing it into the water. She jumped in before it went too far off shore. "Are you coming?" she asked him. Lord Melvin chuckled, the sound gravelly and deep, and Victoria decided she liked the sound. It was warm and honest. So different from how the ton and its elite members often behaved. There had always been something about Paul’s laughter that she never trusted, never thought it quite genuine.

"Right behind you, my lady," he said. He jumped into the vessel, and it wobbled precariously for a moment or two.

Victoria clutched at the sides, not wanting to particularly go for a swim, not in one of her new gowns at least. Her mother would be cross for a week if she did such a scandalous thing. Lord Melvin grinned at her, taking up the oars, and soon they were rowing across the pond toward the island.

"What is over here?" she asked, looking over her shoulder at the tree-filled island. The banks were grassed, and it looked like his lordship's gardener also kept the island grounds well-maintained.

"Roman ruins, as a matter of fact. Quite the find many years ago when my grandfather was planting the oaks. They excavated the site and decided to leave them exposed. The trees, of course, were planted around the site so as not to disturb their history.

"How wonderful. I look forward to viewing them." A few rows farther and the boat scraped along the shore, and they were docked on the island. Lord Melvin helped Victoria alight, surprising her when he swung her up in his arms, carrying her to the grassy bank.

Victoria gasped, having not expected him to do such a thing. No gentleman ever manhandled her in such a way other than her husband and he'd only touched her for six weeks before moving on to someone else. Her stomach fluttered at his sweetness.

Lord Melvin was more unpredictable than she thought him to be, but then that should not surprise her, not really. If he was indeed the gothic romance author she adored so much, then he was well-versed in how to swoop a lady off her feet, keep her from harm.

"Thank you," she said when he set her down. Her hands slid down his arms, strong and surprisingly muscular. He had masculine hands too, some fingers callused as if he held a quill for long hours. She had never particularly liked men having soft hands, they had always reminded her of dandies in London. Paul had been a dandy. She should never have married him.

She glanced back at the house and saw Josh now in conversation with her mama. "You may call me Victoria, Lord Melvin. With Mama giving you leave to call her Sarah, I see no harm in dropping titles when we're rusticating in the country."

Pleasure crossed his features before he schooled his reaction. Even so, she had seen his joy. What an odd gentleman he was, possibly one of the most intelligent and clever she knew, and yet he blushed, stumbled on his words, and shunned social events—an enigma.

"I would like if you called me Albert in return, Victoria," he said, using her given name and making her miss a beat.

She smiled and took his arm, letting him lead her into the small forest and toward the ruins. Through the trees, she could see them now. Foundations really were all that was left. A stone wall here and there, cobbled flooring, but no mosaic. What a shame the ancient tile did not survive the centuries.

"We're here." He stopped them at the side of the ruins. They were rectangular in size and large.

"The family who lived here must have been powerful. The dwelling is quite large, and no doubt there would be others still unearthed, I would assume."

"You are right. My grandfather left those buried, and you can see the trees are planted away from the ruins to keep them preserved. He did not, however, take into account the root system of the Oak tree, and we have had a little damage over the past few years."

"Well," Victoria said, stepping down into the ruins. "At least you have tried your best. That is all anyone can do."

They strode about the space for a few minutes. Victoria kneeled down and ran her hand over a stone, rubbed smooth in a circular way at its center as if it were used for grounding flour or different foods. How wonderful that such things were possible to see even now, after all this time.

"This makes me want to travel and see all the wonderful historical sites around the world." She stood, coming back to stand near Albert, who was leaning against one of the walls, content to let her explore.

"I would like to travel one day. The world is full of adventures if one is game enough to step into the unknown."

She thought about his words a moment, unsure if he really meant such a thing. He certainly didn't appear to be a person who would enjoy travel, meeting new people, the disturbance of it all. "Are you certain that is true?" She ignored his raised brow of surprise. "May I speak plainly, my lord?"

He nodded, his eyes guarded. "Please," he said.

Victoria clasped her hands before her. Could his lordship be saying everything she wanted to hear, but believing none of it? After Paul and all his lies, it was difficult to trust anyone outside of her family. Believe anyone at their word. "For the past several years, I think I could count on one hand the number of times we've seen you in town. You rarely attend events when you are in London, and this house party has a grand amount of guests equalling three. One of whom you've been friends with since you were in short coats. I cannot help but wonder," she continued, "that you're nervous when around crowds. That the London season is too much of a crush, too chaotic for you to bear. And so, I also cannot believe traveling the world would be something you would enjoy. Would I be right in that estimation?"

His mouth opened and closed several times before he said, "You're very astute, Victoria. Is my bumbling about in society so very obvious."

"Not at all. You are a most sought-after gentleman when you do attend events, even if you stumble at times. You enjoy being here at Rosedale, and I can see why you do. The house and gardens are spectacular, but to leave it all, for months on end, travel and mingle as one does abroad, I do think you would hate."

"Oh no," he argued. "I would like to travel. Who would not, but I do see why you would think that of me."

"When one gets to know you, such as I do, as little as that is, one cannot help but pick up on nuances. I want to help you if you would allow it."

"You wish to help me? In what way?"

"I'm a widow, and with that unfortunate event, it also grants me some freedom that other unmarried ladies do not have. While I have no wish to marry again, I think you would like a wife. Is that correct?"

"I have always wished to marry, to have a family, fill my home with love. You think me a foolish romantic, do you not?"

She could never think him so. If only she had married such a man as Lord Melvin and not Paul. What a disastrous mistake and one she could never repeat. "With my guidance and help, my connections, I think I could have you wed before the end of next season. Find you the perfect bride. Are you willing to allow me to train you in the art of courtship? It could also help in building your confidence so you too can travel someday."

Lord Melvin stared out at the ruins a moment, mulling over her words. His lips pulled into a pensive frown. He had lovely lips, supple and the shadow of stubble along his jaw drew the eye. Oh yes, the women would be falling at his feet, panting with want after she was finished with him.

"Very well, we have an agreement."

"Excellent, then we shall start with lessons on how to make you a rake of the first water."

He frowned. "Is it not supposed to be diamond of the first water?"

Victoria waved his words away. "Never mind that, whatever it is, we'll have you prepared for next year's season in no time.

Even if you cannot find a wife, you will be more confident in crowds and open to conversation with people you have just met."

"You're only here for a few days. That will not be long enough, I fear, to help me."

"Leave that with me. I can ask for more time. If Mama thinks that I fancy you, she will want to stay. Not that I am," she reminded him, wanting the rules to be clear before they started. "Do not concern yourself. We shall have enough time."

Victoria wrapped her arm about Albert's, ready to return to Rosedale and to start their lessons. He glanced at her with a knowing look and already he appeared more roguish than she'd ever seen him before Her stomach fluttered. "Come, let us return to the house. We have much to do."

"Indeed," he drawled. "We do."

CHAPTER 8

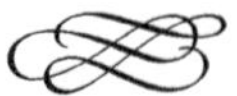

Albert waited for Victoria to meet him in the conservatory the following morning. After dinner the night before, she told him she wished to meet him in that particular room for some suggestions on making a woman more likely to swoon into his arms.

Whatever that meant.

He waited on the wrought-iron seat that sat against a matching chair and small, round table. His conservatory was aflush with flowers, scents, and even a couple of orange trees, a fruit that he enjoyed best.

The sound of slippered feet echoed out in the corridor, and he stood, bowing when Victoria entered the room.

She looked as sweet and natural as the plants surrounding them. Her soft-pink muslin gown accentuated her figure, and he wasn't without so many rakish wiles not to notice she filled her gown out in the most advantageous way. He may be a nervous, clumsy man, but he still enjoyed the sight of breasts on a woman, and Victoria had a lovely handful. He sighed. If only he would be the lucky chap to win her heart.

He'd conclude that with her helping him, it would at least

put him in close quarters to her, and maybe he could have a chance of winning her affection. Not that she saw him as anything but a clown in need of guidance to find a wife. To be more socially capable and travel without having to have his hand held.

"Good morning, Victoria." He took her hand, kissing it. She wore no gloves today, and he reveled in the softness of her skin and the sweet blush that stole over her cheeks.

"Good morning, Albert," she returned, taking back her hand and sitting down on the vacant chair at the small table he was occupied at before. "You are already showing an improvement to your gentlemanly wiles."

He joined her, throwing her an easy smile, while his innards were all a-twist. She did that to him. Made him as nervous as a virgin on her wedding night. What would she say should she know that he had never slept with a woman? He hated to think of such a reaction. Would she believe him? Or worse, laugh?

"I am trying," he replied, ready for his lesson.

"I thought this morning, while Mama is sleeping in, we could have our first lesson." She waved her hand around the conservatory. "This room not only smells divine, but it can also be a place for a tryst between couples. Not that I partook in one. Mr. Armstrong, before our marriage, was quite respectable, I must add for clarification, but the delicious scents, the beautiful outlook, the calming sound of the fountains, which you're lucky enough to have, all help in creating an atmosphere simply perfect for seduction."

Albert shifted on his chair, not realizing with all this talk of seduction from the very woman he'd love in his bed would make his body misbehave. Victoria certainly knew what she was speaking of and could help him. She had been married after all. Not in winning another woman, but winning her. If he found out what she liked, what made her swoon when a gentleman called, there was a chance he could court her, convince her that marriage to him would be so very different than her first.

"Go on," he urged, wanting to know more.

"If you were at a ball and happened to stroll with the woman you intend to marry, and I must stress this, you must not simply walk off to seduce anyone who takes your fancy. That will never do. I shall not like such underhanded, cruel actions toward an unmarried maid."

"I would never do such a thing," he promised, crossing his chest in the hopes that she would believe him.

She studied him a moment, her perfectly straight teeth biting her bottom lip in thought. Albert swallowed hard. Dear God, these lessons would be torture. "Very good. I'm glad you agree. Now, should you stroll into such a room, you may pick a flower, give it to the lady, tell her she is as sweet as the rose you gifted her, or whatever plant that takes your fancy."

Albert couldn't think of anyone he would rather stroll with than the woman before him. "Shall we try it now?" he suggested. “Practice makes perfect, do you not agree?"

Victoria stood, pulling him up to join her. "Oh yes, you are right."

They strolled for several steps, Victoria's arms entwined with his. "Let us pretend that you wish for me to be your wife. That we're at a ball, and you've been courting me for several weeks. Talk to me with what you think a suitor may say to the woman he adores."

Albert pushed down the nervous flutter at having to say anything romantic, especially to Victoria, whom he did, in fact, want as his own. What if she realized what he said was heartfelt? He would never get over the shame should she not want the same. Which from previous conversations, and rumor about town, she did not.

He cleared his throat. "A lovely night for a stroll. Thank you for escorting me here this evening. I know that you risk much by doing so."

She looked up at him, her eyes alight. "Hmm, very good, Albert. And I particularly liked how your voice sounded an octave lower than normal. A seductive quality that you didn't know you had, I would assume."

She would assume right. He hadn't realized he'd dropped his voice to a lower octave. "Have I mentioned how very beautiful you look this evening?" he continued, meaning every word. Even though Victoria was not adorned with jewels or an opulent silk gown, having her here at Rosedale in his arms, she was simply the most perfect lady he'd ever met.

"Thank you. You look very handsome too." She stopped and turned to face him. Victoria reached up to clasp the lapel of his jacket, her hand warm through his shirt and waistcoat.

Could she feel his heart beating madly in his chest? His mind whirled with what she was doing. Was this part of the lessons, or had his words had more effect on her than he thought they would? Shit, he did not know.

"A lady may touch you like this if you have been courting for several weeks. Even so, it would help if you did not give in to your urges. Remain the gentleman always, let the lady decide the pace of courtship."

Albert watched her lips move, but he heard very little. His body had a mind of its own, and all he could think about was kissing those sweet lips that were trying to help him.

"She may even try to lean up and kiss you. Whatever will you do then," Victoria said, leaning upon her tiptoes and placing her but a breath away from him.

His gaze dipped to her lips, and he realized he was holding her hips. "I would kiss her back."

"You could," Victoria said, stepping out of his hold, all business and teacher-like once again. "If you had been courting and you wished her to be your wife. If not, you should excuse yourself and remove your person from the room before you're embroiled in scandal."

The idea of their lessons, of what else she would teach him, made him long for more. The scandal could go hang. He wanted her back in his arms, her sweet lips tempting his.

"Tell me what else I should know when courting a woman. I must know all the secrets if I'm to marry a woman and keep her content."

They walked on, and Victoria picked a rose, handing it to him. "This is for you," she said, "as a token of my affection. You could say something similar. But you cannot send a letter or gift, flowers only. I would suggest keeping your time alone with any lady to a minimum, even with a chaperone unless you do indeed wish to marry her."

"I'm alone with you right now without a chaperone," he couldn't help but add, wondering if she had realized such a thing.

"Oh, that does not signify. I was married and there is nothing that will shock or insult my sensibilities. I think I'm well and truly immune to anything of the sort after Paul."

Albert gave her a half smile, but inside, disappointment stabbed at him. He'd love nothing more than to kiss her, to shock her sensibilities into wanting him. Being so close to her, the desire and need she wrought was unbearable.

"You must know that for me, courting a woman is difficult. I'm not equipped with the easy manners, the words that a lot of gentlemen have when flirting with a lady. I fear all of your lessons, your help will be in vain, Victoria." Especially since he did not want any other woman on his arm but the one beside him, precious in her attempt to make him more suitable to the opposite sex.

"They will not be in vain," she said, meeting his eye. "I'm determined to have you at your best, to show other ladies what I see in you. A lovely kind and attractive gentleman who is ready to settle into a life of domesticated bliss. A man capable and confident. I will not fail in my quest."

Albert pinned an easy smile to his lips as they walked out of the conservatory, but a weight sat atop his shoulders. He needed to figure out a way to use Victoria's lessons to his own advantage, not on others but on her.

CHAPTER 9

Later that day, Victoria sat in the upstairs parlor that Lord Melvin had given her mama to use during their stay. She sat, sketching one of her wolfhounds, Pickle, from memory, but her mind kept wandering to Lord Melvin.

As much as he was interested in her lessons for him, she could not help but feel that his heart was not in it. Did he not want to marry? Or perhaps he had loved another several years ago and lost her to another gentleman. How terrible if that were the case and he was cradling a broken heart all this time, and she did not know it.

It would certainly explain the heroine in his first book, should he turn out to be Elbert Retsek, who had been grief-stricken at the death of her betrothed.

"Darling, you're scowling most severely at the parchment. Your drawing cannot be so terrible that you would glare so," her mama mentioned, catching her eye over the top of her knitting. She was making little mittens for Alice's baby due in several months.

Victoria laid the sketchpad in her lap. "You know that I'm to help Lord Melvin be prepared to court a lady next season. He's terribly shy and awkward in social situations, and I mean to assist him with that floor. But I feel he's a little distracted. He thinks it will not work."

"While I think your motivations are honorable, do remember widow or not, to be alone with Lord Melvin during your lessons does not put you in a welcome light."

Victoria sighed, wondering when her mama would see her as a woman who had married and buried a husband. "Mama, nothing untoward will occur and I am not a virginal miss. Stop acting as though I am."

"Really, Victoria. The way you speak leaves me wondering if you had any lessons in manners at all growing up."

She grinned, knowing she often ran away whenever lessons were held. The thought of Albert flittered into her mind once more. Had she been searching for a suitable match after Paul, she may have considered him herself, but she had no desire to be anyone's property, not a second time. To trust and be so wrong with that gift was not an easy jump to make. The embarrassment she endured at Paul's affairs she had sworn never to subject herself to again. And she would not.

Not that she thought Lord Melvin would be so cruel to his wife as Paul had been. He was kind, honest, where Paul had been deceitful and ungentlemanly. A bastard through and through.

In the conservatory this morning as odd as it was, the idea of kissing him had entered her mind. He was a tall gentleman, fitted her own height well. His superfine coat tailored to perfection over his wide shoulders. His cutting cheekbones, his dark, hooded eyes that stared at her with such meaning that her heat had fluttered.

She shook the thoughts aside. He wasn't meant for her. That was not why she was here. He was meant for someone else, someone who actually wanted a spouse.

"Have you ever considered that Lord Melvin isn't interested

in any other lady? He did, in particular, invite you and your family to his estate." Her mother's knowing smile as she continued her knitting was worrisome.

Victoria frowned, having thought the invitation was due to friendship, nothing deeper than that. That they were now partaking in lessons, an idea suggested by herself, no, her mama was wrong. She shook her head, rejecting the idea. "No, he is not looking at me as a possible candidate as the future Marchioness Melvin. Do not be irrational, Mama."

"What is there to be unreasonable about? You're a duke's daughter, a sister to one. You are Lady Victoria Worthingham. There are not many men in London who would not seek such an arrangement."

"Except you forget I'm a widow to a man most of England despises since he's slept with half our acquaintances wives'. I hate that marriage is so sterile and formulaic. If I should allow a gentleman to court me again, I will only be induced into giving myself to him before God by the strongest, unbreakable love." All things that would never happen, for Victoria was determined never to allow herself to be seduced a second time into a bad match.

Her mama raised one disagreeable eyebrow. "You have been reading too many novels or listening to your sisters too much. While I wish for you all to make love matches, that is not always possible. And not all men are rakes and ravish their brides to be. You should not speak in such a way."

Victoria huffed out a breath, knowing there were no such men left in England. Her sisters had married all the best men in England.

She dismissed the thought as soon as she had it, knowing it for the falsehood it was. Lord Melvin was a good man, handsome and kind, and while he may not ravish a lady, curl her toes in her silk slippers, he certainly had the ability to, should he know what to do...

"Sorry, Mama," she said, hating to disagree with her mama. "But I'm sure you're incorrect. Lord Melvin is merely wanting company and thought to invite one of his oldest friends to his estate. Not that we'll be here long enough for me to train him in the art of courtship. We leave in under a week."

"Oh yes, that reminds me, my dear." Her mama placed down her knitting. "Your brother wants to extend it a month. Lord Hammilyn, a nearby neighbor of Lord Melvin, is having a ball, and there is a country dance at Camberley the week prior to this. Your brother wishes to attend both events, and Lord Melvin has welcomed us staying the few extra weeks."

The news could not be better, and Victoria masked the little squeal of delight at knowing they would be here and have events to attend as well. This would be the perfect time for Lord Melvin to practice all that she taught him in the art of courtship. She would have to double her efforts if she wanted to get him ready for a ball in a matter of weeks.

And, once she had his trust, and he viewed her as a close friend, as close as he viewed her brother, she would be able to ask him about his author life, should he be the man she hoped him to be.

"I'm more than happy to stay here at Rosedale, Mama. The house and grounds are beautiful. This afternoon Lord Melvin has agreed to accompany me on a ride about the estate."

"Hmm, has he, my dear." Her mama's lips pursed into another one of her *I told you so* looks before picking up her knitting once again. "Remember to take a groom with you."

Victoria stood, folding up her sketchbook and walking to the door. "I need to change for luncheon," she said, ignoring her mother's reminder of a chaperone once again. "I shall see you downstairs presently." She left the room, shaking her head and stepped directly into the path of Lord Melvin. She careened into him, her breasts pressing up hard against this chest, sending an odd sensation directly to her stomach.

His arms wrapped around her when she would have fallen. "I beg your pardon, Lady Victoria."

She steadied herself, ignoring the feel of his hands on her back, one on her hip. Or the fact she liked the feel of his hands on her. She shook her head, stepping to the side and out of his hold. Lord Melvin was her friend, possibly her favorite author in all of England. He was not marriageable material. No gentleman was when it came to her.

"It is I who should apologize. I was not looking where I was going."

"Are you going somewhere?" he asked her, his gaze dipping to her lips.

Unable to stop herself, she licked them and spied the muscles in his jaw clench and unclench.

Oh dear. Was her mama right? Did Lord Melvin like her more than just a friend? Did he harbor feelings for her? She hoped he did not. As much as she liked him, she wasn't looking for a husband. The idea revolted her after Paul, even if her sisters seemed so incandescently happy all of the time. She had not been so lucky in love as they had been.

"I'm off to change for lunch. Are we still on for our ride this afternoon?" she asked, hoping that it was so. She had not been on a horse for several days, and it was always refreshing riding about pleasant lands such as Lord Melvin owned.

"Of course, if you still wish to."

She nodded, excited at the prospect of being free for an hour or two. "I do." He stood back, seemingly unable to think of anything else to say. Victoria smiled and stepped around him, heading toward her room. He was so very unsure of himself all the time. They would need to work on that. Why he was so she could not fathom. He had friends. She knew that because Josh had mentioned it in years past. Not that he did much with them from all accounts. He was a man with everything at his feet, and yet to Victoria, he seemed lonely. She did not like that truth. It was time he came out of the shell he had cocooned himself within and live. And she was determined to make it so.

CHAPTER 10

They met at the stables where Albert had saddled a bay gelding, a good sixteen hands, and a steady horse, just as Victoria had asked for during lunch.

He liked the fact that she could ride, was competent and brave, no simpering miss. That she had requested when her mama was busy ordering a cup of tea by a maid that she did not wish to ride side-saddle, but astride, even more so.

Albert swallowed a curse, having thought himself prepared to see her dressed so. He was not. He shut his mouth with a snap, but could not avert his eyes as he should. The feminine figure on display, the long lean legs made a part of his brain think of the sexual positions book he'd been studying. He had never known a lady, a daughter of a duke to be so bold. She was marvelous.

He bowed, biting back his grin of appreciation. "My lady. Your mighty steed awaits you."

She sauntered past him, and he turned to view her as she went by. What was a man to do when a woman dressed in breeches? He could not help but appreciate the roundness of her curves.

Victoria did not use a mounting block. Instead, she reached up to hold the reins and saddle, lifting her foot high enough to enter the stirrup to pull herself up.

It was an impressive mount that even he sometimes found hard to manage. "Shall we be off?" he asked her, gaining his own seat.

"Where are we going? Is there anywhere particular on the estate you wish to show me?" she asked him, her snug riding jacket and the white shirt beneath accentuating her figure. She looked simply perfect, and his stomach clenched with nerves at having her alone for an hour or so.

"There are several fields that give a good prospect over the house and hedge groves if you wish to jump."

"I would enjoy that, thank you," she said to him, all politeness.

Albert led the way out of the yard, heading up toward the western side of the property and the highest points on his land. They rode in silence for a time, not because they were lost in their own thoughts, he at least, but because he could not make his tongue form the right words to say anything to Victoria.

He sighed, hating that he was unable to voice all that he wanted to her.

"Now that we're to be here for some weeks, I hope that you will let me continue our lessons on gaining you a suitable wife. A woman who will inspire sweet sonnets from your hands." She cast him a curious look. "Do you write at all, my lord? A way to a woman's heart is sometimes through the written word."

He glanced at her, knowing he could write several sonnets, sweet notes, and pages-long letters to Victoria if only she would let him. Words that would sweep her off her delicate feet.

"I do enjoy writing and reading. Are you a reader, Victoria?" he asked, wanting to move the subject away from him.

A small, knowing smile lifted her lips as she looked ahead. "I love to read. Gothic romances are my favorite."

At the mention of the genre that he wrote, Albert schooled his features lest she think he'd swallowed his own tongue.

"Any in particular?" Albert prayed she hadn't read his novels. The thought of the woman he wanted to be his wife having read his work sent a whole new set of emotions roiling through him. Fear, pride, but most of all the concern that she hated his books. Dear God, what if she loathed the author him. However, would he move forward with their plan knowing all the while that she hated his books? They were like extensions of him—his book children.

"I adore all the works by Elbert Retsek, but especially the third book in his Beuroguard series. The captain is swoon-worthy while also being quite the scary, forceful character. I would love to meet Mr. Retsek one day, but I doubt I ever will. What with him being such a recluse and wishing to remain anonymous."

Albert listened to her and fought not to crow. She liked his books. Lady Victoria Worthingham was an enthusiast of his work. Such truths were worthy of a few whoops, and arm waving. Instead, Albert smiled, agreeing with her wholeheartedly.

"I enjoy Mr. Retsek's work also," he admitted. As the Mr. Retsek, how could he not agree with Victoria's claim? It pleased him she enjoyed his writing. He strove to make each book better, more action-filled, suspenseful, and darker than the last, so to hear a reader say his books were some of their favorites warmed his soul.

"If only he would come out of the darkness and into the light. Share the joy he gives his readers and relish the accolades that he is worthy of. Do you not think?" she asked him, watching him keenly.

Albert wished he could step into the light as she said, but he knew he could not. It took all his consideration and effort merely to keep a conversation going with Victoria. The idea of going into a bookstore, of talking to readers, and God forbid, reading aloud from his words sent a shiver of horror down his spine. He was incapable of such an act.

"Maybe one day he will. We will both have to live in hope." As much as such a thought scared him, he wished he could be more outgoing and easy about people. He wasn't sure why he was the way he was, but he had to think some of his troubles stemmed from his father's bullying to both him and his mama. His father's death had been a blessing in the end. His years of verbal abuse had ended when he'd breathed his last breath.

"We shall have to, I agree."

Victoria was quiet a moment as they walked up toward the top of a hill that gave a great prospective of the house. "Do you think, should the opportunity arise, that you could ride in Hyde Park with a lady of your choice? Your conversation with me seems very easy. I think that if you relaxed, you could be just so with someone else."

Not that he wanted to be so with anyone other than the lady he was riding with right now. How to make her see him as a potential suitor when he found the words so hard to say. He supposed he could always write her a sonnet. A love letter...

"I would find it difficult, especially if she showed little interest in what I had to say or found my company boring. And anyway," he said, remembering her words from yesterday's lesson. "I thought love notes were frowned upon in society?"

"Society does not need to know everything." She wiggled her brows before taking in his lands with pleasure. "And you are not at all boring, Albert," she declared, sending him a scolding look. "Any lady would be overjoyed to have your affections."

You are not one of them, he wanted to add to his chagrin.

He doubted that many women even knew of his existence, marquess or not. "That is because you are my friend. I have known you for as long as I've known your brother. You are easy to speak with, and I like you more than most."

She chuckled, and he enjoyed the sound of her giggle. He wished to hear it more often. "You would do marvelous, I'm sure, given a little moral support, and that is what I'm here for. There is to be a country dance at Camberley and a ball at Lord Hammilyn's. We are attending both, and I hope to hear you will also. It is a ball in your county, after all. It would be rude not to attend."

He knew of the country dance at Camberley she spoke of. It was the very one each year he was invited to and never attended. Although he ensured the finest musicians came up from London to play for his neighbors and nearby townsfolk. "How could I refuse with you being there by my side." And maybe, if he could bring forth some dutch courage, he could ask her for another waltz and start his courting of a woman in earnest. Not just any suitable miss, but Lady Victoria Worthingham.

CHAPTER 11

Victoria stopped at the top of the hill and overlooked Lord Melvin's estate. The property was very pretty, almost as pretty as Dunsleigh, and she could see herself very happily situated in such a place.

Her deceased husband's estate had been near Blackpool in northwest England. The home had been adequate and large, well kept, but the landscape had been so very different to Surrey that Victoria knew she would rarely visit there. Hampshire, however, could capture anyone's heart, as it had hers.

The matrimonial road had not been a success for her, but that did not mean that Albert should be so unlucky. She wanted him to have love, friendship, and passion in his life. The ball would allow her to help him choose a couple of suitable ladies and perhaps dance with them. There was no reason for him to be worried about the event. She would not let anything happen to him.

"I shall have the ladies fawning at your feet by the end of the night, Albert. You shall be pleased with the results. I promise you."

His visage looked a little green and unsure, and she

wondered why the idea of such an evening made him so uncomfortable. She would seek out Josh and ask if he knew any particulars about his lordship, a little insight into his past that may help her with his future.

"Tell me what other courting particulars you're going to teach me to win a lady's heart."

Victoria thought about his question a moment. "I will impart the need to be confident, my lord. I'm going to speak plainly, as crass as that is, but some things need to be said." She cast a glance over her shoulder and took in account of how far away their groom was. Hopefully, far enough that he would not hear. "You are an attractive gentleman and a marquess. I stand by my promise of having you betrothed before the next Season."

Albert jumped down off his horse, striding to stand under a large oak. Victoria followed him, hoping she had not upset him with her forward words. She could sometimes be a little too presumptuous, bossy even. She did not want to offend.

"I have pushed you a little too much, have I not?" She caught his eye, reaching out to clasp his arm to make him look at her. "Are you angry with me, Lord Melvin?"

He sighed, running a hand through his hair and leaving it on end. The sight of him a little disheveled made her catch her breath. How was it that this man could not already be married? It was impossible to fathom.

"What should I do if the lady, at someplace and time, tries to kiss me?" he asked her.

Relief rolled through her that he wasn't troubled by her help after all, but of the particulars of courtship. "I kissed Mr. Armstrong on the night he proposed." Not that it had been life-altering. If anything, it had been awfully fast and very wet. A shiver of revulsion ran down her spine at the memory of it. "But before that I did not. It is not what is done." She chewed her lip in thought. "I will tell you this, my lord. My sisters had disclosed that they all kissed their husbands before they were married and say it is most enlightening and pleasant. I should think you may steal a kiss or two if you're set on marrying the one particular lady."

His lips thinned into a displeased line. "Your husband kissed you?"

She blinked, unsure where the conversation was headed. "Of course. I was married to him for six weeks before he hied off with his lover."

"He ought to die a thousand deaths for hurting you so. If I had you to kiss every night, no one could drag me from your side."

The breath in her lungs whooshed out at his words. Had Albert's voice dipped an octave or two, and why did the sound of his voice, his words make her feel odd and achy. "That is a very sweet thing to say."

He stared down at her, a dark and hungry light in his eyes that she was unsure the meaning of. "I have never kissed anyone. Pitiful, am I not?"

"Would you like me to be your first kiss, Albert? To practice on me before another lady, one whom you wish to marry, steps before you?" she added as an afterthought, reminding him she was the teacher here, nothing else.

"I would not presume that you would be a willing participant to my kisses." He stepped closer, and the heat of his body warmed her.

She raised her brow, wishing he had not said that. "I'm never marrying again, my lord. My situation in life, fortunately, does not state that I have to. But I would like to kiss you, no matter what you may think. You are my friend and I'm here to help. If you wished to kiss me, I would not refuse you."

The thought of kissing the handsome man towering over her was enticing. "Tell the groom to turn about and kiss me, Lord Melvin."

"John," he called. "Please, turn about for a moment."

The groom did as Albert asked without question.

She watched, transfixed as Albert seemed to will the courage through himself to kiss her. Victoria could feel herself shaking. Oddly she was a little nervous about kissing him. Once engaged, her husband-to-be had kissed her often. Never had she felt the bubbling up of expectation as she did right now. There was something different about the man standing before her, gaining his nerve that her husband never had.

You want to kiss Albert. The thought of kissing Paul was never exciting.

He wrapped his arm around her waist, pulling her against him. She gasped, having not expected him to be so bold. "Last chance, Lady Victoria," he said, dipping his head.

Victoria could feel herself leaning into him, willing his lips to touch hers. Heat coursed through her veins like fire at their first touch. His tentative lips urged and beckoned her to kiss him. It was neither wet nor fast, simply a slow seduction that spiraled her wits to the wind.

She wrapped her arms about his neck, touching the silky hair on his nape, liking the feel of it slipping through her fingers. His hands flexed, clutching tighter against her back, and the pit of her stomach clenched with need. A familiar ache that she recognized as desire. On the few occasions Paul had lain with her after their marriage, his bedding was thankfully much more skilled than his kissing.

Albert deepened the kiss, his tongue tangling with hers. Victoria flung herself into the embrace, wanting more kisses if this was how they were supposed to be. Wicked and delicious. Any wonder her sisters looked flushed and wistful around their husbands.

He moaned, reaching up to cradle her face, and the kiss changed. No longer slow and coaxing, but deep and demanding. Victoria kissed him with everything she had, reveling in the feel of him, his labored breaths, his arduous need. His hand splayed into her hair, sending multiple pins to scatter to the earth beneath their feet.

She cared naught for all of it. All she could think about was his kiss, their first kiss. How wonderful that she could have her first real, passionate kiss with a friend, a man she admired and cared for above anyone else. She closed the space between them, her breasts, her nipples, hard little peaks under her shirt and riding jacket. The feel of his chest teased and taunted, but she could not stop. She wanted more. So much more than kissing, and that in itself ought to give her pause, but it did not.

Albert could not get enough of Victoria. Hell, he'd wanted to kiss her almost from the very first moment he'd met her, and that was several years ago when he was still in short coats at Eton.

The woman in his arms, slender and yet womanly, tall and yet short enough that he had to lean down a little to kiss her. Long, soft strawberry-blonde hair was silky between his fingers. Her skin soft, her mouth pliant and willing and right at this moment, driving him to the point of madness.

He'd never kissed a woman before, hadn't known what to do when she suggested that she be his first. Would she think less of him if she knew all of his secrets? That he'd not only never kissed a woman but had never slept with one either. From watching the few friends he had over the years when they married, their wives were always quite satisfied with their husband's talents.

He would have none of the roguish experience that they did. Of course, he knew the particulars. He had read extensively after all, but doing the sexual act was another beast entirely.

But now, kissing Victoria, something told him that it wasn't something to fear, but long for. Her hands, clutching his hair, her breathy moans when he teased her soft lips with little nibbles and short kisses drove him to the point of madness.

Had he been a rake, a man of the world, he would know how to seduce her, bring them both to a pleasurable conclusion. With her a widow, such an interlude could be a possibility. But he did not know how to do any of those things or even how to go about starting such progress.

Albert kissed her hard, forcing his hands to remain on her hips when she surged against his hard cock. Stars burst behind his eyes, and he went to distance themselves. Victoria made a noise of annoyance, holding him firmly in place.

"Do not deny me," she said between kisses.

Albert forgot all thoughts of where they were. The fact that her brother the duke could too be out riding the grounds and could find them entangled. That the groom was merely a few feet from them. All forgotten at her whispered words.

The kiss turned savage. His body aflame with need, his cock so hard that he was certain he would come should she continue what she was doing.

They needed to stop. One of them needed to end this madness before they tumbled to the ground, and he fumbled his way into having her at the top of a hill with nothing but grass at her back.

He broke the kiss. "We need to end this. Now. Before it is too late."

She stared at him, her eyes wide and glassy with desire. She blinked several times before they cleared, and the woman in his arms was once again the sensible, intelligent Victoria he'd always known.

"Of course, yes," she breathed, stepping away. She checked her riding breeches and jacket before reaching up and pinning her hair back to rights. "Well, that was certainly a very good lesson, do you not think?"

Frustration shot through him that after such a kiss, a soul-shattering one such as the one they shared, that it would be termed a lesson. He stood mute for a moment, unable to form the words to reply.

"We should probably return to Rosedale." Victoria walked over to her horse and gained her seat without help.

Albert shook himself free of the melancholy that threatened his good mood and mounted too. "We shall go this way, it is a shorter way back, but the view is just as good as the one here on the hilltop."

She nodded, turning her horse and starting down the hill. Albert spun around in his saddle and noticed the groom waiting discreetly behind them, no sign on his visage that he judged them over what they had just done.

Which, by the looks of Victoria, was nothing at all. How on earth was he supposed to court her, even if she were not aware of such things, if she was so adamant that marriage was not an option she wished to consider.

He didn't want any other lady whom she would train him to woo. He wanted her, yet even he knew that she would not be an easy woman to win. She would take all his effort, his patience, and the wooing skills he possessed.

Which, unfortunately, were not many.

He kicked his mount on, following close behind Victoria as they snaked their way down the hill back to Rosedale. His mind a whirr of thoughts on how to win a lady who did not want to be won.

CHAPTER 12

Victoria lay in bed later that night, staring at the ornate painting on the ceiling. She had left her curtains open this balmy evening on some of her windows, allowing the cooling breeze off the lake to enter her room.

Her mind would not settle, and it was no wonder after the kiss she shared with Albert earlier that day. She had not particularly known how to act after it and so had dismissed the kiss as a good first attempt at teaching him to be a rake.

She'd never kissed a gentleman like that before, not even her husband while he was bedding her. Could they be soft and slow, a seduction of the senses? Or deep and demanding, taking her breath away and leaving her witless such as the one they shared? Paul's kisses had been awful, nothing like Albert's.

Victoria sighed. Albert had kissed her as if she were precious, as if he wanted to kiss her, not for teaching purposes, but because he wanted *her*.

She thumped the bed with her hands, hating that she did not know which one it was for Albert. Not that she should be mulling over their interlude at all, she reminded herself. She wasn't marrying Albert or any gentleman. The kiss was nothing special, and she was being a fool giving herself ideas that it was for Albert at least.

At this rate she was never going to fall to sleep. Throwing back the bedding, she reached for her dressing gown at the end of her bed and started for the door. A nice, hot cup of milk would do her. She could always ring a maid, but the house had been abed for hours now, and it would not be fair to wake everyone just because she could not sleep.

Victoria checked the hall, and not seeing anyone about, used her candle to make her way to the servant's stairs, knowing these stairs would come out directly across from the kitchens.

This time of night, she encountered no one about. The oven illuminated the kitchen, its bright, burning coals giving her light. She placed her candle on the long, wooden table and turned to the large dresser, finding the milk covered with a cloth to keep out any bugs.

She poured some into the pot, enough for a cup, and placed it on the top of the stove. A stool sat close by, and Victoria sat down, waiting for her milk to warm.

"I did not think a duke's daughter would know her way around the kitchen."

The male voice, familiar and welcome as the cup of milk encircled her, and Victoria stood, pushing down her absurd, enthusiastic reaction to Albert's appearance at the door.

That he was dressed in tan breeches and a shirt, his cravat untied and hanging loosely about his neck, only made him appear more handsome than she needed to think him.

He was not for her. No man was, never again would she be played a fool by a gentleman. Paul had cured her of any ideas of marriage after his treatment of her. She was an heiress, a widow who could direct her own life, go and do whatever she pleased whenever it pleased her. She did not need a husband tagging along, or worse, telling her she could not go or do such things.

But, oh dear, he did look very handsome, all disheveled and

rumpled. His hair appeared like he had run his hand through it several times since she saw him at dinner. Was he also thinking of the kiss, of what a mistake it may have been to tumble over?

Victoria calmed her worries, determined to be as confident and professional as she possibly could around him. He was her friend. They had an agreement. She would help him gain a wife, he would tell her he was the author, Elbert Retsek, marry another and she would go home with her mama and start her widowhood in earnest.

"I could not sleep and hoped a glass of milk might help me. Would you like one?" she offered.

He pulled up a chair and sat across from her. "No, thank you. I heard a noise on my way to bed and thought to come and investigate. I'm glad that we're alone. I want to talk to you about the kiss this afternoon."

Victoria willed the heat to dissipate from her cheeks at the mention of their embrace. She blamed it on the fire in the hearth instead. "There is no need to discuss the kiss, my lord. It was merely an instruction between friends on how you would kiss a wife. I will admit you did a very fine job of."

He cleared his throat, his eyes going wide. Had she shocked him yet again? She was known in her family always to speak her mind, to have opinions that not everyone wished to hear all of the time, and yet, such disapproval never deterred her. She simply persisted with her ways.

"I hope that our kiss has not discouraged you from helping me gain a wife. I would still like your help if you're willing to continue."

Relief poured through her like a balm. "Of course I'm willing to help still. In fact, we can pick up the lessons after breakfast if you would like. Perhaps we could meet in the music room. There is a pianoforte in there, and I would like to give you instruction on what to say and how to act when your particular young lady takes a seat to play for an audience."

His head cocked thoughtfully, and she hoped they could move forward from today. They were friends, after all. Surely male and female fellows could remain so, even after sharing such an intimate act.

"That would be most helpful."

The milk on the stove started to boil, and Albert stood, picking up a nearby mitten before clasping the pot. He poured the milk into her mug with care, not a drop spilled.

"Would you like sugar in your milk?" he asked her, placing the pot in the sink.

"No, thank you. The milk will be enough." She sipped her drink, watching him. "You are sure that you wish to take a wife, Albert? I do not want to force these lessons on you if you're not ready to settle down."

He sat again across from her, folding his hands in his lap, his legs a little parted in his ease of seating. "I am ready to marry. Out here in Hampshire, there isn't much to do most of the year, and the company would be nice. I also long for children to make the house sing with giggles and squeals. I cannot wait for those days to come."

Victoria found herself entranced by his words, his ideals. His future sounded so very pleasant, and once, maybe, there was a time she too wanted such things. Her first days of marriage had been lovely, but it wasn't long before disillusionment creeped into her world. The whispers of Paul and where he spent his nights, the spending, the not seeing him for days on end. Never again would she be a man's property, uncared for and treated like rubbish. Now she wished for adventure—independence above all things, a life of her own on her own.

"I hope you get your wish and with my help, maybe sooner rather than later. I may not teach you everything you need to know to gain a wife. Some things like today's kiss should never happen again. But most etiquette and proper conversation skills I can help with. And my connections, of course, while we're staying here with you in Hampshire, will help draw suitable ladies to your side."

He reached out, picking up her hand. He did not wear gloves, and her attention shifted to his arms, his rolled-up shirt-sleeves that gave her an advantageous view of his muscled arms. His fingers were long and warm, strong, and she shivered, remembering what they felt like against her back, holding her firmly upon his chest.

His eyes met hers, and as if in slow motion, his mouth lowered to her hand and kissed her fingers. She sucked in a breath, feeling his lips, the touch of his mouth against her flesh as if he had kissed her a second time on the lips. Her nipples beaded, and she became aware of how little she was wearing.

Oh dear Lord, what was happening to her? She could not react to this man. Albert was her friend, possibly her favorite author in all the world. She could not lust after him.

That would never do at all.

"I must go," she said, wrenching out of his hold and fleeing the room. "Goodnight," she said at the door, not waiting to hear his reply. Lord Melvin was starting to be a danger, and she needed to calm herself before she saw him again. His reply, husky and low, made longing rip through her. Damn it all, this plan of hers may have been a bad one after all, and she never had bad ideas. Ever.

CHAPTER 13

As agreed, they met in the music room the following morning. Albert walked into the chamber and steeled himself for spending some time with Victoria.

Alone.

She was the epitome of perfection. She stood gracefully beside an open window, the sheer curtains floating past the bottom of her dress, her hair up in curls, several loose and bouncing against her slim shoulder. As for her gown, it fell against her form in the most flattering of ways, revealing her luscious curves and bountiful breasts.

Albert should look away, should not be torturing himself with designs on a woman who did not want a husband, but he could not help himself. She was all that he wanted. He would play her game of instruction if only to win her heart with seduction if need be.

He cleared his throat, and she turned, the pensive, thoughtful expression immediately replaced with one of welcome, her smile warming the room even more than it already was.

"Good morning, Lady Victoria. I hope you slept well."

She nodded once, starting for the pianoforte where she sat on the leather stool. "I did, thank you. I hope you're ready for your next lesson?"

He joined her, leaning over the pianoforte and one that had been in his family since he could remember. "What is it you wish to instruct me on today?"

"Well, as to that. I wanted to talk to you about what you could do to offer help, show interest when the lady you are courting is taking part in a musical night or an impromptu concert after dinner."

Albert knew already what he should do. He knew everything if he were truthful. It was only with Victoria could he be relaxed enough to do what he ought as a gentleman. There was something about her that his soul found comforting, enough to stop his spluttering or his inability to speak at all. Women made him anxious, all but Victoria. She made him nervous. There was a large difference between the two.

"If your lady is called to play a song, you may escort her to the pianoforte, offer to help her with her music while she plays. If you're able, you may even offer to sing a duet with her."

All reasonable suggestions, not that he'd ever been able to do such things. During his first season, he tried to act the part of a marquess searching for a wife, being all gentlemanly and correct. He had offered to turn the music pages, had bumbled the page turn, and the music had ended on top of the lady's hands before falling to the floor.

He had stopped trying to play the part of an able-bodied lord after that.

Until Victoria, that was.

"Let us play a little game. I shall stay here and choose music to play—a duet. You shall come and offer assistance and sing with me. Let us practice to make you perfect when such an opportunity arises for you."

"Very well." Albert walked away and waited for Victoria to

settle herself at the pianoforte. Her music set out before her. He came back over to her, bowing. "May I turn the pages for you, Lady Victoria?" he asked her, his body clenching at the sight of her biting her bottom lip, playing a coy miss, not having expected a lord to ask to help her.

"Thank you, Lord Melvin. That is most kind." She looked up at him from under her eyelashes, and he could almost imagine this was real, that he was so suave and capable of pulling off such a triumph.

"Not at all. You play so wonderfully. It is an honor to help."

She dipped her head, but not before he saw the small grin on her lips.

Victoria started to play *For Tenderness Form'd in Life's Early Days*, the music flowing from her fingers as if the pianoforte were a part of her body, fluid and perfect with each keystroke. For a time, Albert lost himself in the music before her voice broke into song, and he knew what it was to hear perfection.

He joined her, his deeper baritone melding perfectly with her higher octave. His eyes met hers, and he read her surprise, having not known that he could sing. He could do many things. Just his inability to do them well when about the company of others was his issue.

Her lips broke out into a smile as their voices blended to a harmonious, delightful sound. He was thankful that he could sing, for it was days such as this one that he would forever cherish. Being here with Victoria, enjoying her company, turning the pages, and singing with her as if he were the epitome of gentlemanly behavior and breeding made bearing this rogue tutoring worthwhile.

In the book he was penning, he would include a scene like this one, mayhap have the villain in the story come in and ruin the harmonious playing and singing between two lovers.

Would Victoria guess when she read the novel that it was based on this very day? He had never wanted to be prominent.

The idea made him physically ill, thinking about meeting all the people who longed to do so. But would it be so bad if one woman knew who his pseudonym was?

The song came to an end, and with the turning of the last page, Albert could not tear his eyes from Victoria. Her eyes held his, luminous and large. Her lips slightly apart as if she could not quite fathom how in sync they had been.

"You sing beautifully, Albert." Her fingers slid off the ebony keys, settling in her lap.

He wanted to tell her that while he may sing in such a way, she was the one who was beautiful in all ways. A woman after his own heart. Hell, what was he thinking? After his heart? She had captured it a long time ago. If only he could capture hers.

"My singing is nothing compared to yours, and your playing. You are proficient at the pianoforte."

She stood, placing herself closer to him. Albert did not move, merely stared down at her. His stomach clenched, heat swirling in his gut. He wanted to kiss her again. Hell, he wanted to do a lot more than that, even if his virgin body did not know entirely what *that* involved.

Her attention dipped to his lips, and she leaned closer still. She was but a breath from him. Did she want him to kiss her again? He wished he was a rogue and able to make a choice, take what he wanted, but the small voice of uncertainty whispered against his ear, stopping him from taking her lips again.

"How wonderful that you played so well together." The sound of the Duchess of Penworth's voice at the music room door wrenched all thoughts of kissing Victoria away. Albert stepped back, bowing, while disappointment stabbed at him at a lost opportunity.

"Good morning, Your Grace. I did not know you were listening."

She smiled, but her eyes flicked to her daughter. Victoria stood silent, but a blush kissed her cheeks.

"I did not think you knew I was here." The duchess smiled. "Would you accompany me upstairs, daughter? I wish for you to help me pick a gown for our drive about Hampshire tomorrow. I assume we're still going to have the picnic."

"Of course," Albert said, remembering he'd offered to take them on a picnic at dinner the night before. "It does not look like it will storm any time soon. The picnic will be possible, I'm sure."

"Verry good. Victoria?" the duchess said again, pinning her daughter with a *follow me* look.

Albert watched them go, uncertain if the duchess had seen all that had transpired after their duet. She must have, or at least said she had heard the music but had intervened when she noticed their closeness.

Damn it, he did not want to get Victoria into a dispute, nor did he want them to leave early due to his carelessness.

He was so untutored in being a rake he did not even remember or think to close the music room door when they had entered.

Idiot.

Victoria closed the door to her mother's bedroom, steeling herself for the coming conversation, which she was sure would have something to do with the near-second-kiss between her and Albert.

Her mother walked over to the window and stared out over the grounds. "Please tell me that I did not almost walk in on you and Lord Melvin kissing just before?" Her mama turned to her, pinning her to the spot.

Victoria winced, wondering if she should lie or tell the truth and admit her mistake. The second one she was just about to make, not the first. Her mama did not need to know everything.

"You know that I am helping his lordship in gaining a wife. I was merely trying to help him navigate around a musical evening, how to woo a lady while helping her play the pianoforte. Be supportive of her as she plays. You caught us close, and I know what it must have looked like. But we were not going to do anything, Mama. Do not be so silly." So, it looked like she was going to lie to her parent. Better that, before they were bundled up in the carriage and returned to Dunsleigh before her instruction on Lord Melvin was complete. Or her finding out the truth of his life.

"If your brother had caught you, he would have demanded that you announce your betrothal. That is how it looked to me. Do not be forward, Victoria. After the dealings we've had settling your sisters, your marriage that I'm sure society will be discussing for years to come, so abominably did Mr. Armstrong behave, I do not think I could withstand another scandal. Please, if you are considering Lord Melvin as a lover, remain above reproach and ensure such trysts cannot be seen or come upon by anyone."

Guilt pricked her conscience, and she went to her mama, clasping her hands. "I promise, Mama I shall not do anything that will put me or the family name at risk. I am a friend of Lord Melvin's, that is all. With friendship comes a little intimacy, I find. I will not be caught in a compromising position." Victoria crossed her fingers behind her back, knowing that she would have to be extra careful after today.

What was worse was that she had done nothing but think about their shared kiss. Of his lips taking hers. What would happen if they did it again?

The sound of the luncheon gong echoed through the halls, and Victoria reached over and kissed her mama's cheeks. "I shall see you at lunch, Mama."

She fled the room, not entirely convinced her mother believed her words. But she would try, no matter how she responded to Lord Melvin when in his presence, to attempt to tame that part of her that wanted to push him a little. To see if he could be a rake with her as well to his preferred future bride. She would be a liar if she were to declare that a little flirtation with a handsome gentleman wasn't a lovely way to spend a day.

After lunch, she would seek Albert out for further lessons. There was under a fortnight to the country dance, and he wasn't yet ready. But he would be. She would make certain of it, even if she had to use herself as his prop for teaching.

Just as long as her mama never caught them again.

CHAPTER 14

Later that evening, Albert found Victoria alone in the library, a room he allowed guests, when he had them, that was, to use at their own leisure. It was not where he wrote, nor did it hold any identifying manuscripts that guests could see and link to him.

He frowned, thinking of the one page he had misplaced while at Dunsleigh. Had he left it on the desk in the library? The duchess knew that he had used the room. Surely she would know it belonged to him, but would she know what it was that he had left? That he could not say.

He strode into the room, pulling Victoria's consideration from the book she was bent over, a few wisps of her strawberry-blond hair covering her cheek. As he moved closer, he noticed that she not only had hair over her face but was chewing on the end of one curl.

His body hardened at the sight of her lips suckling on the golden lock. Oh dear God, she would kill him before he had a chance to use her instruction against a potential bride.

Not that he wanted anyone but her, but he was still to work

on the particular issue. First, he had to learn to be a rake, and then he could use his skills to win her hand.

"Lady Victoria, what are you reading?"

Her eyes went wide, and she started on the settee, looking past him as if to ensure they were alone. "Shut the door and lock it, Lord Melvin. My mama does not know that I am up, she thought I went to bed an hour ago, but I did not. I snuck in here."

Albert did as she bade, coming back to the chair. "What is it that you're reading?" he asked again, sitting.

She lifted the book, and he felt the blood drain out of his face. She had found the erotic etchings his father had purchased on his grand tour after graduating from university. The very one's he'd been reading for some months. For a moment, he could not speak. Did she think such drawings were his? The idea of such an assumption made his heart stop, and humiliation shriveled it up to a dried prune.

"How wonderful that you have this book. Look, the pictures in it are amazing, and I'm sure should you study them, you may learn the ways of a woman. Become a wonderful lover."

He cleared his throat, stupefied at the image she studied. A man and woman, entwined, but not head to head, it was head to toe, except they were not suckling each other's feet, but their genitals.

He'd seen the book, had looked at it before his first season, and had thought it marvelous, not that he'd had the ability to become rakish as the men in the book depicted.

"It was my father's. He's had it since he was a young man."

"What do you think they're doing here?" she asked, turning the book this way and that.

"Having sex without intercourse," he said bluntly. She looked at him, the light in her eyes curious, and he willed himself not to ask her if she'd like to do such things with him. Had she never experimented with her husband? Possibly not, since the fool found comfort in everyone else's bed except his wife.

Damn, he would adore to have her so.

He ought to study the book more and learn the way of a woman's body and know what to do with his mouth and cock when the time came. The idea of leaving a woman unsatisfied was almost as bad as not knowing his own name.

She turned the page, and the image made her gasp, a sweet sound that went directly to his throbbing cock. The man, this time, was going down on a woman, her legs spread wide, her face contorted into a vision of pleasure. Her arms clenching the bedding, maddening even to look at visually.

"Well, I say," she whispered, shifting a little on the settee. "What do you think the woman gets out of such interactions with her lover?"

Albert had taken himself in hand, knew pleasure, even if he had never found it with a woman. "She would climax from his kiss there. He would suckle and kiss her with his lips and tongue, bring her to a peak of pleasure that is one of life's greatest gifts."

"Married as I was, I still did not know any of this was possible." She stared at him, her tongue darting out to lick her lips. "Have you ever found such gratification in this way with a woman?"

He closed his eyes, willing himself for strength. "No."

She narrowed her eyes. "With yourself then?"

He nodded, unsure how much he should tell her. The conversation was already scandalous, and should her brother even hear of them speaking so, widow or not, they would be before a priest before the crack of dawn.

Which, in Albert's opinion, would not be so bad. As for Victoria, she would feel managed, pressured, and would hate him for it. If she were to marry him, it had to be of her own fruition.

"Yes, it's possible for both men and women."

Her gasp of breath was just audible, and his stomach clenched, the need to taste her lips, suckle her mouth as much as he wanted to do such things to other parts of her body burned through him. As a man, surely it would not be so difficult to learn how to seduce a woman. He was comfortable with Victoria, hell, they had already shared a kiss, and that seemed as natural as breathing.

He wanted more of the same. But how to make her see that he was more than just a friend one could be honest and open with. The man for her, if only she would see him.

Victoria turned her attention back to the book, flipping the page over to a new drawing. Albert swallowed hard. The image was of a woman, on her knees and hands, the man thrusting into her from behind.

Again the woman's face was contorted into one of pleasure, the man's also, showing enjoyment.

"You cannot tell me that this is a position that a couple would partake in." Victoria studied the image, turning the book this way and that. "I do not think this would feel very enjoyable."

She was literally killing him. As a man who had never laid with a woman, to want one as much as he wanted Victoria and have her speak of sex, studying images of the act was torture.

His cock was erect, weeping, and damn it, he wanted her to touch him. He wanted to bend her over the settee where they now sat and take her in such a way until they both found release.

"From what I understand, that act is possible and enjoyable for both."

She glanced up at him, her eyes widened. "You speak as if you are unsure." She stared at him, her eyes narrowing. "Are you a virgin, Albert?"

Should he tell her the truth? Something told him that Victoria held the truth in high regard, and it would do him little favor if he were to lie to her. And there was no shame in being a virgin. If anything, he ought to pride himself on the fact that he hadn't squirted his seed all over London with abandonment.

"I am indeed a virgin. Does that shock you?"

She bit her lip yet again, and his attention snapped to her lips. They were so close on the settee he could feel the heat of her body, the sweet, flowery scent of her hair. He wanted to run his fingers through it. Hell, he wanted to do a lot of things. Kiss her soft, supple skin along her back while he took her just as the image before them depicted.

"No," she said, shaking her head. "I like it that you are."

Albert leaned forward, needing to taste her, wanting her with a need that surpassed the nervousness that usually accompanied him whenever he spoke to a woman. With Victoria, conversation, silence, everything was easier, and he wanted to kiss her again. Had since the moment their last one ended.

CHAPTER 15

Victoria wrenched herself out of the chair. The tome depicting numerous sexual positions thumped onto the Aubusson rug. She stepped back from both Albert and the book, needing space.

"I should probably return to my room. I shall see you at breakfast. Goodnight Albert."

He looked up at her with such longing, such need that her stomach fluttered and clenched with delicious expectation. When they had been discussing the book, her body had not been itself. A maddening thrum between her legs tortured her, a longing she'd never felt with Paul.

Strange ideas of him kissing her at the apex of her thighs, of holding his dark locks in her hands as he pleasured her would not abate.

He stood and bowed. "Goodnight, my lady." He bent down and picked up the book, always the gentleman. Not pushing her for what they both desired. And God help her, she wanted him to kiss her again. A fact that was utterly perplexing since she was determined to remain alone for the remainder of her life. Enjoy her inheritance, her widowhood, travel, and live.

But what is life without pleasure? a little voice teased.

She dipped into a quick curtsy and fled the room. Albert had said that a woman could give herself pleasure. Was he correct? Paul had never stated as much to her, but then when it came to her late husband, he often kept her in the dark.

Victoria could not make her room fast enough, and she locked the door to ensure privacy. What did he mean by that statement? She had never found much interest in herself before, not in that way at least.

She pulled the bedding back and climbed under the sheets, lying and staring up at the darkened ceiling. More research was needed on the subject before she could determine if that were true.

The following morning Victoria ordered a bath and sent her maid downstairs to press her morning gown for a second time. She locked the door and asked not to be disturbed, determined to learn her body more before she confronted Albert of his claim.

She slipped into the bath, sighing at that feel of the warm, fragrant water. Finding the cake of soap, Victoria washed, running it over her beasts. They were large, and she couldn't quite fit one in each hand. Men normally did take in her bust size, but she had always ignored the admiring glances. That was until Albert looked at her. What was it about the man that made her body question all her choices? Her plans for her future.

Her thumb and forefinger slid over her nipples. They peaked under the water, and she squeezed a little, imaging Albert's hand touching her so. Heat licked between her legs, and she lay her head back, closing her eyes.

For all his awkwardness, there had been none present last evening in the library. If she did not know him so very well, she would have imagined him a rake, seeking to seduce.

She slipped one hand over her flat stomach, soothing the need that thrummed between her legs. The thatch of curls tickled her fingers, and she touched herself there. But what was she supposed to do now?

Victoria frowned, placing her hands on the edge of the bath and tapping her fingers along its side. Annoyance ran through her that she felt as though she needed to do something, but what? All her interactions with Paul had been quick and in the dark. A lot of panting, on his behalf, a groan or two and then it was over. He certainly never fondled her with his hands or his mouth as the drawing she'd seen depicted.

Finishing her bath, she stood and dried herself, letting her maid back in to help her dress. She slid on the light muslin gown of mauve before starting downstairs, determined to find Lord Melvin and discuss this pleasure one could have without a bedpartner.

If she were to remain unmarried for the rest of her days, having satisfaction would be a boon she had to have.

Albert heard the determined strides of Victoria long before he caught sight of her. His heart stuttered at the vision she made, her mauve gown accentuating her delectable form, just made for petting and kissing. Her voluptuous bust that he wanted for himself, to suckle and feast upon.

How could she want to remain unmarried when he could make her life fulfilling and enjoyable if only she would allow herself to fall in love? Place her trust in another, but this time, a genuine gentleman such as he.

He was working in a small room at the back of the house that guests normally overlooked. It had used to be his mother's sewing room due to the large windows, but he had now taken it over as a smoking room, although he never partook in such activities. Preferring to sit and read or plot his books when the muse struck.

As it had this morning after last night with Victoria in the library. His next release would be much steamier than his last, and no doubt get the ladies' hearts fluttering and the men's cravats too tight.

"Here you are. I have been looking all over for you."

He smiled up at her, gesturing for her to sit. "Good morning, Victoria. I hope you slept well."

She closed the door, the snip of the lock loud in the room. His body tensed at the determination written across her features.

"No, I did not. I need to know what this pleasure is you speak of that a woman can find. I know this is utterly inappropriate, but nothing that I tried this morning brought me any such thing. Paul certainly did not arouse me in such a way so the idea of bringing oneself to satisfaction is questionable. You must show me what you mean."

Albert choked on the tea he had been sipping. He coughed, bending forward to try to gain his breath and his senses.

"You want me to what?" he wheezed, trying to clear his lungs of his beverage.

"You need to show me pleasure that I can perform myself. I'm certain I'm doing something wrong."

He felt his mouth grow slack while his cock tightened. "You know that I cannot do that."

"I know no such thing," she said, raising a defiant brow. "I want you to touch me and show me. I'm not a virgin nor a debutante taking her first turn, need I remind you. I'm quite determined."

And frustrated if he could read her at all. How much had she petted herself upstairs to place herself in such a state? Much to his shame, he had gone to bed and taken himself in hand, imagined her atop him, riding him, taking her pleasure.

He'd never come so fast and hard in his life.

"And if we're caught, are you accepting of the consequences of us dallying with each other? It would mean marriage, Victoria. It would mean your life of independence would be over."

She paced before him, debating his words for several moments before turning back to look at him. "I'm willing to take that risk. And I imagine marriage to you may not be so very boring if you allow me to do what I want."

He barked out a laugh, but all the while knowing he'd do whatever she wanted if it meant that he could have her as his.

"Where do you wish to start?" The words slipped from his mouth. He could not be about to do this. It was scandalous behavior.

She came over to him, pulling him from his chair. He stared down at her, amazed that by merely being beside her his blood quickened.

"Wherever you wish, so long as I find release."

Albert could not believe what she was saying. This could not be true. The one woman he longed for, wanted in his bed, to be his wife had not just asked him to make her climax.

He wished he knew exactly how to gain that ultimate end for her, but he did not. Nor could he ask his closest friend, her brother, how to manage it.

Damn it all to hell. He was literally living a nightmare caused by his own ineptitude.

"What are your thoughts on starting at the beginning? I fear if we do too much too soon, you may flee."

She shook her head, her chin rising defiantly. "I will never run away from something that I want."

Albert swallowed, thinking back to the books he'd read. Kissing was a good start, and they had already done that, and the act had been enjoyable. He would start there and move on from that position.

He brushed his lips against hers and she sighed into the

embrace, soft and willing. Her tongue teased his lips, and he deepened the kiss, tangling his with hers, searing the feel of her into his mind forever. Her hands clutched at his lapels, no fear for what they were about to do, only passion.

They certainly came together with exquisite ease. How was he to rein in his desires when he wanted all of her? Marriage and a future. Hell, he'd welcome being caught if only it meant they would become man and wife.

All rational thought dissipated when he felt her hand atop his, pulling it from around her waist and placing it on her most private of places.

Albert stilled, breaking the kiss. "Victoria, this is too much. Too soon."

She shook her head. Her lips reddened and swollen from their kiss. "Touch me, Albert. Touch me here where I ache," she whispered.

It was all it took. Her plea and he was lost.

CHAPTER 16

Victoria wasn't sure what had come over her, but what she did know was that she wanted Albert. She needed his touch, craved this sought-after release that the images teased them with. If she could find release by learning how to bring it onto herself, life would be so much sweeter.

It was scandalous of her. Her mother would never forgive her if she brought disgrace down upon all their heads, but she could not pull together the necessary caution to stop.

Albert's demanding kiss stole her wits. He was so very different to how she had always viewed him.

It was in one word... *Delicious.*

He kissed like a man starved. His little murmurings of pleasure, of need, spurred her to mimic him, kiss him back with all that he made her feel.

And it was quite a lot.

Her body was aflame. Her cunny was wet and weepy. She moved his hand from around her waist and placed it over her breast. The sensation made her knees tremble, and before she knew what was happening, Albert had scooped her up into his arms and sat on a nearby settee, placing her firmly across his legs.

Their tongues continued a dance of desire, seeking, teasing. His fingers ran along the top of her gown, teasing her flesh. Little goosebumps rose on her skin before he dipped one finger beneath her bodice.

She gasped, clutching at him as the pad of his finger grazed her nipple, taut and longing for touch. The sensation was wonderful and she wanted more of it.

The term greedy would suit her very well right now.

"That feels so wonderful." She pushed boldly into his hand like a cat after a pat.

"I ache to touch you." He kissed her cheek, jaw before moving down her neck, suckling at her earlobe. It tickled, and she giggled, undulating on his lap.

"More, Albert," she admitted, meeting his eyes quickly before he dipped his head to her neck, his lips sending a shiver of delight up her spine.

"I know that you do." He kissed his way across her bodice, his hands at her back, working the buttons on her dress. Within a moment or two, the gown gaped at the front, and Albert used the opportunity to push the bodice down, exposing her breasts.

Heat kissed her cheeks, even though she wanted him to see her. Wanted him to kiss where his finger had just teased. But she'd never been with a man that she had not been married to. As liberating and scary as that truth was, she did not stop him. Instead, she forced herself to relax and enjoy what was to come next.

Albert bent over one breast, his tongue flicking out to tease her pink, beaded nipple. Victoria clasped his face, holding him captive so he may never stop.

"Oh yes, Albert. More..."

His tongue flicked at her puckered nubbin before he covered her with his mouth and suckled. The sensation spiked need between her legs, and she barely bit back a moan. She squirmed on his lap as his mouth lathed and teased her until she could stand it no longer.

"The other one, please," she implored him.

He pushed her down onto the settee, covering her. Albert took little time in pulling the gown down to her waist, exposing her fully.

"I have admired your breasts for some time. I could kiss them forever," he admitted.

Victoria enjoyed the admiration, reaching back and holding the settee armrest, flaunting herself to him with little embarrassment.

There was no time for awkwardness. Not anymore. Not when she knew he could make her feel alive. Something she had not felt for years.

"I am yours to do with as you please," she declared, her voice huskier than she'd ever heard it before.

Albert groaned, coming over her. Their lips met, held, and he took her mouth in a demanding, punishing kiss. Their tongues meshed, teeth mashed as the kiss turned wanton.

And then he was gone, his mouth over her second breast, his free hand teasing and kneading her other.

Victoria moaned, her body not itself. He teased her toward something that she'd never experienced before. It remained aloof, close, but not quite there.

"Melvin? Are you in there? I'm looking for Victoria, but I cannot find her. Have you seen her about the house?" The handle of the door rattled as Josh tried the latch several times. "Melvin? Did you hear me?"

They both stilled at the sound of her brother's voice. Albert moved first, wrenching off her and dragging her from the settee before she could fathom what was happening.

"Turn about. Your gown needs to be put to rights," he whispered, physically turning her and pulling up her dress, his fingers working madly on the buttons of her gown.

"I won't be a moment," he yelled out to Josh. He turned her back around, cringing at the sight of her hair. Victoria reached up and realized several pins had fallen out.

"You need to hide." He looked about the room. Victoria did too but could see nowhere that she could remain hidden.

"In the window, there is a little ledge. Sit on that, and I'll cover you with the curtain."

She looked at the window. The ledge, if one could call it, was extremely narrow. "I do not think I will fit in there."

He ushered her over there, securing the last of her buttons as he did so. "You will." He pulled the curtain aside, helping her to sit on the seal, before he wrenched the curtain past her face, blocking her view from the room.

Victoria huffed out an annoyed breath, both because she was being hidden away but also because when she had entered this room, she had needed Albert. Now with her brother interrupting them, she was even more in need since they had not finished what they started.

She glanced down at her gown, correcting it more when she heard the lock of the door give way before it was opened.

Victoria recognized her brother's footsteps, holding her breath as he walked in and about the room, his steps coming too close to the window. She held her breath, expecting at any moment for the curtain to be wrenched aside, her brother's disappointed visage staring back at her.

"I do believe I saw Lady Victoria head out into the gardens after breakfast. Should we head outdoors and see if she is still taking the air or is on the terrace?"

For a man who prided himself on honesty, and there were no falsehoods when it came to Albert, he certainly knew how to fib very well. Had she not known the truth, even she would have believed such tales. Her brother did not reply straightaway but continued to walk about the room with a casualness that made her armpits damp. Did he suspect she was in the room? Is that why he had not left yet?

"The garden, you say?" Josh said, his footsteps determined once more, and headed toward the door. "Let us go and fetch her then. Mama wishes to leave soon for the picnic."

"Of course," Albert said, closing the door and leaving her alone.

Victoria bit her lip, having forgotten that they were to go for a carriage ride before lunch and picnic somewhere on Albert's estate afterward.

Retreating footsteps sounded down the hall, and Victoria took the opportunity to escape, leaving through the back of the house and using the servant's stairs to make her room, just as her mama came to fetch her.

"Ah, you're back from your walk. Very good, shall we go? I believe the carriage will be brought around soon."

Victoria picked up her bonnet and cardigan, forgoing the shawl, and followed her mama. She breathed a sigh of relief as they came downstairs, into the foyer just as her brother and Albert came in through the front door.

"Ah, there you are, sister. I have been looking for you."

"Not very well," her mama said, throwing her only son a warm smile. "She was in her room."

Her brother opened his mouth as if to say something but then thought better of it, holding out his arm to escort them to the carriage. "I must not have looked very well at all. Shall we?" he asked throwing Victoria a pointed stare.

Victoria dared not meet her brother's eye or look in the direction of Lord Melvin for fear of giving herself away.

She did, however, feel the heat of Albert's gaze burning down her spine as they made their way outside to the awaiting vehicle.

It seared her just as his touch had.

CHAPTER 17

They traveled a mile from the estate and stopped on the opposite side of the lake to Rosedale estate. Here they had a picturesque locality that ensured a better view of the Roman ruins that sat on the island on the lake.

Two footmen stood beside numerous blankets set out on the grass under the shade of an oak tree. The day was warm, with only the smallest bit of wind. As they made their way to the blankets, Victoria was thankful for the shade the old oak cloaked them in.

Albert and her brother talked incessantly about London, their estates, and improvements both of them wished to do over the coming months away from town. Not that Albert should have issues arranging repairs about his estate or on the tenant farms, for he rarely left Hampshire as it was. A gentleman was always accessible to his staff and farmers.

Victoria sat across from Albert, watching him, and knew that her mama watched her, but she no longer cared. The man intrigued her, and after his kissing and petting earlier today, she realized he quickened her blood like no other before him.

She turned her attention to the servant who opened the carriage door, helping her alight. They strolled to the blankets and sat, Victoria taking her time to set out her dress. Another odd thing for her to do. She'd never before wanted to impress any gentleman, but again, Lord Melvin made her preen.

It was utterly ridiculous since she had promised herself a future that included no husbands. No ties or children clinging about her skirts.

Paul had cured her of that absurdness, no matter how lovely Lord Melvin was turning out to be. Or how wicked his kisses.

She bit back a grin as Albert came and sat beside her, his warmth and presence making her stomach flutter. She cast him a look and found him watching her, his heated gaze warming her skin.

Her brother cleared his throat, passing her a glass of champagne before taking his seat with them all. The servants passed plates of food of cold meats and cheese, bread and tarts.

"There is a strawberry field just beyond, and also an olive grove that my mother planted during her first years of marriage. She had traveled to Italy as a child and enjoyed the little fruit. You're welcome to explore if you would like."

Her mother held out her hand to her brother. "Help me to stand, my dear. I should like to see the olive groves. I have heard of your mama speak of them at balls and parties and have long wanted to see what they were about."

Albert chuckled, the sound deep and gravelly. Had he always sounded so very handsome before? Could a voice be termed in such a way? After today, Victoria had to admit that it was possible.

"Would you care to join us?" Josh asked them.

Victoria shook her head, popping another lemon tart in her mouth. "No, I would prefer to stay here in the shade. You go on. We will watch you from here."

Josh glanced at Albert, his eyes narrowing a little before turning and escorting their mama toward the olive trees. Was that a warning that passed between her brother and Albert? Maybe Josh had suspected her in the smoking room earlier today after all. She started when she felt Albert's hand cover hers, linking their fingers.

"I'm sorry that we did not get to finish what we started." His dark-blue eyes held hers, and she was powerless to look away. However was she to deny herself him when he was so very desirable? This was a complication in her life she had not planned on. Widow she wished to remain, but never a wife and she knew Albert would not abide having her as his mistress. "I long to be alone with you," he whispered.

Victoria took a calming breath. The memory of his hands, of what he had been doing to her before being interrupted, taunted her needy self. There was something serious misplaced within her. She could not turn into a wanton. Only lightskirts acted so, but here she was, a duke's daughter who could think of nothing but having Lord Melvin's clever mouth on her breasts, kissing and petting her aching flesh.

"Tonight, where should we meet?" She moved his hand to hide under her skirts, glancing behind her to see where the footmen were, happy to see they were over near the carriage taking their luncheon repast.

His eyes darkened, the muscle in his jaw clenched as she slipped his hand over her leg to her aching core, pushing him against her. Her dress hid most of what they were doing, but it could not hide her face, nor Albert's. Their ragged breathing, the need that shone in his eyes that she knew hers replicated.

He pushed against her, and she gasped, closing her eyes. Her body ached, thrummed, and she would do anything to be alone with him. Excited to see what else they would do when they were. She longed to be away from prying eyes so he could give her what she wanted.

"Oh," she gasped. He teased her in a circular motion. She longed to lie back upon the blankets, to open up to him, to let him have his way with her. So this was what she should have been doing with her hand in the bath...

How wonderfully wicked it would be when they could finish their interlude.

Albert could not stop, nor could he tear his hand from her cunny. Damn it. He was surely going to hell touching a lady in this way—his friend's sister. The duke would call him out, and rightfully so should he catch them. They were walking a fine line of both scandal and desire. He watched Victoria with something akin to awe. She was so beautiful, so innocent, and utterly reckless. He'd always known she had a little rebellion in her blood, but this... Taking his hand and placing it against her sex floored him.

She utterly spellbound him, and he wanted her.

A virgin he may be, but after being around her, he was starting to think that having sex, taking pleasure from each other would not be so hard after all. It was more natural than unnatural, especially when it was with a woman one desired more than anyone else in the world.

The sound of the duke laughing in the olive grove pulled him to his senses, and he moved away, fisting his hands in his lap. Not only to keep them off her person but to stop anyone from noticing his erect cock straining against his breeches.

"Meet me in my smoking room tonight as you did today," was all he said as Victoria's mother, the duchess, and brother rejoined them.

Thankfully they did not move back toward the carriage for some time, content to finish lunch and the two bottles of champagne his cook had chilled and packed for them. Victoria stood and, taking her mama's arm, strolled about the area, looking at the olive grove herself.

Josh studied the champagne in his hand, a quizzical frown on his brow. Albert schooled his features, hoping that he did not suspect that he was overstepping his bounds with his sister. Which he certainly was doing. And tonight, would even more so.

"How is your courting of Victoria progressing? It seems she likes your company better than most. Why, before I left London when Armstrong's courtship had just begun, she never showed much emotion with the chap." The duke lay down on the blanket, watching his sister and mother promenade. "With you she's all smiles and laughter. A shame that Armstrong was not able to keep his cock in his own breeches. What a gem he lost the day he overstepped his bounds."

To be a duke's daughter and be cast off for a maid, was not something that was done to someone so high on the peerage ladder. Victoria did not deserve such treatment. No one did.

"She sees me as a project, I believe, more than a possible husband. I will continue to try and dissuade her of that ideal in the coming weeks."

"So long as your persuasion is chaste, I wish you well with your endeavors. But I will not have you use her for your own misdeeds, Melvin. Victoria is my sister, and I will protect her at any cost to others."

Albert swallowed. Friend or not, the duke would not take kindly should he find out what they had done already during their "tutoring". It was anything but a game for him, but for Victoria, he was not as certain. To her, he believed she still saw him as a little fun, a gentleman to help her gain her wants and desires and nothing more.

Even knowing this, he wanted her to have feelings for him, both physical and emotional. She was such an independent, strong woman and would be a well-fought-after and victorious lady to catch should he secure her heart.

"My intentions are honorable, I promise, Your Grace," he said, meaning every word. As for Victoria's intentions being so, he was uncertain at this moment. But time would tell, and he would either end up with the woman he adored, or he would be sporting a very broken heart that he feared would never recover.

CHAPTER 18

Victoria bathed and dressed for bed later that night, wishing her mama and brother goodnight before locking herself away in her room. She had taken a silly risk this afternoon on their picnic. When she thought about what she had done, she still could not believe she had taken Albert's hand and placed it on her person. And not just anywhere on her body, but between her legs.

She slumped down on the settee before the fire in her room, glaring at the flames licking the wood. It was all Lord Melvin's fault when she thought about it in truth. He had left her in a state of need, more than she had when she'd come to his silly smoking room the first time.

When she could not find this pinnacle by herself, well, she had little choice but to make him find it for her.

She pursed her lips, wondering if it were late enough and if her family would be asleep by now. Josh had departed for the local town to try out the tavern and had attempted to persuade Albert to join him. Thankfully the marquess had cried off, stating he needed to catch up on some paperwork, but wished her brother a good evening.

Victoria stood and crossed to the door, impatience nagging at her. She slipped a dressing gown on and slippers and cracked the door open just a bit. The hall was dark. No candle burned in any of the sconces or candelabras. Only a small, flickering light illuminated from under her brother's door. Victoria made her way through the house, memory guiding her this time before she came to the smoking room door. Checking once again that she was alone, she looked up and down the hall and could see no one. Stealing into the room, she closed the door quickly behind her and found nothing. Not even Albert.

She frowned.

Where was he? No fire burned in the grate, and the room was dark, save for a little moonlight that stole through the windows.

Victoria called out to Albert, or whispered more like, but there was no response.

Had he reneged on his own plan and decided not to come and meet her?

She huffed out a breath, tracing her steps back to her room, not seeing anyone on her way. Where had he disappeared to? Disappointment stabbed at her as she climbed into bed. Lord Melvin would want a very good reason for standing her up, but somehow she knew he would not. No doubt her brother had persuaded him to go to the tavern. The idea of him there, surrounded by women looking for a little fun with a lord, left her uneasy. She glared into the darkness of her room, listening out for their return, the sound of horses, anything so she could confront him over his movements.

What was she thinking! He was not her husband. He owed her nothing. Still, it took her several hours to fall to sleep.

. . .

Albert was foxed. The tavern room, rank with smoke, sweat, and the foulness of stale beer rent the air, and still, it was not as terrible as he thought a night out at a tavern would be.

Several gentlemen estate owners joined him and the duke, drinking, some whoring the night away upstairs. For an hour or so, Albert had lost sight of Josh, but then he returned, his cravat less poised, along with his hair.

The duke slumped into the chair beside him, grinning from ear to ear. "Lovely company here. I'm surprised that you do not darken these doors more often."

More often? Albert had never before stepped foot into the premises. That he was missing his rendezvous with Victoria because her brother would not take no for an answer also did not help his mood.

Even so, the beer was refreshing, company amusing, and to sit and watch the play of people had been enjoyable. As a writer, picking up people's nuances and mannerisms was always helpful.

"Look here, that woman over there. She is watching you keenly," the duke said, sipping his beer and grinning.

Albert shook his head, having no interest in the lady. "If I am to win your sister's hand, you should know that she would not approve of me being here or if she heard of me bedding any of the ladies selling their wiles tonight. I thought you would've known better, Your Grace."

The duke chuckled, leaning back in his chair. "Oh, I know better, but when there is fun to be had, what of it? And you're not married yet. What would it hurt?"

Albert did not like this talk or the thought of touching another woman, not when he wanted Victoria above all else. "I am content to drink beer with you, my friend, but that is all. I will not be sewing my seed around here this evening."

The duke watched him a moment before clapping him on the back. "That is very good then, my friend. I'm glad you would remain true to your course, that being my sister. I like you even more now than I did before."

"You were testing me?" he asked him, not entirely sure he liked to be tested. The room spun, and he clasped the table to steady himself.

"I have been, but you passed. Now, shall we have another drink?" the duke asked, summoning more beer.

Albert tried to dissuade His Grace of the notion of more alcohol, but then again, it was a very good brew, so why not.

Victoria woke to the sound of doors slamming open before shutting just as loudly. She went and checked out in the corridor, her eyes widening at the sight that beheld her.

Her brother was nowhere to be seen, but Lord Melvin was standing before her door, his eyes glassy and unfocused, his body reeking of beer and smoke.

"I missed you tonight," he said, louder than he ought.

She shushed him, pulling him into her room and closing and locking the door behind him. "Be quiet. You'll wake Mama."

He stumbled over to the bed, lying down with an *oomph*. Victoria wasn't sure what she should do. Should she ring for her maid? Or try to maneuver him back to his room without anyone seeing.

For all that she would like him to touch her, she still did not wish to be anyone's wife. No matter how much being Lord Melvin's wife was becoming more and more appealing every day. He was kind and sweet. How could anyone's heart remain immune to such a gentleman?

He stared at her through eyes that struggled to stay open. "I missed you this evening."

Victoria crossed her arms, staying a good distance from him. "Yes, I know. I found the smoking room empty when I went down there, and you nowhere to be found," she said sarcastically. "But I can see what you've been up to tonight. I hope you enjoyed yourself, my lord."

He groaned, fighting to sit up. When he'd finally managed it, he reached for her, but she darted out of his reach. "Do not be angry, Victoria. I wanted to stay home. Your brother would not take no for an answer."

All understandable, and Josh did tend to get his way when he wanted something. "Well, I'm sure the women at the tavern were much more skilled than I am. I do not blame you for going out. You are a man, after all, and they seldom do anything that warrants gentlemanly behavior. My late husband no exception. You appear no different."

He clapped his hand over his heart. "You wound me, my darling Victoria. I did not sleep with anyone. Hell," he mumbled, flopping back down on the bed. "I've never slept with anyone, and I'm not about to start with a whore plying her trade."

His words comforted her and made her like him even more. "You should leave my room before you are caught in here alone with me."

He slumped an arm over his eyes, groaning. "Oh yes, better not be caught with me. Or you may be made to marry me, and what a terrible disaster that would be." He sat up, leaning on his knees. "If I had you in my bed every evening, Lady Victoria, let me assure you, it would be anything but terrible."

A shiver stole down her spine at his words, intoxicating as they were. His gaze burned up and down her nightshift, and she covered her breasts, realizing she wasn't wearing a dressing gown.

"You need to go now, Albert," she whispered, with one last plea for him to do as she asked before it was too late.

CHAPTER 19

Albert wasn't sure why he was in Victoria's room, but what he did know was that it was spinning at an alarming rate, and he ought to leave. He was foxed, stank, even he could smell his clothing, yet he could not bring forth the energy to get up and go as Victoria asked.

Instead, she kept speaking, and he kept answering in the most inappropriate ways. Alcohol was not made for appropriate conversation. It would seem.

She clasped his hand, pulling at him. He wrenched her close, and she tumbled over him. His cock twitched, the breath in his lungs seized. Hell, she was pretty, so damn sweet that she made his jaw ache.

He reached up, sliding her golden locks behind one ear, needing to see her face. "You're so beautiful, Victoria. Do you know how beautiful you are to me?"

She bit her lip, shaking her head. "You're drunk, Albert. Can you even see straight, my lord?"

"Do not call me my lord. I'm Albert to you. Always Albert." He leaned up, closing the small space between them, and kissed her. She met him halfway, their mouths fusing, taking from the other in a kiss that stole what little wits he had left. Which, in his current state, were not many.

She undulated on him, her legs slipping over his hips, and he reached down, grinding her against his aching cock. Her ass was tight and small and made him instantly hard. She gasped through the kiss, moaned his name.

And then she moved, rolling her hips over his cock, the buckskin breeches he wore. The thin lawn nightgown no barrier to their needs. He held her there, helping her tease them both.

His cock ached, strained against the buttons. He wanted to release himself, take her, take them both to heights yet to be explored, but he could not. Certainly not tonight. He was a drunken lout, in his cups in her room. He would not stoop so low as to take her here like this.

"Oh," she gasped against his lips. "Albert. This feels..."

He slid against her core, the heat between their bodies scalding. "It feels good," he breathed, fighting the urge to come.

"You're so hard, and ahhh, I ache for you. Tell me, is this what happens when one has pleasure without intercourse?"

"Yes," he breathed, rolling over to settle between her legs. "I promise I shall not take you, but I need to be closer."

She nodded, giving him leave, and he wrenched up her gown, exposing her mons to his view. She glistened from desire, the scent of need filling his nostrils. Like the image in the book, he wanted to lay his lips against her flesh, kiss her, flick her sweet nubbin with his tongue until she cried out his name.

She tried to push her gown down. Her cheeks kissed with a rosy hue. "Do not be embarrassed. You're beautiful to me. All of you."

Albert leaned down, kissing her deep and long until he felt her relax under him. He broke the kiss, kneeling between her legs, and ripped at the buttons on his breeches. His cock sprang free, thick and long, and her eyes widened.

But the brave, curious Victoria he adored reached out and slid her finger along his length. Albert swallowed a curse, wishing her finger was her hand, wrapped around him, pulling him toward release.

He closed his eyes, reveled in her touch. No, he wished it was her mouth, suckling him, taking him deep in her throat.

He groaned. "Allow me to bring you pleasure," he pleaded, unsure what he would do should she say no.

She lay back and let him do what he willed. "I trust you," she said, her eyes burning pools of need watching his every move.

Albert guided his cock against her heat. It felt so good, too good to be bad, scandalous like it was. He slid against her, teased her engorged nubbin until they were both breathing hard, Victoria's legs wrapped about his waist, her arms holding him close as he kissed her, teased her. He wanted her to come, to soar under his touch.

She moaned, gasping and pushing, stretching and undulating against him with increasing ferocity. The feel of her against him, wet and wanton, left his wits to spiral.

He was so close. Just a few more strokes, and he would shatter.

"Albert," she gasped, her eyes opening wide and wonder crossing her features as she climaxed. Her fingers slid over his back, her nails scoring his skin.

He groaned and joined her, spilling his seed over her mons and stomach. Terribly crass, but he could not care. They had found release, together, and there was nothing more marvelous.

They lay like that for a time. Both lost to the euphoria of what they had done before he rolled and slumped beside her. Without urging, she turned on her side, staring up at him.

"That was utterly unexpected. I had no idea that was possible. You may think me naive, but Paul never did anything of the sort in our bedchamber. When he bothered to be there that is."

Albert hated the bastard even more for his treatment of Victoria. He pulled her closer.

He had no idea it could be like that either. When he'd taken himself in hand, it had never felt as good as it did just before with Victoria. Already, the thought of her made his cock twitch, and he wanted her again.

He smiled, meeting her wondrous gaze. "It has never felt like that for me before either. You had better take care, my lady, or I shall become addicted to you, and there will be no getting away from me then."

She chuckled, stretching out across the bed. "It is you, Lord Melvin, who ought to be careful, or I'll make you my mister."

He barked out a laugh, and yet at her words, a little hope expired within him. How could she share her body so intimately and still only see him without any emotional connection? He certainly wanted more from whatever it was that they were doing—tutoring him in how to be a good husband. He did not want to be a good husband to anyone unless that anyone was Victoria.

"It is you who ought to be careful, or you'll be made my wife." A little crow of satisfaction shouted in his mind when she paused at his words. He would not look upon tonight as a misguided, utterly reprehensible action that he'd done, but a step to making her see they fit like kid leather gloves. She may not see just yet, but she would. He would win his Victoria still, and tonight had been the first official stepping stone along that path.

The following morning Victoria sat at the breakfast table and fought not to think about what the marquess, who sat at the head of the table eating bacon, eggs, his steaming-hot black coffee to the side, had done to her.

What they had done together last night in her room.

Her stomach knotted at the memory of her release. It had been different to her times with Paul. The intensity had been higher with Albert, even thinking about it now made her squirm. Her body had broken free at that moment. She had become a woman free of restraint, of wifely duties. She was simply a woman who had found pleasure with a man, and it was Lord Melvin who had driven her there.

She stirred her tea, wondering how they could go forward after such an event, how she would steer her instruction of him toward finding a wife and not toward finding a vacant room in the house and making him make love to her.

"Darling, I think your tea is stirred," her mama said, pulling her from her thoughts. She dropped the spoon, and it clattered on the small dish the cup sat on.

Heat crept up her neck, and she looked to where Albert sat and maddeningly found him behind his paper, ignoring the commotion she had made.

"Apologies," she said, her brother watching her intently. Victoria picked up her tea and sipped it, a congenial smile pinned on her lips. "What are we doing today, Mama? Should we travel into the village and cast our eyes over the shops?"

"That sounds like a lovely idea, my dear. I shall have our carriage brought around after breakfast."

"May I join you?" Albert asked, folding his paper and laying it on the table. "I feel as though I have not been out of the house in an age."

"Really?" Victoria queried sweetly. "I thought you and my brother were out only last evening?"

Her mama cast a curious glance at Josh before turning her attention to Lord Melvin. "Did my son take you out last evening, Lord Melvin? I hope he was not too much of a bad influence on you," she teased.

Josh sputtered, affronted. "I would never be a bad influence on my oldest friend. We had a beer at the local tavern, and it was an enjoyable night all around."

"It was indeed," Albert said, his gaze catching hers quickly.

Need, hot and senseless, thrummed through her, and she wished they were alone. Victoria swallowed, schooling her features. "We shall be looking for a modiste, my lord. Are you sure that is what you would like to escort us to?"

Albert's lips twitched. "I shall accompany you if only to escort you as I should since you are my guests. I will, however, leave the modiste up to you to visit alone."

"I wonder if they have any gowns fit for the country dance, Mama. I do not wish to look too high in the instep."

Her mother raised her brow. "Really, Victoria, your gowns are lovely and new. While we shall look, I do not think you need a new wardrobe."

Victoria stared out the window in the breakfast room. She had not been looking for a new wardrobe, just a gown that was less opulent than the ones she owned. She would stand out against the townsfolk and local gentry, and as much as she adored her family, sometimes blending in helped a little. Made one's night much more pleasant, and she wanted to be approachable for Lord Melvin's potential brides. If they were scared of speaking to her, she would not be able to vet them for the position of his wife.

CHAPTER 20

Albert greeted some of the townsfolk who wished him good morning as he strolled before the modiste's window waiting for Victoria and the duchess.

The groom held the horses while the driver sat atop the box, waiting patiently for them all. He wasn't so patient. He needed to speak to Victoria and be alone with her if he could manage such a thing before expiring. He did little these days but think of her, and tonight he would have to make an effort to ride out to his hunting box and get some words down on his next manuscript. The muse was well alive within his mind, Victoria giving him plenty of ideas and plot fodder to write onto the page. It would also help keep his hands off her person, which he was wont to do at any opportunity that arose.

He started back up the pebbled path before the shops and inwardly groaned when he spotted Miss Nancy Eberhardt, only daughter and heiress to a local gentleman and whose mother had passed during her birth. The young woman was pretty and sweet-natured, all the elements a gentleman would want in a wife, but unfortunately for Nancy, he had never had eyes for her.

The only woman he'd ever taken note of was currently looking at gloves near the window of the modistes.

Miss Eberhardt spied him and smiled warmly. He bowed when she came to stand before him, her broad smile and bright eyes putting him on guard. Her maid, a sickly little creature, stood back, demure and quiet as always.

"Lord Melvin, how wonderful to see you about. I was only telling Papa the other day that the townsfolk do not see you enough. What brings you here today? You look as if you're loitering about if I'm honest." She chuckled.

He smiled, gesturing to the store. "I'm merely escorting my guests to the modiste."

Miss Eberhardt's face lost a little of its brightness at his words. "Oh, you have guests? Do I know them?"

Albert had little idea if she knew Victoria or was associated with the Duke of Penworth's seat. "My good friend, The Duke of Penworth is staying, along with his sister and mama."

"Lady Victoria is here?" She smiled, looking toward the shop windows. Albert did the same and could not see Victoria anymore.

"She is, yes."

Miss Eberhardt clapped her gloved hands, her smile back on her pretty visage. "I shall love to see her again. As you know, Papa fell ill during the last few weeks of the Season, and we had to return home early. I was unable to meet with her before we left."

"I did not know that. I hope Mr. Eberhardt is doing better now?" he queried, liking the older gentleman, his straight talk and no use for nonsense, similar to himself in that regard.

"He is doing much better, thank you."

Just then, the door to the modiste opened, and Victoria stepped outside. Her attention slipped from him to Miss Eberhardt. "Nancy?" she queried. "I did not know you lived in

Camberley. How did I not know that?" Victoria said, pulling Miss Eberhardt into a quick embrace.

Albert watched with interest, not knowing the two ladies were acquainted and looked to be close friends.

"We're situated but a mile from here and from Lord Melvin's estate. I did not know you were staying close by, or I would have called on you." Miss Eberhardt clasped Victoria's hand, squeezing it. "How are you? I feel we have so much to catch up on."

Victoria chuckled, her eyes bright with pleasure. "I am very well and all the more pleased at having seen you again."

"I see you are visiting our local modiste," Miss Eberhardt stated. "Were you able to purchase anything in the store to your liking?"

"A dress for the country dance. Are you attending?"

Miss Eberhardt's eyes brightened, and she all but bounced where she stood. "I am, yes. How wonderful that you'll be there. We shall catch up properly."

"You're more than welcome to visit me at Rosedale. I should like some female company other than Mama." Albert smiled at her teasing. How he admired her. She was so friendly and warm, so different to other ladies of his acquaintance of lesser rank when speaking to others. And Miss Eberhardt, no matter how wealthy, had no peerage in her family, no titles or elevating connections, and yet still, Victoria treated her like an equal. A friend.

He marveled at her. Admiring her all the more for her warmth and good heart.

"If you're in agreement with that, my lord?" she asked him.

Albert smiled at them both, knowing that he would do anything if it meant that it made Victoria happy. "Of course, you're welcome to visit."

"Thank you, my lord," Miss Eberhardt watched him for

longer than he would term appropriate before she turned her attention back to Victoria.

He hoped she did not have romantic designs on him. As much as he liked the young woman, she had never stirred his blood. He had always seen her as a affable acquaintance, but not for him.

"We shall be home the day after tomorrow if you would like to luncheon with us," he offered.

"I would love that very much." Miss Eberhardt's attention shifted past him, and he turned to see her father waiting in a carriage. Albert gave a cursory wave to the gentleman.

"I must be off, but I shall be at Rosedale the day after tomorrow."

"It was lovely seeing you again, Nancy," Victoria said, sincerity echoing in her words.

"And I you. Both of you," Miss Eberhardt said, casting one last smile at Albert before she was off.

He ignored Victoria's stare, and the knowing grin on her lips that he could discern from the corner of his eye. He opened the carriage door, helping her up. He followed her, seating himself beside her.

"You look very beautiful today. I have missed you," he said, reaching for her hand.

Her fingers entwined with his, her eyes darkening with a need that he too felt. Would it always be this madness, this undeniable want that sizzled between them? If they were alone, her mother not mere feet away from them in the store, he would be tempted to wrench her into his arms and kiss her soundly.

"I did not think you would remember last evening. You were hardly in the state to have such a sound memory."

"I may have been foxed." He picked up her hand and kissed her gloved fingers. "But I remember everything of what we did."

"Really?" she teased, pursing her lips. "What did we do. Remind me?"

He pushed down on the need that ran wild and hot through his blood at her words. Memories of her crying out as he made her come, as his cock slid against her cunny left him hard and aching.

He leaned toward her, his lips but a breath from her ear. "I made you come. I want to make you scream my name, maybe even one day in a carriage." He felt her shiver, the small gasp of shock at his words.

The door to the shop tinkled its little bell, notifying them the duchess had left. Albert sat back just as the groom opened the door for the duchess. He offered his hand to Her Grace. "Let me help you," he suggested.

The duchess took his hand and settled herself across from them, two small packages placed beside her by the groom.

"Your gown will be delivered tomorrow, not that I think you needed another, but now that I've seen what they had, the best for a country dance such as the one we will attend, I understand your plight."

"Thank you, Mama," Victoria said.

Victoria's reply revealed not an ounce of her being affected by his words, his touch of just before. How was it that she could remain so calm and unaffected?

He could not be further from such a stance.

"I am looking forward to the dance. It has been many years, not since before my coming out, that I have attended such an event." The duchess's words were warm at the memory.

"I saw Miss Eberhardt, Mama. She lives close by and will be attending the dance and calling on us the day after tomorrow." Victoria considered Albert a moment, and he fought not to fidget under her gaze. "She's a lovely woman of means and will do well as a wife. Although, since her papa is a widower, I think she would be happily settled if she were close by to her home."

Albert inwardly groaned, already foreshadowing where Victoria's thoughts were taking her and who she thought quite perfect for his future bride.

He did not comment on her words, not wanting to be rude, but Miss Eberhardt, no matter how aggregable, was not for him.

"Do you not concur, Lord Melvin?" Victoria asked him, her innocent smile hiding a devious matchmaking mind he did not particularly like.

"Miss Eberhardt is a kind, considerate woman. I wish her well with whomever she marries. I'm sure she will make him very happy." But it would not be him.

Victoria's eyes narrowed, and he ignored her ire, deciding this conversation was over, and the view outside the carriage window was much more to his liking.

CHAPTER 21

"What is wrong with Nancy, Albert? She is quite perfect for you. She is from Hampshire, her father lives close by, and she's an heiress. If one dare says it, I would suggest she is the answer to your prayers. You ought to court her at the forthcoming country dance, see if you have anything in common other than your wealth and similar upbringing. You may be pleasantly surprised and find you like her very much."

After finding him ensconced here after they had returned from the village, Victoria slumped down on the settee in Albert's library. He had been oddly quiet on the way back to Rosedale in the carriage, and even though she and her mama had kept the conversation going, she could not help but wonder if he was put out with her in some way.

He did not look up from where he sat at the desk, looking over a pile of letters and estate account books. She may be interrupting him, but she could not leave him now. Not when they were so close to finding him the perfect woman to fill the position of a wife in this beautiful house. He would be a fool indeed to let such a wonderful opportunity such as Nancy slip through his fingers.

Victoria did not know a nicer or sweeter-natured woman in London. Other than her sisters, of course.

He sighed, throwing the quill onto the ledger open before him with more force than necessary, spilling a little of the ink. "I have already stated I am not interested in Miss Eberhardt in a romantic sense. Had I been, with us living in such close proximity, I would have already courted her to see if she returned my affections, Victoria. Please know that I shall not be pursuing her."

Victoria came over to the desk, leaning against it. She narrowed her eyes on him, not understanding why he was such a pain about it all. "You wanted my help in finding you a wife. Of teaching you how to go about courting a lady and being less awkward and shy around them. You did very well this morning with Miss Eberhardt. You are improving daily. I do not understand what we're doing if you're not going to take my advice when a suitable lady steps before you."

He leaned back in his chair, running a hand through his hair. She ignored the flutter the action made in her stomach or how ruggedly, flusteredly handsome he looked right at this moment. How could anyone not want to marry him?

Albert was a hidden gem among all the rough stones in society for all his nervousness around women.

Then why do you not have him for yourself?

Victoria thrust the thought aside. Her future was secure, set, and she had already started planning her first trip abroad. That travel did not include a husband and a gaggle of babies holding her back. Marriage was a mistake she would never make again.

"I do need your help in helping me navigate courtship with a woman. I did well today because I have known Miss Eberhardt for many years, and while I do not like her romantically, she is a friend. That is the only reason why I did so well. Place me in London, and you will see how awkward I still am."

Victoria wiggled to sit up on his desk, scrunching up some of the papers beneath her skirts. "Is there no one that you already know who you think will suit? You must be open to meeting new people, making connections for this to work."

"I am open to the possibility, but Miss Eberhardt is not one of them. I'm sorry to disappoint her if she harbors feelings for me. Mine are what they are, Victoria. You would not like to be forced toward a gentleman you only saw as your friend, would you not?"

"Well, no," she admitted.

"If I," he said, standing and coming to stand before her, "followed you about at every ball, forced my affections on you when you did not return them, you would dislike it very much. It is no different."

She supposed he had a point, but still, a small niggling worry kept poking at her mind that Albert viewed her as his future wife, the woman he wanted and he should not. Her heart was no longer capable of such trust, not with Albert or anyone. She thought she had known her late husband. She hadn't known him at all. Albert wanted children, a wife content to live in the country. She was none of those things. The world had opened up to her as a widow. She could not run back down the aisle to repeat a mistake that had humiliated her more than even her family knew.

"Very well, I shall try and help you dissuade Miss Eberhardt in thinking there is a future between you, but you must promise me that you will try with someone."

His lip twitched into a devilishly handsome grin. Victoria found herself reaching for the lapels of his jacket, pulling him close. Realizing her mistake, she dropped her hands, mentally chastising herself for giving him ideas of them.

"Thank you," he said before striding for the door and leaving her sitting on his desk to watch him go. She frowned after him, unsure if she was put out or relieved by his departure.

Stupid fool that she was, she did not know which one it was.

Later that evening, when everyone was abed, Albert stole out to the stables, saddled his gelding, and rode out to his hunting lodge. He was behind on his words and needed to get down several pages before he fell behind on his deadline.

The lodge was quiet and dark, and he took a few moments starting the fire and lighting almost all the candles he had there, needing light above all else. He would normally travel down here through the day and leave before nightfall or just after, but due to his guests, his routine was all at odds.

He sat down at his desk, the words flowing from his fingers for several hours, his mind transported to the dark, dank streets of London, the story taking a menacing turn where the heroine was in search of the hero after footpads had kidnaped him.

The sound of birds chirping pulled him from his pages, and he looked up to see the kiss of dawn on the landscape outside. He leaned back in his chair, stretching and yawning, wondering how he would get through the day playing host while needing to sleep.

"Albert? Are you out here?"

He swore at the sound of Victoria's voice, throwing the manuscript pages into a leather folder and locking it away in the bookshelf behind him.

He went over to the decanter of whiskey, drinking from the bottle to freshen his mouth just as the door opened. Victoria poked her head around the wood, a warm smile forming on her lips.

"Ah, so this is where you were hiding all night. I did try to find you to partake in more lessons but could not locate you. A servant told me you had ridden out to the hunting lodge."

What was he to tell her? That he wrote the very books she loved to read out here? That he was her favorite author? Albert chose neither.

"I needed to check on the lodge. There have been reports of poachers and thieves in the area," he lied, having never cared if people walked his grounds and took wildlife from him to feed their families.

She closed the door behind her, walking about the lodge and taking in the thick Aubusson rugs under her leather boots. She was wearing trews again and her tight riding jacket that accentuated her figure. The kiss they shared the last time she was attired so rose up in his mind and he took a calming breath, cooling his desire.

He followed her progress with something akin to a man starved of sustenance. He was starting to think he was a little obsessed with winning her love.

She flopped down onto a settee, kicking off her boots and undoing the buttons on her riding jacket, throwing it aside. She wore a white linen shirt beneath, hemmed prettily with lace. "This is as good a place as any for more lessons." She reached into a bag that he had not seen over her shoulder, pulling out the book of sketches of sexual positions.

She opened it to the last page they had looked upon. "I thought we should start here, Albert. Discuss what I liked about what you did to me the other evening, and how perhaps what you can have with your wife when the time comes."

He inwardly groaned but joined her, sitting close by, reveling in the fresh scent of her. Had she bathed already so early this morning? He wanted to kiss her, kiss her skin and see for himself if she tasted as sweet as she smelled.

"Very well," he agreed. Feeling bold, he pointed to the sexual act of the man kissing the woman between her legs. "I should like to know if my wife would enjoy such touch. Would you be brave enough to let me practice on you, Victoria?"

He held his breath, knowing it was wrong what he was asking her. He ought to be horsewhipped. Her brother ought to put a bullet through his skull, and still, he did not back down. Merely waited for her to reply.

Her chin rose defiantly, and he knew her answer before she uttered it. Of all her siblings, Victoria was never the one to back down from a challenge, certainly if it were asked as such.

"Of course. I said I would help you, and I will. Shall we start now?"

Liquid-hot desire rushed through his veins, and he stood, pulling her to stand. "Let me help you with these," he stated, untying the buttons on her breeches. Dear God, she was magnificent, and the idea of what they were about to do was beyond his dreams. He just hoped he performed it as well as she hoped. He would hate to disappoint his future bride.

CHAPTER 22

What on earth was she doing? She should not be allowing such intimate acts with a gentleman she had no intention of marrying. But the dark, hungry gaze of Albert's pushed away her nervousness and allowed a boldness she never thought she would possess to take charge.

Even if she were known in her family as bold and outspoken, she was not a woman of loose morals. Not until Albert Kester came into her world. Being a widow had made her lose her sense of morals.

With a care that left her trembling, he flicked open the last of the buttons on her breeches and slid them down her legs. Victoria watched as he took a calming breath, a muscle working at his temple with each beat of his heart.

Her own pumped fiercely as she let him start with the ties at the neck of her shirt. There were only three before he lifted it from her body, and she was left with nothing but a corset and shift beneath.

"You may sit back down," he suggested, his voice deep and raspy as if the words were hard to speak.

She did as he asked, gasping when he kneeled between her legs, pushing them open with a determination she did not expect from him. Victoria bit her lip, wondering what this was going to be like. How on earth was she allowing such liberties with her body? Albert had muddled her mind in more ways than she first thought.

His large hands and strong fingers slid up her legs, massaging her muscles as he glided ever closer to her sex. Her body ached, her senses alive and needy.

She realized with no small amount of shock that she wanted to see his mouth on her, watch him make her reach pleasure as they had the other night.

His hands grasped the backs of her knees, and he pulled her toward the edge of the settee. His heavy-lidded eyes fixed on her core, and he licked his lips. Victoria let out a huff of breath, having not expected to like his reaction to her so much.

"You're so beautiful, Victoria. I ache to taste you."

Her eyes spied the book, open on the page of the sexual act they were about to perform, and she shivered.

He kissed her leg with slow, torturous strokes, and Victoria moaned with need. She was so open to him, a shiver of vulnerability stole through her, hoping that he approved of what he saw, would not shy away from her after they did what they were about to do.

Although she did not want to marry, she did enjoy Albert's company, liked him very much. She wanted to help him, but something told her that nothing would ever be the same again after they did what they were to do.

Would she be able to walk away from him, stand by and watch him marry another? Know that he would make love to another lady night after night, and that lady would not be her?

He kissed along her leg, his warm breath marking her skin. His fingers flexed on her thighs, pushing her wider. He marveled at her a moment before dipping his head. She gasped, biting her lip as his lips touched her, and then his tongue flicked out, caressing her most private flesh.

Victoria leaned back, closing her eyes, reveling in his touch. He kissed her, flicked her aching, throbbing nubbin with his tongue before suckling and sending her wits to flee. His mouth devoured her, taking his fill. His muffled moans of enjoyment met her ears, and he kissed her cunny with abandon.

It was too much. Too wonderful. How had she never known with her husband that such acts were possible. For all of Paul's rakish wiles, he knew very little at all. Or did not want to do these things with her.

She pushed the unhelpful, hurtful thoughts aside, lifting herself toward his mouth. Ignoring the wantonness of her action. He scooped her legs over his shoulders, taking her with a need that surpassed any she'd ever known.

Victoria reached down and ran her fingers into his hair, holding him to her, grinding herself on his face like a woman out of her mind. And perhaps she was a little out of her mind with need.

Pleasure teased her senses. She was hot, clammy, and wanted to shatter to a million pieces. Albert flicked his tongue across a sensitive place, and finally, she tumbled over the edge. Stars burst behind her eyes, and she undulated against him, not caring how she looked, how much she moaned, his name a chant of pleasure.

He kept her against him as the last tremors of her release echoed through her body before ending how he began, kissing along her legs, watching her through heavy-lidded eyes that burned with his own need.

Victoria could not move. Every muscle felt lax and as heavy as a case of gold. Albert reached over, taking a rug from the settee, and laid it over her legs as he came to sit beside her, picking up the book that lay on the floor.

"What did you think, Victoria? Should I not disappoint my future wife?"

Victoria shook herself free of the muddling pleasure that cloaked her to what Albert was saying. Disappoint his wife? The idea made ice run through her veins. She sat up, taking the book and flipping the pages, anything but to dissect why it was his words upset her so much.

"I think your wife will be most pleased, and today, when we return to the house, we shall sit down and play cards, learn how to interact together in that setting. It is not only in the art of lovemaking that you require tutelage. You also need to feel confident and sure when hosting and courting during the season. We cannot lose ourselves in this way when there is still so much to learn."

"Instead of cards, what do you think if we partook in an archery contest? Or lawn games. There is a chance next season that I will host a house party here at Rosedale, and I know ladies like to take part in that pastime."

"We can do that too. We have a few days to fill before the country dance, but tonight I think cards would be best."

"Whatever you think," he said.

Victoria shuffled out of the chair and dressed quickly. She could not look at him, achingly aware that he watched her every movement. Just as she, too, was aware of him and his presence. The memory of her climax an occasion she doubted she'd ever forget.

Albert was taking up too much time in her mind, but she could not help herself. Whenever she saw him, she wanted to be near him, even if only to converse and spend time. If that conversation and time led to pleasurable interludes, then all the better.

It was out of character and unhelpful to her plans.

She wrenched on her boots, tying them quickly before

looking about for her riding jacket. She stilled, swallowing the need that coursed through her blood when she spotted Albert holding it aloft with one finger, a small smile playing about his lips.

He was a devil, and he knew it. He was also becoming quite the rogue. Well, what she assumed a rogue was like. Men of that ilk seduced ladies in hunting lodges during daylight hours.

Which reminded her, if she did not return to the house soon, she would be missed at breakfast, and her mama would be concerned or suspicious.

Victoria stepped over to him, taking the jacket, and slipped it on. "Thank you. I shall see you back at Rosedale."

"Is that all?" he queried, his brows raised.

Nerves fluttered in her stomach. "What else do you want?"

He growled, wrenching her close. He took her lips, and all thoughts of getting out of there, away from him, vanished. Victoria kissed him back, tasting the tart taste of herself on his lips. It was not displeasing. If anything, it made her long for more of what they had started with each other.

He broke the kiss, his eyes dark and stormy with need. "I want everything, Victoria."

Victoria chuckled, but her insides seized with panic. What did everything mean? Did he want a future, to marry her, for her to have his children, and a life together? She wanted none of those things, not after her disastrous first marriage. The idea of being anyone's property, to be treated with no respect revolted her sensibilities. She shook her head, an impossibility she could never do again.

But a life with Albert would be different. You are different around him.

Victoria stepped out of his hold, striding to the door, and the freedom the outdoors beckoned. "I want lots of things too, but I do not always gain them. I shall see you back at the house," she called over her shoulder, shutting the door on his handsome, if not disappointed, face.

Their little tutoring game was getting out of hand. Emotions were becoming involved and awful and alarming as it was, Victoria was not sure that it was all Lord Melvin who was feeling them.

CHAPTER 23

Albert strode back into the foyer of Rosedale and directly into the path of the Duke of Penworth. Penworth greeted him warmly before they started for the parlor upstairs.

"I saw Victoria earlier at breakfast," His Grace stated. "She mentioned you were hosting a card night this evening. Would you mind if I invited some local friends, gentry that I know in this area, and you too, I should imagine?"

Albert rang the bell for tea as they entered the room, warming himself before the fire since the day had turned cooler than expected. "You may invite whomever pleases you. Anyone in particular?"

"Lord and Lady Hammilyn are at home and are close enough to attend. They will, of course, wish to bring their daughter. I hope that it suitable."

"I give you leave to use my desk to write to them. Have a groom ride over and deliver it. I should think they will attend."

Penworth sat on a nearby chair, crossing his legs as a footman came in with tea and biscuits. "I will pour, thank you," Albert said to the servant, dismissing him.

He poured Penworth a cup before doing the same for himself before settling down on the chair opposite his friend. "I cannot help but wonder if your interest in Lord Hammilyn has anything to do with his daughter, which from what I hear is a beauty and one that many a young buck are looking forward to seeing next season in town."

Penworth shrugged, sipping his beverage. "I have never laid eyes on the chit, and I would never marry a woman so young."

"Ah, but remember, Lady Sophie is not so young. She spent several years abroad with her brother, who lives in Spain with his wife. They will return, of course, when he inherits, but until then, I believe they live in Cadiz."

Penworth frowned at this information, clearly confused. "How old is she?" he asked, unable to mask the curiosity in his words.

"I believe she is two and twenty."

"A perfect age for you, Lord Melvin. Maybe you will go into a contest with my brother and court Lady Sophie yourself."

Albert coughed, choking on his tea, having not known Victoria was listening to their conversation. She waltzed into the room. The scent of lavender soap and her usual perfume of jasmine wafted through the air. Albert fought not to take a noticeable breath, the memory of what they had done only hours before clear in his mind.

Penworth grinned but did not comment as his sister sat. "What else are you two gentlemen discussing other than the ladies you're going to court?"

"Nothing of interest, merely the card games to be played this evening. I thought to invite Lord and Lady Hammilyn and their daughter, who Melvin tells me is back from abroad. Do you know Lady Sophie, Victoria?" her brother asked.

She shook her head, leaning back on the settee, clasping a nearby pillow, and holding it on her lap. The scene was reminiscent of a domesticated family enjoying the morning together.

Albert could imagine such a vision of Victoria joining him for tea, discussing future events at Rosedale with visitors such as her brother. He watched her, sipping his drink and wishing he could convince her that to be married to him would not be a chore. That he would do everything in his power to make her happy and content, even if that meant they traveled for years before starting a family. Convince her that he would never break her heart.

"I do not know her at all. Although I do believe Elizabeth may have met her some years ago."

Josh finished his tea, placing the cup on the table before them. "I shall write to them and hope that they will attend. You would like Lord Hammilyn, Victoria. He has wolfhounds like you."

She grinned at her brother, her eyes lighting up at the mention of her favorite breed of dog. "Oh, well, I shall like him very much, and I will always have a conversation subject to swing to should the worse happen, and I find dreaded silence has ensued between us."

"Just right," Penworth said, standing. "I shall be back soon. But I want to get that missive off before it grows too late."

Albert listened as the duke made his way down the hall, heading to the library downstairs.

"Is something the matter?" he asked her at her silence, hoping he had not pushed her too far out at the hunting lodge. When she had turned up at his door there, he had not expected they would progress to such acts, but now that they had, he would never regret their actions.

He wanted her as his wife. He would seduce his wife with actions similar to what he had performed on her. There was no shame in that. Not unless she refused him when he gained enough confidence to breach the taboo subject that she seemed to detest.

She shook her head, but worry clouded her emerald eyes.

"Not particularly, but I do think you ought to consider Lady Sophie for your wife. Tonight if she attends, you must try to use the tools that I have given you to see if there is a connection there."

"And if your brother is interested in the lady?"

"Then you shall both try, and we shall all see who the victor is. But you do not have to marry her this evening, merely see if she is pleasant and suitable to your character. Suppose you can converse with her without getting tongue-tied and anxious all the better. I shall be there with you too. I shall not let you fail."

A cold, hard stone lodged where his heart beat. "You are determined as ever to have me married before the end of the next Season. Not every female that I meet is someone whom I want to shag for the rest of my life."

Her cheeks heated, and he was glad of it. He frowned, starting to dislike being pushed toward women he had no interest in whatsoever. He knew whom he suited, whom he adored and wanted by his side for the rest of his life, and it was the very woman telling him to marry another.

"I know that. I'm merely trying to help. You did agree to my aid."

"Of course," he acknowledged. "But can I not tell you should I find a woman who sparks my interest and then move forward with a plan? This throwing women at my head at any available turn is starting to grow weary."

"But we have only just started, and we're only using these women as practice. Do not be so prickly, Lord Melvin. I am only trying to assist you."

"And I suppose you are still determined to die old and alone, never marrying due to being broken hearted by an ass."

She gasped, and he regretted his hard words immediately. "Victoria, I—"

"Right, the letter is off to Lord Hammilyn. I should think

they will attend. When I ran into him yesterday in the village, he was doing nothing but rusticating at home."

"Sounds delightful," Albert mumbled, watching Victoria, who sat glaring at him. "I shall have cook do a light supper this evening instead of a meal."

"That sounds just the thing," Penworth said, sitting back down on the chair he vacated only minutes before with not a clue his sister and friend were at odds.

"Cheer up, Victoria. Lady Sophie will be good company for you. Keep you occupied since I know you tend to grow bored."

"I'm not bored," she said defensively, throwing a quick look in Alberts's direction.

He poured himself another tea, wishing it were something stronger like whiskey or brandy. He could use a little fortification right about now. Should Victoria grew bored did not bode well for his plans and hopes. Would she find life here at Rosedale beyond her endurance? Would she never settle or always wish for adventure?

He would love to travel if he found the right woman to go with, but he could not be away constantly. His estate, his writing required him to be in England several times a year. The idea of them, of being her husband, grew ever smaller in his mind's eyes, edged a little further out of reach.

"You could have fooled me," Josh teased, grinning. "Maybe while you're trying to fix up Melvin or myself with Lady Sophie, you could think about your own future. Of who else in London would suit you now that you're available once again."

"No one will suit me." She shot out of her chair, striding for the door, her gown swishing about her legs as her forceful steps carried her away. "I'm going to die old and alone without family. That is what I'm going to do. To hell with men and their needs for a family and bed partner. I'd rather love myself, trust in only myself before anyone else."

"Victoria, that is uncalled for," Josh said, standing, scowling at his sister, who stormed down the hall before a door slammed somewhere in the depths of the house. Her bedroom door Albert supposed.

"I do apologize, Melvin. I say I was only teasing her. I do not know what could be upsetting her so."

Albert knew what had sparked such a temper, but he could not be sorry for it. The truth sometimes hurt, and that she continuously told him no, that she did not want him for herself, no matter how much pleasure they may give each other. How well they got along. At some point, he would have to accept that truth and move forward.

"Do not concern yourself. I'm sure she will be back to rights this evening. We're all entitled to a moment or two of temper."

"I suppose," Penworth said, frowning at the door his sister had left through. "But I am interested in seeing what this rumored beauty Lady Sophie looks like. Let us hope she has a pleasant disposition as her face is said to be."

Albert smiled, but inside, his gut churned, hating the fact Victoria was angry and upset. That was not supposed to happen. He never wished for her to be so. "I think you shall be pleased, Penworth. Maybe it is not I who will marry first after all my schooling, but you."

Penworth chuckled, shaking his head. "She would have to be a rare gem to tempt me, but we shall see."

"That we shall," Albert agreed. "Tonight."

CHAPTER 24

Albert made sure to pay attention to their guests, especially Lady Sophie, whose beauty had caught him unawares. She had grown in height and beauty since he'd seen her last. Granted, she had been quite a distance from him when he had spied her.

Even so, Penworth continued to remain amusingly tongue-tied when around the woman. Which, if anything, made being near her entertaining. Not that he wanted the chit for himself. He was only talking to her more than he would normally because Victoria had asked him to.

Victoria stood beside her mother, watching his every word. He studied Victoria a moment, unable to make out if her visage was one of curiosity or displeasure.

He hoped it was the latter. That him talking to Lady Sophie, who next year would certainly be a success in London, vexed her. More the truth of the matter was that she found fault in his conversation and was working out how to correct him when they were alone.

"Are you looking forward to next season, Lady Sophie? I understand you're making your debut," Albert said, surprised by his confident tone. Mayhap Victoria's lessons were working in his favor.

"Not particularly. If you were in my shoes, Lord Melvin, would you care to be auctioned off to the highest bidder? I think not."

He bit his tongue, fighting to keep the laugh that wanted to bubble up and out of him.

Penworth wasn't so successful in hiding his amusement at the lady's words. If Albert were a betting man he would lay blunt down that the duke's interest was piqued.

"I would not care for that, no. I suppose it is why I rarely go to town."

"Do you not?" The lady studied him a moment. "Well, I suppose it is because you're always too busy scribbling in that book of yours."

Albert choked on his drink, looking about to see who had heard Lady Sophie. Penworth narrowed his eyes, and with terribly bad timing, Lady Victoria joined them.

"You are all looking like a jolly fun party over here. What are we discussing?"

"We were discussing why Lord Melvin does not attend town. I merely mentioned the books he's always scribbling in."

"Really?" Victoria said, her tone interested. "And what book is that, Lord Melvin?"

He shrugged, not willing to tell anyone, certainly Penworth and Lady Sophie, what book he was always scribbling in. How on earth Lady Sophie would know to say such a thing was beyond him. Had his staff been talking about him around the village? He did not care for such things, if that was the case, and would put a stop to it immediately.

"Father tells me he often sees you riding out to your hunting lodge. He has called on you a time or two there, but you've always had your head down at your desk, scribbling away, and so he has not disturbed you. Our property line, you see," Lady

Sophie explained to Victoria and Penworth, "is very close to Lord Melvin's hunting lodge. Father often rides the boundaries, and that is when he noticed you, my lord. Please do not think he is stalking you, for he is not." She chuckled, a tinkling laugh that grated on Albert's nerves.

"How interesting." Victoria watched him a moment before she said, "And what makes your father suspect that it is a book that his lordship is scribbling away in?"

Lady Sophie shrugged, her attention shifting to other parts of the room and showing she was losing interest in the conversation. "Oh, he is merely guessing. Was it a book, my lord? Or merely a letter?"

Albert cleared his throat. "A letter. I should be so clever to write a book."

Victoria thought over the words a moment before she said, "Lord Melvin, now that the other guests are busy playing cards, I thought we should have some music and dancing. I will play the pianoforte if you like and Josh may dance with Miss Eberhardt who looks a little lonely over by the fire."

They all turned to look at the miss, only to see her fiddling with the bodice of her gown.

Albert cleared his throat. "Of course. A lively tune, if you please, Lady Victoria."

She dipped into a curtsy, heading over to the pianoforte. He watched as Penworth followed his sister and discussed something before crossing the room and asking Miss Eberhardt to dance. The young woman looked a little star-struck at having been asked to dance by a duke.

They danced for several minutes to a reel, and Albert found it wasn't so bad to be sociable, take part in the conversation, and listen to people's lives. He so often was stuck in his own little world that it was hard to step away from the lives he created and live in the one gifted to him.

Albert caught sight of Victoria while she played the

pianoforte, her straight back, her smile at the dancers as she played. A proficient who did not need to look at the music sheets to know the notes. He hoped she had not listened too much into what Lady Sophie had said about his writing. That side of him was so personal, an element he hadn't shared with anyone. To tell Victoria of his writing persona, his books, he would need to be sure she was the woman to be his wife. No one other than his bride could know. It was part of the secrecy, the mystery of Elbert Retsek, the unknown. To be known, even by one person, was a serious undertaking and not to be taken lightly.

Victoria played a minuet and watched her brother lead Miss Eberhardt about the floor. The young woman looked half in love with her sibling already, and the dance had only just begun. Poor lass, she would not get all that she dreamed of regarding her brother. Her brother's constant glances at Lady Sophie told Victoria he had become a little spellbound by the woman's beauty.

As for Albert, he seemed to be progressing well, certainly conversation between himself and Sophie hadn't stalled, not even when her idiot brother became mute and could not speak for a full five minutes after their initial introductions.

Josh had never acted like such a fool. Maybe he was in love.

She hummed to the music, her mama and the other guests present in the adjoining room playing cards, their laughter, and the murmuring sound of chatter notifying the night a success for Albert.

Pride rose in her at her accomplishment for his lordship. He was capable, and when prodded, willing to do his part as a peer of the realm, entertain and make pretty ladies blush.

Lady Sophie reached up to hold Lord Melvin's shoulder, and

Victoria missed a key. She checked her position on the pianoforte and continued, hoping no one noticed her fumble.

The song continued for several more bars, and with each one, just as the music was lively, so too was Lady Sophie's exploits. Was she smiling up at Lord Melvin a little too brightly now? Why was he laughing?

The pit of her stomach twisted. She would not be jealous of Lord Melvin finding another to converse with and company to enjoy. He appreciated her companionship too, and he needed to find a wife. She had told him often enough that she would not marry again.

A little niggling doubt settled in her mind that she was jealous of Albert and Lady Sophie. That seeing them together had sparked discontent in her she hadn't thought would arise.

She didn't want him for herself. She had plans. Countries to visit, her inheritance to spend. A life to live without being made a fool of by a runaway husband. Didn't she?

The song came to an end, and she smiled at the short applause from the guests before making a hasty exit from the room. She swallowed hard, heading for the back of the house and the servant stairs, not wanting to come across any guests. She could not breathe, her corset too tight, her gown restricting.

A hand reached out and spun her about, just as she swiped at her cheeks, horrified that she was upset.

What was she so unsettled about? She was being a silly little ninny who needed to remember all that she wanted in life. It was certainly not the man gazing down at her with so much kindness in his dark-blue orbs that one could get lost in. Quite willingly, in fact.

"Let me go, Albert," she said, hating the whiney voice that had uttered those words.

He reached up, cradling her face with his hands, his thumbs

wiping the tears from her cheeks. "What is wrong? You left as if the hounds of hell were nipping at your silk slippers."

"A megrim, that is all. I think I shall retire for the night."

He did not let her go. Victoria fought not to revel in the feel of him coming after her. The care that shone in his eyes and what he made her feel whenever she was around him. Bliss, amusement, safety, all of those things.

"I think we know each other well enough that you know I know when you're lying. Are you still angry with me after our disagreement?"

Victoria had all but forgotten their disagreement, but she nodded anyway, needing to get away. To calm her racing, jealous heart. For that was what she was. A jealous cur ready to scratch out the eyes of the beautiful, wealthy Lady Sophie, who looked more than pleased to be in Albert's arms.

"I am, and I need time to work through my displeasure with you. Please let me go."

He stepped back immediately, and she missed his touch almost as quickly. She closed her eyes, hating that she was a kaleidoscope of mixed emotions and needs.

"Of course," he uttered, his voice heavy with concern.

Victoria looked up and met his eyes, hating the pain she was causing him. He deserved better than her. Better than how she was in his arms when he touched her and made her yearn. To how she was acting now. Cold and aloof. Angry at him for making her feel too much when she's sworn to never feel anything ever again. If one could not feel, one could not be hurt.

She turned about and fled to her room—a coward as well as an ass.

CHAPTER 25

At breakfast the following morning, Albert watched Victoria fuss with her food while eating very little of what was on her plate. Her light-blue muslin gown was pressed so perfectly that not a crease dared mar the fabric. Her hair did not have one curl displaced. The little diamond earbobs on her ears taunted him. To Albert, she was a perfect gem, flawless in every way, noble, wealthy, and educated, and yet, he knew her intimately. She was the woman he wanted to marry, the woman he'd brought pleasure upon. He never wanted her to leave.

Victoria did not look at him. In fact, she did not take part in any of the conversations at breakfast. Merely pushed bits of scrambled egg around her plate. Was she making some face with it?

"I'm sorry for being late, but I must ask that we postpone any invitations or plans for the day. I have a terrible megrim, and I cannot understand as to why," the duchess said, sitting down at the table and requesting tea immediately from a footman.

Albert hid his grin behind his coffee cup, knowing only too well it may have been the overindulgence of champagne the duchess had imbibed the night before that made her so out of sorts today.

"Mayhap coffee would be better, Mother," the duke said, throwing a knowing smile at Albert before calling for a footman to pour coffee for the duchess.

He cleared his throat. "I do not believe we have anything planned today that cannot be altered, Your Grace."

Albert turned to Victoria, who continued to be uninterested in the conversation going on about her. "Lady Victoria, do you not agree?"

She looked at him then, and he fought the urge to go to her. She looked wretched. Was she, too, ill? Was there an illness in the household that he did not know about? Perhaps the duchess was not suffering the implications from too much wine.

"Pardon?" she asked, looking to her mama for clarification. "What do I agree to?"

The duchess grimaced. "That today, I think we should postpone any invitations or callers. I am not feeling the best, my dear."

"Oh." Her eyes widened, as if only now noticing her mama's paleness. "I will write to Miss Eberhardt immediately after breakfast and ask her to come tomorrow." Victoria placed down her fork, signaling she had finished her meal. "Would you like for me to keep you company today, Mama? I'm more than happy to."

Albert supposed if Victoria were going to be busy with nursing her parent, he would walk out to the hunting lodge and write for the day. He was still several pages behind on where he would like to be, and he had left his heroine in a most awkward predicament that he needed to write her out of.

"That is not necessary, darling. I shall feel better after a tisane and some peace and quiet."

Breakfast was a silent affair after the short conversation. Victoria sipped her tea, lost in her own contemplation. The duke declared he was off to the Camberley, and the duchess finished her tea and some toast before taking herself upstairs.

Albert sat at the table, trying to form the words to ask Victoria what was troubling her. He did not want to push her too quickly and frighten her off. For all he knew, he may have already scared her away after what they had done together. Not to mention their disagreement over her choosing women to throw at his head.

Last evening, she was upset after his dance with Lady Sophie, but Victoria did not want a husband. Was she fighting with her own convictions? Her own hopes and dreams?

"If you'll excuse me," she said, fleeing yet again from his presence. He stared at the empty door she had all but ran through and frowned, slumping back in his chair.

What on earth was he to do?

Albert pushed back his chair. He called for his cap and cane and started for the hunting lodge. His mind was a chaos of ideas and thoughts of fixing what was so obviously broken between them.

But then, maybe she did not want to fix the rift. Was this her way of leaving him, letting him move forward in life without her by his side? Without her guidance in his so-called quest to find a wife.

He whacked a flower on the field, sending the yellow bud flying across the ground. He didn't want any other woman but her. This whole wife charade had gone on long enough. He needed to tell her the truth of how he felt about her. That he wanted her and no one else, let her decide his fate as only she could.

She would either fall into his arms or leave him.

He ran a hand through his hair, at a loss, his stomach in knots. Damn, he hoped it was the former. He wasn't sure he could live if it were the latter.

. . .

Victoria stayed in her room for as long as she could before the four walls and furniture, no matter how prettily decorated, started to grate on her nerves. She rang the bell for her maid and ordered the horse Lord Melvin had allocated to her for their stay to be saddled for a ride.

Her fear was unfounded. For days she had been worried she cared for Albert more than she should. That she wanted him for herself, but she did not. There was too much in her future to look forward to, to be worrying about how her friend made her feel when in his arms.

He gave her pleasure. They had given each other pleasure, that was all. To be worried about satisfaction equating to deeper emotions was a silly thing to do. Women had lovers all the time in London. She knew of several widows who enjoyed the company of men after their husbands had died. No one was declaring themselves so in love that they wanted to marry again.

She could be like those women. Not in the sense that she would take many lovers, but that she would enjoy being with Lord Melvin while he remained unmarried.

Her maid entered the room just as she was picking up her whip, notifying her that her horse was saddled and waiting at the stables.

Victoria made her way out to the stables, dismissing the need for a groom. She cantered out of the yard, into the surrounding forest, and directly toward the hunting lodge.

Somehow she knew Albert would be there, scribbling away as Lady Sophie had said. Somewhere in that building, he hid his author persona, his manuscripts. If there were any deeper feelings between them, Albert would have disclosed that little secret. It had not been declared, and it only added another layer of fortification that she had been wrong to worry Lord Melvin felt more for her than she wanted him to.

That she felt more for him than she ought. Her jealousy had

been because she did not want to share him at present. Not with anyone, not when he could give her so much satisfaction while she was a guest here.

But that was unfair to him and the lady who would eventually become his wife. She needed to be more immune to seeing him with others. After Albert married another, she would survive. Move forward and be happy in her life.

"I will," she yelled aloud.

Victoria slowed her mount as she came close to the lodge. Smoke billowed out of the chimney, and she knew Albert was there. Wanting to see for herself if he were scribbling away in a book, she tied her horse to a tree a little away from the lodge and walked the rest of the distance.

Feeling like a thief in the night, she tiptoed up to the cottage, not wanting to make a sound. Albert did not come to the door, and she hoped that meant that he had not heard her. As slowly as she could, she peeked through the glass window and watched him for several minutes.

He was bent over his desk before the fire, his shirtsleeves rolled up, exposing his muscled forearms. His hand was indeed scribbling with a speed that told her he was far away in another world and telling of the tales there.

Her heart did a little flip that her Albert Kester, Marquess Melvin, had to be Elbert Retsek. Not that it mattered if he were not. But the page that she found and now this sneaking away at all times of the day and night to write seemed too much of a coincidence.

She bit her lip, wondering how she was going to bring up that conversation. She was a forthright person. Her best approach was probably direct and without delay.

He sat back, stretching, and she jumped back out of sight. She warred with herself to go inside, to break his concentration when he seemed so involved with his words.

But then she needed to speak to him, away from her mama

and brother. Tell him that she had let him down last evening and that her slip in concentration would not happen again. That she would no longer throw women at his head unless he wanted an introduction. She was his friend and would be a help, not a hindrance, until the day she watched him marry.

Only, she could not make herself knock on the door. Instead, she stared at it for several minutes before slipping away. She would speak to him after the dance in Camberley. There was little point in doing it now when Albert was so close to moving forward with his life and without her in it to complicate matters further. Plus, he was busy with his work. All excuses she was willing to use if it meant postponing the inevitable.

CHAPTER 26

A few days later, the country dance at the local village was in full swing when their carriage rolled to a stop outside the hall's front door. Several other carriages lined the street. Other gentry of the area waiting for their turn to come to a stop before the double doors to the hall so they may disembark.

Her mama's attention was fixed outside the carriage window, watching the guests who strolled along the cobbled streets, mentioning the gowns and jewels, who had partners, and who walked with older chaperones. That several young ladies were wearing dresses from last year's belle assemble, which seemed to shock her mama so much so that she mentioned it several more times before it was their turn to alight.

"I'm sure if the young ladies had the opportunity, Mama, they would have ensured their dresses were up to London standard," Victoria drawled, one of the many things that vexed her when it came to the *beau monde*. How very vocal they were when one was so unfortunate to wear a dress from the previous season. "Do not forget we're in Hampshire. I'm sure they try to keep up with the latest fashions as best they can."

Albert, who was sitting beside Josh, grinned at her across the carriage. On the other hand, Josh looked less than pleased to have to wait their turn to exit.

"What is taking so long, do you think? Mayhap the hall is full, and they're turning people away."

"Unlikely," Albert said, adjusting his cravat and checking his hair. "The hall is one of the largest in the country."

Was the man nervous? It was his first time out in society since her lessons had commenced. And although they had covered several situations that his lordship may come across during courtship, mostly they had been unable to keep from slipping into each other's arms. A most peculiar situation that Victoria needed to handle with care.

She liked Lord Melvin very much, and to hurt him with her choice of future, one that did not involve a second husband, was the last thing she wished to do.

"I'm sure we shall arrive soon, and then we may meet the local populace, dance until our feet are bruised, and drink until we're merry."

"You shall do only two of those things, Victoria," her mother chided. "To drink until one is merry is not a pastime that you are ever to take part in."

Victoria chuckled just as the carriage lurched forward several yards, and it was their turn to roll to a stop before the doors. "How wonderful. We're here," she declared, not bothering to answer her mama, who sometimes thought all her children, even the married ones, not yet old enough to know their boundaries.

Two young men ran to the carriage door, one opening the door while the other quickly lay down the steps. She supposed the ducal crest on the side of the carriage pulled not just their attention but several guests who mingled outside.

The music, lively, the hall full of laughter and conversation, floated out onto the street. Victoria stepped down from the vehicle and adjusted her gown as she waited for her mama. Albert and Josh stood nearby, both of them watching the guests outside scrutinize their every move.

"Come, Mama," Victoria said, taking her arm and walking up the short path to the doors. Albert nodded and spoke to several people, introducing them to the duke and his family before they stepped inside the hall.

It was a large building indeed. Albert was not wrong about that. An orchestra sat on an upstairs balcony, gifting the room with music without taking up the ballroom floor space. The room was a mixture of people of all social statuses. A servant announced them to the room, and several families started toward them, one being Miss Eberhardt. Unfortunately, the one woman whom Josh seemed almost desperate to meet again, Lady Sophie, was nowhere to be seen.

The introductions, the conversation took several minutes. Still, it felt like hours by the time they had located themselves halfway into the room, watching the dancers be carefree on the floor, enjoying their night of revelry.

"You see, Lord Melvin, it is not so very bad to be sociable. You are enjoying yourself, are you not?"

He stood beside her, clapping his hands in time with the music. "I find it most charming, and even more so since I have you by my side," he teased. "Will you dance a set with me?"

Victoria smiled, seeing no harm in one set. She took his hand, not caring how forward the action may appear. Albert was her friend, and she would hold his hand if she so wished. "I would love to dance. I did not think you would ask me."

Without warning, he dragged her into the throng of revelers to take part. They laughed, twirled, twisted, danced, and waltzed through several sets. The room was cloudy with smoke, sweat, and a multitude of perfumes.

Victoria was pleased she had worn a gown of less-conspicuous means. Had she worn one of her gowns from the season just past, they would have looked untouchable and unapproachable. As it were, several guests did not come up to speak to them, even to wish them well, but certainly, the local gentry seemed delighted that they were not so high in the instep that they would forgo such an event.

This was good for Albert too. He needed to learn how to interact with others, even after she returned home to Dunsleigh. "You must ask several young ladies to dance tonight. I insist, or I shall think that all my lessons were in vain."

He shook his head, looking less than pleased to be asked to do such a thing. "What would you say if I said I only wished to dance with you, my lady? Would you deny me?"

She could no sooner deny him than she could deny herself a sweetmeat—her favorite dessert. "No, I shall not deny you, but please, Albert. Do this for yourself if not for me. You must practice. And the people here care for you. You will not be denied a willing dance partner. I'm sure of it."

He spun her into a turn during a minuet, coming to stand at her back. His breath whispered against her ear, and she fought not to lean back in his arms, revel in his closeness.

"Whom should I choose that would please, my lady? If you so wish, I shall dance with whomever you like."

Victoria glanced about the room as best as she could. Several young ladies were watching them, and she could see the admiration, the small amount of jealousy in their gazes at the marquess, their local lord dancing with a woman who was not one of them.

"What about Miss Thompson, whom I was introduced to earlier this evening? She seemed lovely and not at all unfriendly to anyone, not even those who are less fortunate than the heiress." The young woman's father had made a fortune in coal, and as dirty as such an industry was, money still rose just as well in society as a title.

"I shall ask her to dance next if it pleases you. Now, will you please enjoy what is left of our time? Or will I need to ask you for a second set this evening?"

To dance with Lord Melvin was an honor, but she knew she could not monopolize his time. He was here for one reason and one reason only. To meet suitable, eligible young ladies to fill the role of Marchioness Melvin. The notion left a sour taste in her mouth, but at the end of the dance, she fixed a smile on her lips and watched as Lord Melvin led Miss Thompson out onto the floor for a waltz.

She was a tall woman, similar in height to Victoria. But where she was fair-haired, Miss Thomson was as dark as night. Her long, dark eyelashes fanned out over bright, almond-shaped eyes.

The woman was striking, and Lord Melvin seemed to be engaging her in lively conversation that they were both enjoying.

"Are you going to let him waltz off into the sunset with another young woman? Are you not the least bit envious, sister?" Josh prodded her, watching his friend as well. "I thought when you fled from the pianoforte the other evening that you disliked seeing Lord Melvin in the arms of another."

Victoria sighed, schooling her features to one of pride instead of the unease she felt bubbling up in her soul. "Lord Melvin wishes to marry, and I do not. It would be wrong of me to keep him from his desires when we are only friends."

"Friends, you say?" her brother said, rubbing his chin in thought. "The man is in love with you, and you're only friends?"

The word love twirled around in her mind. Lord Melvin was not in love with her. Lust, yes. But love. No. They did not feel such things. It was impossible. He knew that she was his friend, helping him. He would not be so foolish to allow himself to fall in love with her. Josh was addled and nothing more.

"Do not be absurd. Lord Melvin is, right as we speak, putting into practice all that I taught him. Why would you suggest such a thing about your friend? That is unkind."

"It is more unkind, sister, to steer a man toward affection and rip it away as if it is not returned. When everyone who sees you together knows that it is."

"I adore Lord Melvin. He is my friend."

Her brother shook his head. "You are now dishonest with yourself, which is even worse than being false with Melvin. You had better not learn your mind too late, Victoria, and come to regret your stubborn designs on life. Do so, and you may rue that choice and never recover from it."

"What are you saying?" she demanded, although a small part of her knew what Josh was alluding to. That she was so fixed on her course that she may miss the greatest opportunity gifted her.

Josh stared down at her with a patient smile. "I know you wish to remain alone. I do not blame you to protect yourself after Armstrong. Your desires to travel the world, remain a widow protect you from life. But think about that life for one moment, many years from now, when you're elderly, your family have all married and are busy with their own families. What will you have then? I fear that you will be lonely. I do not want you to be unhappy in your older years."

"I will not be unhappy. I shall have all of your children to keep me company and those of our sisters." Victoria loved her brother for his kindness, his concerns, but they were unfounded. No matter what her future held, one thing she was certain of, and that was her decision never to have children. It just wasn't in the cards for her, wasn't something she desired. She hoped her family would accept this fact and move on from pressuring her.

"You will not have family around you all the time, Victoria. Do please think rationally over this."

Victoria fought not to glare at her sibling. She glanced back to the dance floor only to see Albert leaning down as Miss Thompson whispered something in his ear. She narrowed her eyes. Was the lady truly interested in Albert? She supposed she would be. Anyone would be. It should not surprise her that just as men chased women about town, that ladies would show their interest as well.

She took a calming breath, stemming the emotions that roiled inside of her at seeing him so close to another. It was a reaction she needed to heed and squash.

She did not like feeling left out, and, with her brother chastising her on her wants for the future, the enjoyment of the evening diminished somewhat.

"If you'll excuse me. I think Mama is gesturing for me to attend her." Victoria moved away, not looking to where she was going, only that she knew she needed air. She spied her mother and ensured she went in the opposite direction. If Josh saw her maneuver, she did not heed.

The front doors to the hall beckoned, and without looking back, she left, strolling around the side of the building. Outside, the moonlit night bathed the surrounding park and grass in dappled light. There were several groups of people mingling outside, taking the air. Victoria spied a seat a little along the wall, just where the shadow of an elm tree blocked out the moonlight.

She sat, gazing out into the park beyond, thinking over her brother's words, thinking of Albert.

Tonight was supposed to be so easy. She was to help him toward marriage, yet thinking of him with another left her at sixes and sevens. She did not like seeing Miss Thompson in his arms, happy and too familiar after such a short introduction.

"Victoria?"

She jumped at the sound of her name before liquid warmth flowed through her at the sight of Albert standing only a few feet from her. He was so tall and broad, and devishly handsome. She inwardly sighed, hating that she would hurt him. Mayhap not tonight, but soon.

"I saw you hasten outside, and I thought something may have upset you."

He came and sat beside her, laying her shawl over her shoulders that he'd been kind enough to claim for her.

"I am well. My brother is insistent I do my duty for a second time and marry. He even went as far as to say that you're in love with me and that I should consider you for a husband. If you can believe that," she said, hoping he would dissuade her of the thought. He barked out a laugh, but even to her it sounded as hollow as her own words.

Albert thought furiously on how to answer Victoria. What to say to a woman who had declared what he was feeling. He wanted her as his wife, loved her most ardently, and nothing, no matter how many ladies waltzed in his arms, would change that.

Even while dancing with Miss Thompson, he knew Victoria's whereabouts, who she was speaking to, and when she had left. "Your family is seeing a possibility of us because we're spending so much time together, that is all. I suppose they know me, and it's only normal that they would think we suit," he said, keeping to their original plan for lessons on how to court a woman when one was as awkward as he was around the opposite sex.

He'd done very well this evening. His conversations with Miss Thompson were distinguished, and he'd not made a fool of himself once. "You would be pleased with me had you been dancing alone with Miss Thompson and me. I asked her about her likes and dislikes, her favorite flower, and dance. What her ancestral home is like and if she is attending London next Season. And I did it all without choking on my words out of fear of her reply."

"And did she reply to you?" Victoria asked him, meeting his gaze.

He reached out, smoothing the small worry line between her brows. "She did. In fact, she was more than forward with her responses."

"Do you think you would like to court her in town next year?" she asked, biting her lip.

Albert checked to see the location of the other guests and delightfully found this side of the hall now deserted. He leaned down, closing the space between them, and kissed her, stopping her from biting the sweet, plump lip of hers.

She melted against him, reaching up to run her hands into his hair. He loved the feel of her taking what she wanted, holding him close so she could kiss him back with as much fire as his own had been.

The kiss turned in an instant, demanding and hot. His tongue tangled with hers, their bodies thrust against each other, seeking contact and fulfilling a need that burned as hot as the sun. She tasted of champagne, a heady flavor intoxicating his mind. "Victoria, we should stop. We'll be caught," he said, taking her lips yet again, wanting to snatch her up and sit her on his lap.

Damn, he wanted to do a lot more than that to her. He wanted her in his bed now and forever.

"Do you think that Miss Thompson would kiss you so? Or that Lady Sophie would satisfy you as I do?"

"No, I do not. Nor do I think about them in such a way," he admitted, even though he knew he should not. He could not allow Victoria to believe that he, too, just like her brother, wished for them to be more than friends. For now, they needed to retain the teacher-student relationship they had settled into, if only to give him time to win her.

"You make me question my decisions, Albert. I do not know what I shall do when you're looking at me the way you are now."

He stared down at her. To him, Victoria was the most beautiful woman he had ever met in his life. He had based several characters on her and had wanted her with such fierce desire that sometimes sleep eluded him.

"I do not mean to make your life challenging. I know what you wish for in your future, and we have an agreement for lessons on etiquette and courtship. I should like to continue those. Come," he said, pulling her to stand. "Come inside and dance with me. There is to be a second waltz soon. I do not wish to dance with anyone else but you."

She grinned, allowing him to pull her up. She placed her hand atop his, and they started back indoors.

"I would like to dance with you too," he heard her say, and hope seized his soul.

Perchance there was a possibility for them if he stepped carefully about Victoria. The risk was certainly worth taking.

CHAPTER 27

Albert swept Victoria into the waltz, moving effortlessly around the throng of dancers partaking in the dance. She stared up at him, his sweet, handsome face lovely to gaze upon and admire.

An overwhelming deluge of emotions washed over her with how much she adored him. His friendship and honesty, his sweet, understanding nature. He made her question her dreams. If only he had courted her before Armstrong. The sting of that man's deception would never have happened. Perhaps then she would not be so wary of the marriage state. Or the fact that no matter how much you thought you knew someone, it could all be a mask—a lie.

Something told her, however, that marriage to Albert would be different, for he was different. But how could she be true to herself, give up what she longed for just because the man guiding her about the room made her want other things too?

She closed her eyes a moment, forcing her thoughts to clear. She would not debate her life right now, this instant. Instead, she would throw herself into the Camberley dance, this waltz, and enjoy herself until the sun broke on the horizon.

Albert pulled her close for a spin, his hand grazing the small of her back. His thumb brushed her spine, and she shivered, savoring his touch. The man had an uncanny ability to draw her in—a dangerous gift for a woman such as herself, set on her way and refusing to detour.

"Will you meet me later tonight? We could go over what you thought of my conduct here at the dance this evening. Guide me on what you think I could improve on if you like."

She grinned up at him, looking forward to when they would return home so she may be alone with him. Do what she so desperately wanted to do with him right now. Kiss him, tease him, learn new things with him from the sketchbook.

"I think you're doing very well already, my lord. You could, I suppose, hold me a little closer."

His gaze burned into hers, and heat licked up her spine. "Like this," he asked, pulling her the tiniest bit nearer to him. Her breasts brushed the lapels of his coat. She sucked in a breath, advancing closer still to tease her body the way she liked.

"Yes, just like that."

A muscle worked in his jaw. Victoria wanted to reach up and clasp his face, kiss him, no matter what scandal broke after the fact.

"Have you been studying the book?" he whispered, leaning down toward her ear. His warm breath tickled her, and she shivered. "Is there anything in particular that has caught your attention you would like to try? That you think my future bride would enjoy?"

There had been one drawing in the sketch that she had looked at and studied for many hours. That of a woman, kissing a man's erect shaft. Smaller illustrations showed the woman taking the man fully into her mouth. The memory of him kissing her between the legs made her ache, and she supposed it would be the same for him. Or at least that is what she assumed.

"There is one thing that looks to be safe to try." And she supposed when he married, he could ask his wife to perform a similar act if she were so inclined.

His lips twisted into a wicked grin. "And what is it?"

Victoria pushed her hips to graze his buckskin breeches. Albert's eyes widened, but he did not say anything, merely stared at her in a way that made her want to leave the dance right now.

She looked about, checking they were as alone as they could be during a waltz. "I want to kiss you. But not on your lips. I want to kiss you here," she admitted, moving against him yet again.

Albert let out a huff of breath intertwined with a groan. "You cannot do that, as much as I would enjoy the lesson."

Victoria shrugged, determined to get her way. She licked her lips, already imagining what he would do when she took him in hand, guided him into her mouth. Would he moan her name, clasp her hair as she had gripped his? When he spent his seed, what would he do? Would it spill into her mouth, or would he make her stop?

"Oh, I'm going to start and finish the lesson, my lord. That is part of the deal, is it not? For us both to learn while we're able to do so."

He spun her in the dance, and she laughed, catching sight of her mother, who looked upon them with a warm but calculating gaze.

"Mama is watching us, and if I can read my mama as well as I believe I can, I do think she believes we're courting."

He raised his brows, setting Victoria a respectable distance from him again. "I suppose we do look comfortable enough in each other's company that people would assume that is the case. But your mama knows you are helping me navigate the marriage mart. I'm sure she's merely pleased we are enjoying ourselves."

"I would be enjoying myself more should we be alone and back at Rosedale."

Albert missed a step in the dance but righted them before being noticed. "Do not say such things, Victoria."

She let her hand slide up his shoulder, her finger tracing the back of his neck. "I want to see you shatter under my kiss, Albert. Just as I shattered under yours."

Albert fought for calm, his body a riot of wants and needs. He wanted to drag her from the dance, out into the carriage, and have her in all the ways imaginable. And more if she agreed.

As it was, he was glad there were several minutes left of the waltz due to his raging cock in his breeches that should anyone look closely enough, would undoubtedly notice.

He wanted to see her plump, supple lips wrapped about his phallus. He wanted to see her work him, suck him hard until he spilled in her mouth. The idea that is what she wanted to do to him left him incapable of calm.

"What if you do not like it?"

She lifted one delicate shoulder, looking up at him under long, dark lashes. She was so pretty it made him ache just being near her. With a need that went beyond the physical, he wanted her to be his, to have her in his bed every night so he could give her pleasure. Watch her shatter under his touch again and again.

"I shall like it. I know I will. And there is no danger in what we are to do. I cannot become *enceinte* by being with you in that way."

No, she could not. But that did not mean that it made her wholly safe. For him, at least, each time they were together, either like this, conversing and alone or giving each other pleasure, his heart became less independent of her.

He was in love with her, had been for years if he were

truthful with himself. How was he to watch her leave him when she tired of the lessons and thought him prepared for the world, the London season. A life without her?

He could not continue with the lessons indefinitely. Eventually, she would return home, and he would have lost her.

The dance came to a regretful end, and he led her over to her mama.

"I think I have had enough of the dance, my lord," Victoria remarked, as she joined her mother and brother, who was speaking to Lord Hammilyn just a little ways away.

"I agree, my dear. Shall I motion Josh that we're ready to depart?"

Victoria nodded just as loud shouts and the sound of shattering wood sounded near the back of the hall.

"Quickly, to the carriage," Josh said, ushering them toward the doors. "Two local men have started brawling."

Albert looked to where the commotion occurred and noted several other men had now joined in the fray, and the scene represented a day at Gentleman Jackson more than a country dance. "We must leave," he agreed, helping the duke separate the ladies from the danger.

Albert helped the duke as he searched for the family carriage. Thankfully it was not blocked in, and they were soon on their way back to Rosedale.

"Well, I say. Tonight was going so well too. Several young gentlemen wished to dance with you, Victoria. I suppose we shall have to wait for Lord and Lady Hammilyn's ball for them to ask for your hand."

"Mama, I hope you have not been singing my praises to everyone who should walk by you. You know that I find such interfering unpalatable."

"Really, dear. How else am I to have you find a husband when you do nothing to draw them in? If I need to converse with young men in your stead, sing your praises, then I shall. When you are happily settled, I shall stop."

Albert watched as Victoria rolled her eyes before meeting his gaze across the darkened carriage. He fisted his hands at his sides. The idea of Victoria being courted, of having sweet, hollow words whispered in her ears, left him to want to do physical damage to anyone who dared courtship with her.

She could not want anyone else. Certainly, from what she said, she did not want any man. The urge to reach across, wrench her onto his lap, and start what she had promised him the night would encompass overwhelmed him.

"In any case, I suppose it will not be tonight." The duchess yawned, covering her mouth with the little silk fan that hung on her wrist. "I am to bed when we return home."

"I agree," Victoria said, a mischievous light in her eye. Albert knew she would do no such thing. Expectation thrummed through his veins, and he counted down the time until she was in his arms and his bed.

Later...

CHAPTER 28

Upon returning home, Victoria ordered warm water to her room and bathed quickly. After the dance, the smoke and scents from the night left her in need of a wash. Her maid helped her, brushing her hair and setting it into a long knot that slipped over her shoulder.

Victoria dismissed her maid for the night before getting under the covers of her bed. The house soon quietened, the sound of the last servants going about the halls and rooms, dousing the candles and collecting any dishes that may have been used in the parlor upstairs.

Victoria sneaked out of bed, opening her door to check into the hall, pleased to see it cloaked in darkness, only slithers of moonlight stole in from the bank of windows at either end of the hall.

She checked her brother's door, saw no light coming from under it, and sneaked out of her room, closing her door as quietly as she could before tiptoeing to Albert's suite.

Without knocking, she entered and found herself riveted to the spot. Albert stood before his washbasin, stark naked. His bottom, toned and a lovely muscular shape stared directly at her.

Victoria remembered to close the door and snipped the lock, wasting no time in going over to him. He bent over the bowl, seemingly unfazed that she was seeing him in his full glory.

And what a glorious sight he was to behold. With husbands such as Albert to come home to after a ball or party, one would have to wonder why one would go out at all.

Or travel abroad as a widow when one could have such a man warming one's bed.

Victoria came up behind him, running her hand over his bottom. Goosebumps rose on his back, and she kissed him there, along his spine, wanting him with a need that scared her.

She should not be here or igniting a rendezvous, but blast her scattered mind, she could not leave. Could not do the right thing by the man before her.

"You are lovely to behold, my lord." Emboldened, she reached around, running her finger around the underside of his shaft. His manhood jutted out, erect and eager. She felt him, teased him and her stomach clenched, wanting him with a madness that would not be sated.

He turned, staring down at her. Her attention snapped to his muscled chest and she ogled it without indiscretion. With every breath, it rose and fell, tightened, and glistened from the little amount of water from his wash.

"You make my heart stop," he cooed, his voice husky. Albert scooped her up in his arms, taking her lips in a kiss that made her forget all her troubles. Her future, the decisions she had to make melted away as he carried her over to the bed, laying her down.

He joined her, and she pushed him to lay on his back, a question in his blue orbs over what she was doing. "Tonight, my lord, it is my turn to learn what you like. Enjoy you as much as I want." Victoria ran her hand over his chest, her attention feasting on his manhood. A purple-blue vein ran along its length, his shaft thick and long.

Whenever Paul had come to their marriage bed it had been dark and she scarcely viewed his manhood in the six weeks they were married. Certainly, they had never learned each other as privately as she was becoming to know Albert.

He lay his arms beneath his head, watching her, an amused light glinted in his blue orbs. "Do you like what you see, my lady?"

She smiled, biting her lip as she moved down the bed to come face-to-face with his shaft. Victoria touched it softly, marveling at its silky softness. "I love what I see, Albert. I'm going to kiss you there now," she admitted to him.

She heard him suck in a calming breath, but he did not move or try to stop her. The first taste of him, earthy and a little salty was not unpleasant, if anything, she liked the essence. She kissed the tip of his manhood, smiling as it jumped at her touch. With care, she wrapped her lips about the head of his shaft, sucking. "Is this right?" she asked him.

His fingers spiked through her hair. "Yes," he gasped.

Victoria could feel every muscle in Albert's body tighten. A little part of her crowed that she could make him mad with desire.

She took him into her mouth fully then. The feel of him, hard, but velvety was unlike any sensation she'd ever experienced before. He quivered each time she took him farther into her mouth.

"Yes, like that, my darling," he breathed, his voice tremulous.

Victoria watched him as she gave him pleasure, their eyes met, his ablaze with a need that sparked heat at her core.

"I have another idea," he groaned, sitting up and holding her at bay.

She sat back on her haunches, unsure what this idea would be. "Tell me what it is?"

Albert reached for her nightdress, pulling it from her body in one swift movement. She sat on his bed now, as naked as he. The cool night air kissed her skin, and she felt her nipples pucker under his inspection. He traced her pinkened flesh, laying a sweet kiss on each of her breasts.

She sighed, holding him close.

"While you're taking me in your mouth, let me bring you to climax. Let me taste you too but at the same time."

"Is that possible?" Her body hummed at the idea of Albert kissing her cunny while she pleasured him. Moisture flooded her core at the idea of such naughtiness.

"It's in the book. Trust me, it's possible."

She bit her lip, nodding. "I'm willing if you are."

Albert chuckled, pulling her close. "You know I'm more than willing. Now, come."

Victoria shivered, hoping he meant that literally as well as figuratively.

Albert lay back down on the bed and took several calming breaths as Victoria straddled his body, placing her sweet cunny before his face. He'd never partaken in the sexual position, but he had admired the sketching in the book on several occasions.

The thought that Victoria trusted him enough to allow him such liberties with her body left him honored. He clasped her ass, slipping her against his face, and kissed her.

There...

She was hot and wet, her gasp of pleasure as he kissed her weeping flesh making his cock rock hard. Without inhibition she undulated against his tongue, taking her pleasure, her gasps and moans pushing him to the brink.

She sucked his cock with vigor, enjoying herself as much as he. He teased her, flicked her nubbin with unrelentless strokes.

She did not shy away, lose herself in her pleasure, but took him deeper into her mouth, rose to his challenge. He clasped her ass, holding her against his face and fucked her as well as she deserved, pushed her toward climax.

She moaned about his cock as he felt the first tremors of her climax thrum through her body. The knowledge spiked his release, and he came, hard and strong, pumping his seed until he was spent.

For a time, they lay as they were, their breathing ragged, their bodies damp with sweat and sex. Victoria rolled to his side and he smiled at her satisfied chuckle.

"Well, I must admit that position may have become one of my favorites, my lord."

He slapped her on the ass, electing a squeal from her. "Albert, not my lord. Not after that." He gestured between them.

"True." She smiled, meeting his gaze. "What other delightful positions are in that book of yours? If they are as good as the one we just tried, I'll be counting down the hours until we're alone again."

He would, too, count the hours. But a little tidbit of despair prickled his soul. He did not want to have to wait for the house to be abed. Have to wait for them to steal away to unoccupied rooms. He wanted to be able to make love to Victoria whenever they wished. He wanted her to be his wife, his to love and cherish forever.

"There are others we can try," he found himself saying. "Meet me here this time tomorrow night, and we'll explore more of what we can do together."

She flipped about on the bed, slumping over his chest. She kissed him, a slow, intoxicating kiss that left his heart aching. "Tonight was my choice. Tomorrow I shall let you choose what we do."

Marry me then, Albert wanted to ask. Instead, he raised his brow, giving her a mischievous grin. "A dangerous game, Victoria. Are you sure you wish to keep playing?"

"Oh yes, I like this game," she said before kissing him soundly once again, and they lost each other to several more hours of pleasure. And Albert lost a little more of his heart to the woman in his arms.

CHAPTER 29

The following day dawned one of the hottest of the year, even though the summer months were giving way to August's chill. Victoria wore a dress of white muslin and ordered lemonade out on the terrace as she caught up with her sister's correspondence.

She told Alice of her time here, her enjoyment, and the town dance, but she did not tell her sister everything that had taken place within the walls of the Rosedale estate.

Her mama sat across from her, waving her silk fan before her face as she gazed out on the lawn.

"You and Lord Melvin seem to be fast friends. Is there a possibility with you helping him gain his feet in society that you have not fallen at his?"

Her mother's question pulled her from her thoughts, and she glanced up, noting her mother's serious visage.

"Of course not," she lied, knowing that was far from the truth. She had come to not only enjoy Albert's company but longed for it. The idea of leaving, traveling for years about the world without him, left her cold instead of excited.

It was a turn of events that she had not assumed would

happen, and she wasn't entirely happy about her muddled thoughts. All of her conflicting emotions could be laid at her bastard late husband's feet. His cruelty and scandalous lifestyle would be enough to scare anyone for the hills and never wish to marry again. She was no different, even though Albert was nothing like Paul.

"We are friends. Nothing more, Mama."

Her mother let out a little annoyed huff of breath. "Please, my dear. I may be older than you, and my first season may have happened some years ago, but this is not my first foray into a ballroom. I know when two people are more than friends."

Victoria continued to scribble words down to her sister, but as to what she was writing, she could not say. Her mother's words distracted her to no end. "Lord Melvin wishes for a wife. You forget that I do not wish for another husband."

Her mother clicked her tongue in annoyance. "You cannot travel the world on your own, my dear. Even if you are a widow and heiress, a daughter, and sister to a duke. You will get a reputation as being fast and our family will be looked down upon. Is that what you want?"

She sat back in her chair, throwing down her quill. "What do you mean I will gain a reputation? I will do as I want, and no one will stop me. I married the man you all thought fabulous and look how that turned out. He ran off with a maid six weeks into our marriage, and then continued to whore his way about Europe before a husband shot him. No one will censure me for wanting to remain alone, not after Paul."

"I do believe your brother will want you to reconsider your plans."

"Not when he knows how important it is to me," Victoria argued, hating the idea of being told what to do by anyone, even her family. This was her life. Hers to live and enjoy. What was life if one hated all that it encompassed? "And I can do as I please. I'm not a debutante anymore, Mama. I'm a widow, such as yourself. Please try and remember such facts."

When Paul had run off, after the initial shock had passed, anger replaced any sadness she may have felt. As a man he was free to do as he liked, sleep with numerous women without thought to his wife. She had promised herself that she would never be at another man's beck and call. Never give them the power to hurt her, humiliate her as she had already endured.

The world was large and getting bigger by the day. So much to see other than English countrysides, grand estates, and the London Season. To change her plans simply because she had found pleasure in another man's arms was illogical. No matter how much she cared for Albert, the life he wanted was so different to the one she coveted.

She could not settle again.

"I know Mr. Armstrong caused you pain and embarrassment, but Lord Melvin will not. You have nothing to fear from marrying his lordship."

"Nothing but the fact that I shall be stuck here in Hampshire for the rest of my life. Every year pushing out another child that will keep the family happy, so long as at least one is a male."

"You speak as if you are a broodmare."

"Am I not?" she argued. "Is that not what we're all expected as ladies to be? Women of privilege. Marry men of equal value, tolerate all their vices and mistresses they have in London while pushing out their children, putting our lives at risk each time we do so. I do not want that kind of life. I do not want children or a husband, Mama."

There, she had admitted it. Her mother's face paled, and anyone would think the woman had seen a ghost. Her mother did not speak for a moment, even though her mouth opened and closed several times.

"You cannot mean what you say," she eventually gasped.

Victoria stood, packing the letters she was reading and

writing in the little writing box she had brought down from her room. "I do mean every word. You do not need me to have children too. Or to marry again. You have three other daughters already married with children. Josh will be next, and he will do his duty to the family. I do not see why I should have to as well. It is unfair to ask this of me when you know how against it all I am. I cannot trust anyone, Mama with my heart. I will not have it broken for a second time."

"Victoria, darling, it will not," her mother cajoled, but Victoria wasn't hearing it.

She turned about, striding down the terrace stairs and starting for the lake. She mumbled expletives, hating to argue with her mama but also disliking what was expected of her, even after all that had happened with Paul. It was utterly unfair. Determination spiked through her and she huffed out a breath. It was not to be borne, and nor would she bear it. Never again.

Albert heard Victoria coming through the trees before he saw her. Her mumbling to herself, words such as vexing family, stuff and nonsense, expectations just some of the few terms she pitched out into the world at no one in particular.

He sat at the short dock, his feet bare and dangling in the water on this hot day.

She came into view and skidded to stop when she spied him. He waved, smiling at her and her shoulders slumped before she joined him, kicking off her silk slippers and pulling down her stockings without care to dangle her feet too in the water.

"Something the matter?" he asked her, knowing that there was.

She shook her head, staring down at the dark water of the lake. "Nothing that I am not handling." She paused. "I will say that had I never married Paul my troubles would be naught," she teased, throwing him a self-deprecating smile. "What are you doing down here at the lake all on your own?"

He pointed to the tackle and rod behind him. "I was fishing. Your brother was here but wanted to go for a ride before it grew too warm."

Victoria raised her face to the sky, giving him the perfect view of her profile. His heart did a little thump at how much he cared for her. How much he longed for Victoria to care for him in the same way.

Was his dream for them a fantasy? Hell, he hoped it was not so.

"It is sunny today. It is probably why my mama is so vexing. She does not like the heat," she admitted.

Albert did not push her to find out what had happened, and instead, offered an idea to please instead. "Would you like to swim? The water is not chill."

Her eyes widened, and she looked back toward the house.

"No one can see us from here," he offered when she looked to refuse. "And I've told my servants not to disturb me."

A mischievous grin lifted on her supple lips. "Will you help me with my gown?" Victoria turned, giving him her back.

Albert unclipped the tiny buttons at her back, admiring her creamy-soft skin beneath her shift. "You have a very kissable back." He caressed her neck, nuzzling just beneath her ear.

She pushed back against him, reaching up to clasp his hair. "Come, let's swim."

Victoria stood, the gown slipping to her feet before she ran and jumped off the end of the dock, eliciting a squeal as she hit the cold water. Albert wrenched off his waistcoat and pulled his cravat free before throwing his shirt onto the dock with all of their clothes. He left his breeches on and then joined her, jumping in beside her.

She laughed, swimming over to him and wrapping her arms around his neck. For a moment she stared at him, the droplets of water sitting on her long eyelashes. Her green eyes were fierce with the lake surrounding them, and then she kissed him. Albert pulled her legs about his waist, holding on to the dock to keep them afloat.

The kiss was as wild and demanding as the woman in his arms. Untamed and wicked. Love welled up inside of him. She was his life, and he needed Victoria to realize that he was hers. That being married to him did not mean she had to give up her dreams, just let him be part of them. He would compromise if it meant they were to be married.

Until then, he would play this game until she muddled through her thoughts, forgave the past and welcomed the future with open arms.

Victoria needed time, and he was in no rush. He'd wait forever if he needed to.

CHAPTER 30

The days passed by, followed by nights of scandalous awakenings. Victoria could not remember enjoying herself so much before at any house party in all the years she attended them.

But Albert was a very special host and paid particular attention to her. Her wants and desires. He was utterly addicting and wicked, and she savored every moment in his arms.

The carriage rolled to a stop before the estate of Lord and Lady Hammilyn's home. The house wasn't as large as Rosedale and was quarter the size of Dunsleigh. Even so, the earl's property was grand and very pretty with its sandstone walls, glistening windows, and lanterns that lined the oak drive up to the house.

Josh this evening looked particularly dashing, and she wondered if he had set his cap on Lady Sophie and dressed to impress the heiress. She was very beautiful, but cold, Victoria could not help but think. Josh needed a kind and cheerful lady like his character, and Victoria wasn't sure they suited all that well.

Her mama spoke very little. Still a little put out after their disagreement several days ago. She supposed she would have to make peace with her mama, but how to do so when she was determined to live her life as she saw fit?

"We're here," Josh stated, slipping his top hat onto his head. He jumped down first, helping Mama and then Victoria to alight. Albert joined Victoria and took her hand, placing it on his arm as they walked up the short flight of steps into the house.

Several friends from London were guests in the ballroom and after introductions they joined them. For some time, Victoria chatted about fashion, London, who had returned to their estates and what scandals were brewing in town. Thankfully she was no longer the topic of conversation regarding that subject. Albert, by her side, maintained conversation well with people of his social sphere. He had come such a very long way since their first lessons. He would do splendidly next year in town.

She pulled him aside, smiling up at him. "I know you do not want me to introduce any ladies to you, but I see Miss Marigold Scottsdale has arrived with her brother, and no one has joined them. Being one of the highest-ranked gentlemen in the county, maybe you could go speak to them and make them feel more welcome."

"Was not Mr. Scottsdale embroiled in some scandal last year?" Albert asked her, not moving away from her side.

Victoria frowned, thinking over the past season. "I do not believe so, but then I have not circulated in their group of friends. Either way, that they have been invited here, I'm sure whatever you heard is unworthy of concern."

He ran a hand across his jaw, an uncertain look crossing his features. Victoria steeled herself to observe him with Miss Scottsdale. This what he needed to do if he were to move forward with his plan for a wife. This was what he wanted in life. She could not stand in his way simply because she enjoyed his company and the delights they shared when in private.

"Go and speak to them, Albert. I shall be perfectly well here with my friends."

He nodded and reluctantly started toward the two guests. Victoria returned to her group, moving aside somewhat so she could watch Albert's interactions. Relief was evident on Mr. Scottsdale at the marquess's presence, and Victoria could not help but feel sorry for the pair. The *ton*, when anyone stepped out of line, could be so harsh in their criticisms. Maybe Mr. Scottsdale had been in a little trouble and had not been fully forgiven for it yet. She knew all too well how it felt to be a pariah, even though she had been the innocent party of her husband's whoring, the *ton* had not seen it that way.

"Lady Victoria, you are here with Lord Melvin and your brother the duke, of course. It is good of you to join our small society here in Camberley. I know that you are not used to such menial events."

Victoria turned to Lady Sophie, nodding in welcome. "There is nothing menial about Camberley at all. I have enjoyed myself immensely while staying here."

Lady Sophie raised a skeptical brow. "Really? Lord Melvin and his penchant for privacy, a homebody of sorts I did not think would suit your character or your social calendar."

"Lord Melvin has been friends with my brother for some years, and Mama and I had no fixed engagements, so thought to join the duke on visiting his friends after the season." Victoria pinned a smile to her lips. "I did not think you would be interested in my social calendar."

"My father knows of everyone's whereabouts or at least those he chooses to know. My father, you see, has designs on me marrying a lord or a duke. I am yet to make up my mind which one I want."

Victoria narrowed her eyes, a prickly sensation rising along her skin. "You are yet to have your season. Would you choose before you attended London?"

Lady Sophie lifted one delicate shoulder into a shrug. "My father is determined to see me married, and so I shall. If I marry, I do not wish to ever be in reduced circumstances, and so I think I have two options to satisfy both mine and my father's wishes."

"And what is that?" Victoria could not help but ask, even though she knew she would not like the answer.

"Why, I shall choose between Lord Melvin and your brother the duke. Two of the wealthiest men in England. While the duke has been more forthcoming in his interest, Lord Melvin is certainly curious, do you not think? And handsome, which a husband should be if one is so lucky."

Victoria swallowed the ball of fire that lodged in her throat. "Do you care for Lord Melvin?" Not that Victoria should ask such a personal question, but Albert deserved a lady who loved him, adored him in every way. She would never allow Albert to marry a woman who did not care for him, only his money, even if she did not want marriage herself.

"Does not matter if I do not. He would be marrying me for my dowry and to have his children. Love is not a requirement."

"And your thoughts on my brother?"

A small smile played about Lady Sophie's mouth, and Victoria decided she did not like her. The woman was calculating, and next Season, whoever ended up married to the chit would need all the luck in the world to make such a marriage work. She would not be an easy woman to be hitched to.

"I'll be a duchess. There is nothing more to say than that."

Victoria cleared her throat, forcing the words she had to speak. "You do understand that I am the duke's sister and that Lord Melvin is a family friend. After what you have said, I wonder if you're suitable for either man at all."

"Really?" Lady Sophie laughed. Victoria stared at her,

nonplussed and not quite believing the woman found her words so amusing.

"Why are you laughing?"

Lady Sophie waved her hand before her face, the amused farce carrying on too long. "You are amusing, my lady, and I find it surprising you would care that I would see marriage as a binding agreement. You are the one who has sworn off marriage, after living through a disastrous one. I would have thought you would agree with me and urge me to guard my heart against any spouses who have little respect for their wives. Marriage is a contract and without love, one cannot be hurt. If I was unfortunate enough to marry a man such as your late husband, well, if I did not love him, I would not care if he were shot on foreign shores."

Victoria glanced about the room, discombobulated by Lady Sophie's words. Was she right? Is that how society saw her now? Like a woman sworn off men, of marriage as if it were some dirty institution to be pitied and ridiculed for those who chose that path?

To her shame, there was truth to Lady Sophie's words. Marriage was not something she longed to endure a second time. Nor the children that followed the wedding day. But then, when she looked across a ballroom such as the one where she now stood, watching Lord Melvin, the small lines at the corner of his eyes creasing when he smiled and laughed, she could not imagine not seeing his face every day. Of not having a future with him.

"I do not see you as a foe, Lady Sophie. I merely want more for my brother and Lord Melvin than a cold wife unable to love. While I may not be searching for a husband, that does not mean that I do not believe that love is real and can be found between people. My siblings are proof that the emotion can be found and nurtured."

"But you still do not want it."

Not with men such as her late husband had been, she did not. But with men such as Lord Melvin, well, that was a vexing issue she had been debating for weeks. Not that he'd asked her to marry him, even though he had hinted a time or two that he would be willing to travel with her. Give her freedom.

She narrowed her eyes. But would he really? Men were very agreeable during the engagement, and then once the marriage had taken place, they were known to change their character and minds. Paul's true character—a cheating snake—had not taken long to slither out of its hole and strike at anything in a skirt.

Victoria did not think Albert was such a man, but then she had been wrong before. Her life was all such a mess, choices coming at her, decisions she wasn't ready to make. She needed time to think. That was all.

"I wish you well next season, Lady Sophie."

Victoria bid her good evening and went to find her mother, or better yet, a whiskey decanter. She needed a little toddy before continuing this ball. A few minutes later she found herself headed for the library and, thankfully, welcome peace from the bustling room. Once she had steadied her racing heart and stopped imagining everyone was still talking of her in the way Lady Sophie had mentioned all would be well.

CHAPTER 31

Albert cast his eyes over the guests bustling about the ballroom and could not find Victoria. He stood with her mother, hoping she would return so he may dance with her, but after several minutes and she still did not appear, concern bit at his gut and would not relent.

He left the duchess speaking to a group of matrons, all of them watching their charges like hawks. He moved through the room, taking care not to be pulled into a conversation that he could not remove himself from.

Penworth stood talking near the supper room doors with Lady Sophie, and something about his friend's visage made him wonder if the duke was enjoying the conversation with the young woman as much as he would like.

He moved on, leaving the room and walking past the ladies' retiring room and the men's salon set out for their use during the ball. Victoria did not appear near either of these spaces, and he stood in the hall for several minutes, wondering where she was.

Was she safe? Had she become unwell?

He started back downstairs, striding toward the rear of the

house, and skidded to a stop before the library doors. They stood slightly ajar. Inside he could see Victoria standing beside a sideboard where the whiskey decanter stood, pouring herself a glass.

"Victoria? What are you doing in here?" he asked, coming into the room and closing the door behind him.

She spun about, a little of the liquid spilling onto the floor. "I needed time away from the ball." She sipped her drink. "Oh, and Lady Sophie is not the lady for you. Trust me, should you marry her, your marriage will be as miserable as my first one."

His life would be miserable no matter whom he married if that woman was not the one standing before him.

"I do not want to marry Lady Sophie. Your concerns are moot."

She sighed, going over and slumping against the desk. "Well, thank heavens for that. I suppose now I only have my brother to worry about."

Albert did not think she did in truth. Penworth looked to have formed his own opinion on the lady in the past hour since their arrival. He reached out and took the whiskey glass, downing what was left of the drink.

"Never drink alone," he teased her, stepping against her to reach behind and place the glass on the desk.

His body, close to hers, soared with desire. Without caution, he reached out, placing her onto the desk. Her eyes darkened, a wicked light entering her jade orbs. She did not shy away from his touch but reached for him, settling him between her legs.

"I want you so much," he admitted, kissing her deep and long. Victoria sighed, taking all that he could give her. The demanding kiss stole his breath and wits, and he knew he had to feel her.

Tease her sweet flesh until she shattered in his arms.

He shuffled up her silk ballgown, pooling it at her waist. The soft skin of her thighs making him burn, his cock hard and aching to have her.

"Touch me, Albert," she begged him. "Please, touch me."

He could not deny her. He slipped his hand between her legs, teasing her bud, wanting to make it bloom. She was wet, achingly so. Feeling bold, he teased a finger into her hot core. She clamped about him, making stars flash before his eyes.

He moaned, wishing it was his cock that had taken her instead.

"Oh yes. Touch me, tease me."

His cock ached, and he could feel himself on the brink of orgasm at her breathy pleas. He fucked her with his hand, pushing her toward a climax they would both enjoy. She clutched at his shoulders, her head thrown back, lost to her pleasure. He kissed her sweet neck, reveling in her scent, her breathy sighs, and pleas for more. She rode his hand, taking all that he made her feel before the first tremors of her release drew at his finger.

Her body milked his digit, and he rubbed her nubbin as the last of the tremors wilted from her.

As the haze of pleasure subsided and Victoria came back to the present, he grinned, knowing he would never tire of the sight of her during climax. "That was unusual, but I do believe we've just covered another act within our sketchbook," he declared, helping her to sit up.

She smiled up at him her eyes hazy with the aftermath of pleasure. She adjusted her gown and settled her skirts about her legs. Her cheeks kissed with a rosy hue, she resembled a lady well-pleased. "Hmm, I do believe you are right, my lord."

He stepped back, and she slid off the desk, reaching up to check her hair.

"Would you like the same service performed on you, Albert? I'm more than willing to touch you here," she suggested, placing her hand on his cock.

He groaned, running a hand through his hair. He wanted her touch. He ached for it almost constantly, but here and now was not the time. As it was, they had risked Victoria's reputation by being here alone.

Should they be caught, she would be forced to marry him, and he did not want their union starting in such a way. He wanted her to willingly marry him or not at all. Of all the times they had been alone, he was surprised that they were not already before a priest.

"Not here. Later," he suggested, taking her hand and walking from the room. Thankfully they did not encounter anyone from the ball, and they returned to Victoria's mama just as supper was announced.

The meal was enjoyable, with fare that would rival the best balls in London. Albert talked and contributed to the conversation, but he could not stop the niggling concern that Victoria would not change her mind.

Was she so determined to cry off marriage, a life with another after her disastrous life with Armstrong that he could never win her heart?

They had been intimate for some time now. Certainly, he cared for her above anyone else in the world. He loved her dearly and wanted her as his wife.

Did she now feel the same? Did she want him for her husband? Or was she as unwavering as she had always been? How he wanted to break the stone tomb she had enclosed around her heart into a million pieces.

"Do not forget to dance a set with Miss Scottsdale, Lord Melvin. She has not been able to keep her attention from turning to you all supper. I think you have won her over already with your charm."

The duchess turned to her daughter before looking for Miss Scottsdale. "Are you certain that Lord Melvin wants to dance with Miss Scottsdale? You ought to be sure your matchmaking is wanted before pursuing it," she said, a look of apology on her face at her daughter's words.

"Lord Melvin knows that I have nothing but his best interests at heart."

Albert inwardly swore, having the answer to his question delivered without asking the awkward question at all.

How he wished Armstrong was alive so he could pummel the bastard to a pulp. Punish the rake for the hurt he caused Victoria, and the hurt against him should he not be able to win her hand after everything that they shared due to his misbegotten ways.

Victoria heard the words spilling from her mouth, yet she could not wrench them back, no matter how hard she tried. Miss Scottsdale was a sweet young lady, that was true, and she appeared quite taken with Albert. Still, after all that they had done together these past weeks, only half an hour before in the library, how could she request that of Albert?

She was the worst of people. He ought to shove her aside, tell her to cry off, and leave him alone. And yet, he never did.

He was too good for her, not by society standards, but moral ones. She was a vixen, a tease, some may say. Was her mother, right? Would she become scandalous and have a name of ill repute? When had she fallen so low?

Each time she suggested a lady to Albert, she read in his eyes the hurt. The continual disappointment that her words wrought within him. She was hurting him, and she hated that she did.

The remainder of the ball went remarkably well, considering her heart was no longer in the mood for dancing or conversing. All she wished for was to return to Rosedale, or maybe even Dunsleigh.

This game they were playing had gone on long enough, and no one was the winner. She needed to speak to Albert, and in the morning, she would. They could not continue to be together so intimately without consequence. She was not ready to give him her heart. Maybe she never would be. Victoria stood beside Josh, listening as he spoke of Lady Sophie, whom he seemed to be disappointed in for whatever reason, and watched Albert dance with Miss Scottsdale.

For Albert to find a wife, to move forward in his life, she could no longer be around him. He needed to form an attachment with another, and if they could not keep their hands off each other, their physical desires overpowering the rules of etiquette, then she had to go.

She had to leave Hampshire. England if she could manage it.

And sooner rather than later.

CHAPTER 32

Albert had no time to hide the pages he'd been writing when a knock sounded on the door at his hunting lodge the following morning. Victoria poked her head about the wood, a small smile on her supple lips. Although there was a concern, a cloud of worry in her eyes that gave him pause.

He sat there, unable to move and unsure what to do should his hasty filing away of his work cause interest from her. Make her question what he was doing at his lodge all times of the day and night.

Instead, he stood, coming over to her and leading her away from his desk and the words that a keen reader and lover of Elbert Retsek would distinguish.

"Victoria, I did not think you would come here today. I thought you may still be abed after the late night we all endured from the ball."

She cast a curious glance at his desk but did not ask, merely let him lead her over to the settee, the very one he'd given her pleasure on. He pushed the memory from his mind, sensing she did not come here to find release in his arms but some other quest. Was she about to admit to having feelings toward him?

He hoped that was the case. He wanted nothing more than to be hers from now and forever. The idea of not having Victoria in his life was unfathomable.

She sat on the many cushions and throw blankets, looking lost and a little unsure of herself.

He sat beside her, silent and waiting.

"I owe you an apology, Albert. I acted atrociously last evening. After what we did in the library, to ask you to dance with Miss Scottsdale was unforgivable. I've been throwing every eligible young lady at your head since we started your lessons. At the same time, I have been getting in the way of your progress by being intimate with you. I hope you're able to forgive my abominable behavior, and you can move forward with your desire for marriage, but with someone of your choosing, not mine."

Albert slumped back in the chair, staring at the ceiling, praying for patience. How had he allowed this charade to carry on for so long? How could she not see it was her that he wanted, not Miss Scottsdale, Miss Eberhardt, or Lady Sophie. None of them.

"Victoria, as much as I enjoy our lessons, God knows they've been enjoyable," he added, throwing her a rue smile. "I have concluded that I do not wish to marry just anyone who suits the role of the marchioness."

"Pardon?" She stared at him, not comprehending his words.

Albert decided enough was enough. They could not continue this game, not when they would either be caught and forced to marry, or she would leave, and he'd be a wreck for the rest of his life, having lost the only woman he ever loved.

"Albert, whatever do you mean?" she asked after his continued silence.

"I've been lying to you, Victoria, and I ought to be horsewhipped for it. In fact, I could understand if you do not want anything further to do with me, but if you do choose that course, know that it would be unbearable pain for me to endure."

She shook her head. A curl slipped loose and bounced about her shoulder. He reached over, placing it behind her ear, a diamond earing glistering in the morning sun.

"I have allowed your lessons to continue because they enabled me to be near you. I have wanted you for as long as I can remember."

"Why did you never say? Why did you not try to court me when Mr. Armstrong made his suit known?" she asked, a haunted look entering her eyes.

"Because you were Penworth's sister, and I knew that I could only court you if I were ready for marriage. I wasn't at that time. Other things were occupying my mind." His writing, his publishing contracts that she still was unaware of, the death of his father. "But I am ready now. When you suggested to help me, all I wanted was to take you up on your offer. I thought I could seduce you into marrying me. That by being with me, you would change your mind on marriage, grow in affection for me and marry me after all."

Her mouth opened and closed several times, but her continual silence echoed like a death knell. Blast it. She was still, after all they had done, against marriage.

Surely not!

"Oh, Albert, I do not know what to say other than what I have always stated from the first. I do not wish to marry again." She reached out, taking his hand when he flinched at her words. "While I do like you so very much, and being with you makes me feel wonderful, I have plans and dreams. A second marriage, a husband and children would stop all of those from coming true."

While he did not want to ruin her dreams, could there be room for him in them? "We could travel together, see the world for as long as you wish, so long as we called into England every few months. Is that too much to ask?"

She nodded, casting her eyes down on the floor covered with an abundance of Aubussons rugs to keep the chill out of the flagstone floor. "It is. To travel with you sounds so wonderful and free, but children would inevitably come. They always do, and I do not think that is what I want in life." She paused, meeting his gaze and his heart crumbled at her words. The unshed tears in her eyes that told him she meant every word she spoke. "I cannot be the reason you do not gain all that you desire in life. A wife, children of your own. I know that is what you want, but I do not. You hate me, do you not? You think I'm wicked for wanting what I do."

"I do not think you're wicked." He could never think that, but it did not make it easy for him to accept either. Damn Armstrong and his underhanded means, his lack of respect for his bride. "I merely think you're missing out on an opportunity that could turn into one of life's grandest adventures. But I will not force you. I will not disclose to Penworth all that we've done simply to marry you. But know that I do wish for you to be mine. Now and forever."

“Albert,” she pleaded, “please do not make this any harder than it already is.”

There was nothing harder than losing the woman he loved. “I love you, Victoria. That I will tell you before you leave me.”

Victoria did not know what to say. Albert was so honest, so open with her, but still, she could not give him what he wanted. It broke her heart that she could not. She was certainly going to hell for being such a wicked woman. "I do not know what to say.” Panic assailed her at his disappointment. What could she say? Nothing would help the situation they found themselves. "Our lessons must end, and we must stop what we're doing."

He nodded slowly, taking in her words. "Our lessons do need to come to an end before there is no stopping what happens between us. We have been lucky so far not to be caught, but that luck will only hold for so long."

She met his gaze, the need and longing she read in his eyes crushing her soul. She was a terrible person. Albert was one of the finest gentlemen she knew. One of the best her family had ever known. Any lady would want to marry the marquess, and yet, she could not.

No matter how much pleasure they gave each other, that was not worth giving up all her dreams for, nor his. One day Albert would realize his love was nothing more than infatuation. When the right woman walked into his life, he would know that today she did the right thing by him, as hard as it was at this moment to believe that. He would have his children to bring laughter to the many rooms at Rosedale and he would know Victoria gave him that gift this very day.

"I do not mean to hurt you, Albert, but I cannot marry again. Each time I think that I may wish to consider the state in my future, my throat closes over and my stomach pains me with dread. I lived with a man for six weeks before he ran off with one of my maids. Made me look the biggest fool in England. Society pitied me for months and discussed my husband at balls and parties with scorn, forgetting I was there, listening to their every word. That I could not divorce him, that I was at his mercy, when Paul had none, I knew that never again would I endure such embarrassment."

"I am not Paul, Victoria," he stated, his voice thick with emotion.

She reached out, clasping his hands. "I know that you are nothing like him and it's a credit to you, truly. But I just cannot marry you or anyone."

He shook his head, a muscle working in his jaw. "May I kiss you goodbye?" he asked.

She met his kiss without hesitation. His lips crushed hers, their tongues tangling. Liquid heat pumped through her veins, down into her stomach, to settle between her legs.

She would miss this. This hunger that he made her feel every time they touched. Albert would be the last man she would ever be like this with again in her life, and she would kiss him, take her fill of him until there was nothing but fond, delicious memories of what they had to keep her warm at night.

You're a fool, Victoria, a little voice in her mind taunted.

She pushed it aside, just as Albert wrenched away, standing and striding to his desk and packing numerous papers into a leather satchel.

"You should leave, Victoria. Go now, before we're caught, and you're forced to marry me. I will not have you in that way."

She stood, her legs a little unsteady. His dismissal of her pinched at her heart, but she did as he asked, walking silently to the door.

"I am truly sorry, Albert. I shall ask Mama for us to leave. I will say I have a letter from Alice begging us to return home. Something to do with the baby. Are you in agreement with this plan?"

He nodded, a muscle working in his jaw, and yet he would not look at her. Instead, he remained focused on the papers on his desk, his eyes overly bright and glassy. Horror clutched at her heart that he was upset, more than she'd ever thought possible.

Had she broken his heart?

She took a calming breath, forcing her legs to move out the door and toward her horse. She did not look back.

. . .

Victoria found her mama in her room back at the house, still suffering from the megrim from partaking in too much champagne at the ball. Victoria sat beside the bed, shaking her mama's arm a little to wake her.

"Mama, I'm back from my ride and have received a letter from Alice requesting that we return home. Nothing is wrong, but she would like us closer with the baby due now in only a few weeks."

Her mother shuffled up on the numerous cushions at her back, blinking away her sleepiness. "Alice wrote again? I received a letter only yesterday stating all was well."

Victoria shrugged, not liking the fact she was lying to her dearest mama, but knowing it was necessary. "I do not know about the letter you received. I only know of the one that she sent to me that arrived today." She stood, going over to the bell pull. "Should I ring for your maid to have the packing started? I have already instructed mine to ready things for home."

Her mother tossed back the blankets, and Victoria knew they were going home. If there was one thing her mama prided most about her role in life, it was that of mother, and if her child needed her, made up or not, she would return home and cluck over her for weeks.

"Of course, ring the bell, dear. We shall depart today. It is not yet noon, and if we hurry, we should be home just after nightfall."

Victoria rang the bell, only too ready to return home to Dunsleigh.

Oh, who was she kidding? She was not returning to Dunsleigh. She was running away like the coward she was. And not only did she know it, but she was also certain Albert knew it as well.

CHAPTER 33

"Can someone please explain why the carriage is preparing to leave for Dunsleigh? I saw our driver helping with the loading of trunks," Josh asked, walking into her room.

Victoria looked up from her desk in her room where she had been sitting the past half hour, hoping her escape from Rosedale would occur before Lord Melvin returned from his hunting lodge.

It was rude of her to leave without saying a formal goodbye, but the one she had endured with him at the lodge was bad enough. She could not face him again.

"Mama and I are returning to Dunsleigh. Alice has requested that we return home." And she just hoped she was able to talk to her sister before she arrived at Dunsleigh's door and Alice outed her lie for what it was. Her mother would never forgive her that she had made them flee Rosedale when there was no valid reason to do so. Even if Lord Melvin knew of her excuse, her mama could never know the truth of it.

Never know that her daughter had been partaking in scandalous liaisons with a man, not her husband. And not only that but then to leave without marrying him as he wished.

"This hasn't got anything to do with you and Lord Melvin does it, Victoria? I know that he has been courting you. He asked for my permission to court and propose when the time came. I gave him my blessing, of course. He is a man of honor and good standing. You are not running away, are you?"

How on earth did her brother know her shameful truth?

"I do not wish to marry Lord Melvin, and it is unkind to him to allow him to believe that I do so. While I have been instructing him in the art of finding a wife, working through his nerves when about ladies and crowds, he has somehow seen me as his future bride and not another in the middle of it all. That cannot happen."

Her brother crossed his arms, a pronounced frown between his brows. "And why can it not happen? He's a kind and honorable gentleman. More so than Armstrong ever was or even myself. He's titled and not a gambler or a violent man, a good match for you, whom I love. You ought not to be so quick to dismiss his affections."

Victoria took a calming breath, knowing all of this already and having been warring with herself the whole morning. She thought of her sisters, their happy marriages. Wondering if she'd done the right thing. If she were acting foolish.

"Will you be returning home with us, Josh?" she queried, ignoring his continued defense of his friend. How could she not try to change the subject? She had no defense against her brother's words, for everything he said was true.

Albert was wonderful and she was running away.

"I have ordered the carriage to be returned to the stable. We shall leave tomorrow and not run off like highwaymen in the night." Her brother sighed, coming over to her desk, staring down at her with something akin to pity. "Armstrong did you wrong, sister, but that does not make every gentleman after him ineligible or incapable of standing at the end of an aisle to marry you and mean every word that they say. To honor and love. You are Lady Victoria Worthingham, a duke's daughter and sister to one. Do not let that bastard late husband of yours ruin your future as well as your past. You do not deserve to live alone and without love." He reached out and chucked her under the chin. "Let Melvin love you. I know he will not disappoint you."

Victoria's eyes burned at her brother's words, and she blinked to clear her vision. Swallowing the lump that formed in her throat. "Even if what you say is true, Albert wants children. That is no longer a desire within me. I want to travel. He has an estate in Hampshire that needs to be overseen. We are not compatible even if I wished it so."

"You want this solitary life so strongly, Victoria? Truly, because I fear if we leave tomorrow, Lord Melvin, after all your tutoring of him in the ways of courting a lady, will marry by the end of next season. He is an honorable catch. Are you willing to stand by when you return from your travels to see him settled and happy?"

The idea of seeing Albert so made her catch her breath, but this was for the best.

"I am willing to let him go and marry another," she heard herself say. And while her mind calmed, her heart was another matter entirely. It twisted to a painful degree, and she cringed, wondering if it would ever untangle itself to beat normally again.

Something told her it never would.

Albert returned to Rosedale late that evening, having decided to miss dinner and continue writing. So he was surprised when he walked into the foyer and found his butler waiting for him.

"My lord, the duchess and Lady Victoria are to depart in the morning. Her Grace wanted you informed the moment you returned."

"Of course. Thank you," he said. He had thought they would have gone today after Victoria returned to the house, and guilt pricked that he had not returned as host to dine with his guests.

He supposed he would have to apologize to them when they broke their fast in the morning.

The house was quiet, and he requested his dinner in the library. The fire burned brightly upon entering the room, and he was relieved to see Penworth had not waited up to speak to him. No doubt he would want to know why his clandestine courting of his sister had not worked.

He flopped down on a chair, kicking off his boots and warming them before the fire. The night was chillier than normal, and his stomach rumbled when the butler entered with his tray of roast lamb, vegetables, and his cook's delicious gravy.

He dismissed his staff, sending them to bed at this late hour, and ate his meal. Going over to the decanter of whiskey and pouring himself a hefty glass, he drank it down, deciding instead of pouring another, he'd just take the bottle over to where he was settled and drink as much as he liked.

The alcohol would numb the pain coursing through his heart. He had hoped and thought that with what had happened between himself and Victoria that she would come to feel something for him. More than benign friendship. That her emotions were not so injured from her previous marriage that she may come to feel something for him.

Were women able to hide their sentiments so very well? He had been schooled that they could not, that they were emotional creatures, likely to fly into a fit of rage or an abundance of tears.

But he no longer thought that way. Victoria was the opposite of such women.

He finished his meal and the sweet vanilla biscuits that were left on a side plate before pouring himself another glass of the amber, dulling liquid.

He lay back on the settee, watching the flames in the grate, sipping his drink. Well, at least he had tried, which was more than he used to do. Victoria had given him that gift at least. He could take what she had taught him, his newfound confidence that he would work on making stronger in the coming months before the London Season next year. He would return to London and try to find a woman who sparked his desire and challenged his mind. A rare gem and one who would not be Lady Victoria Worthingham. For no doubt, she would not even be there.

She would be living her dream life on the continent, seeing and meeting all kinds of people while guarding her heart from feeling anything for anyone ever again.

He poured another glass, the room spinning as he drank it down—until he saw and felt nothing at all.

CHAPTER 34

Victoria was foxed. A disgraceful act and one she was not proud of. Still, nevertheless, she had imbibed too much wine at dinner, followed by proclaiming she was going to bed early, only to then sneak out to the upstairs parlor where she found another bottle of brandy that had been sweet and tempting.

She wandered through the house, no longer caring who came upon her or what her brother and mother would say if they knew she was three sheets to the wind. That Albert had failed to arrive for dinner was her fault. She had made him feel unwanted and alone in his own home. By telling him of her wishes, breaking his heart, he had not been able to face her. She had made him feel a fool, unworthy of her.

Would he ever forgive her?

Albert was sweet, charming, and made her feel things no other man ever had. To throw him aside was not an easy choice. She hated that she had hurt his feelings. In truth, he should never forgive her for her callous actions.

The memory of his touch taunted her. His kisses, his warm body against hers, touching her, making her scream. His laughter and smile. She shivered, knowing that she would miss him even with all the adventures that lay before her. Adventures she would have alone with only her servants for company. Miles of travel, and no intimate interludes to make the distance shorter. No romantic strolls or dinners on foreign shores.

Alone. Alone. Alone.

She downed more brandy from the bottle, only to find nothing but a dribble left. She held it up to the moonlight coming in through large windows in the foyer and realized she'd drank it all.

Oh dear Lord, she would pay for her trouble tomorrow, and she had a carriage ride to endure.

Victoria stumbled into the library, the only light illuminating the room coming from the fire that burned in the grate. Her heart stopped at the sight of the sole occupant seated alone —a pensive look on his profile.

Albert...

Her stomach did a little flip, a nervous titter that he may not want to see her. That his inability to attend dinner had been purposeful. That he disliked her now more than anyone on the planet.

He ought to. She was a terrible person.

She hoped that was not the case. She liked him very much, even if their wishes for the future differed. They could still be friends.

Would he allow her even to ask?

Victoria shut the door and stumbled over to the settee. Having thought to be alone, Albert jumped at her less-than-accomplished appearance before his visage shuttered like a book.

Closed and read to completion.

"Leave, Victoria. There is nothing more to say between us. And need I remind you, should we be caught alone in a closed-off room, you will be my wife, and no matter how much you want your freedom, that will not happen after the fact."

His words were a little slow compared to how he spoke normally. She slumped down beside him, ignoring his warning, and met his gaze. His eyes were glassy and unfocused. "Are you foxed as well? It seems we both have drowned our sorrows into a bottle this evening."

He shifted away from her, and she hated that he did not want to be close to her. A little voice reminded her this was a good thing. She did not want him for herself.

Even so, the move pierced her pride.

"I do not wish for us to be enemies, Albert." Victoria realized she was still clasping the brandy bottle to her chest. She placed it down on the floor. Albert watched her with quiet calm. More than what she could say for herself. Being near him again, alone and in the middle of the night, left her hungry for his touch.

There was something off about wanting a man for what he could do to her but not want the commitment of the action. Maybe one day, women could live life so, but she could not, and being here, she was risking her future alone.

She ought to leave as he said, but she could not make herself move an inch. "Please do not hate me. I could not bear that," she whispered.

He lay his head on the back of the settee, staring up at the ceiling. His throat moved as he swallowed, and she followed the lines of his jaw, the cutting edge to his handsome face, the stubbled jaw after a day of not shaving. He looked disheveled and handsome. And he was telling her to leave.

"I do not hate you, Victoria, but you do not want me. Do not be caught in here and then be forced into a union you do not want. I could not stand it if you viewed our marriage as bad as your first."

She understood all that he said, but still, she did not move. No one was up. They were perfectly safe. And while she did not want to be his wife, she did not want to be anyone's wife. That did not mean she did not crave his touch. His sweet, intoxicating kisses left her breathless, kisses that would keep her warm at night for the many years to come when she was alone.

That word again...alone.

"We can spend some time together before I leave tomorrow, Albert."

A growl of disapproval tore from him. If he meant to dissuade her, he was mistaken. The sound merely made her crave him more. "Do not say such things. They are unfair."

The despair she heard in his voice wrenched at her heart. She did not want him to be sad and disillusioned with her plight, but she also did not want to leave him alone. But she was unjust. Her actions these past weeks all had been.

Maybe you wish to be his wife and have adventures with him and not strangers in foreign places?

She met his gaze, and time stood still. Her body shivered with need, alive with want of him. His eyes burned with a hunger that ought to scare her away, but it did not. Victoria took a calming breath, steadying herself as much as she could as Albert watched her with a longing she'd never seen before.

"Even after your denial of me, I still want you. I am selfish enough to want to have you, even if I must let you go upon daybreak," he said, a deep gravelly plea. He reached out and traced her jaw with his finger, sliding his thumb over her bottom lip. She kissed his digit before he pulled his hand away, forcing it at his side.

The words, an appeal, called at a part of her no longer willing to adhere to rules. She wanted the man before her but without the constraints of marriage. What was wrong with that?

Nothing.

Victoria closed the space between them and kissed Albert. She sighed as their lips touched, meshed into a conflagration of emotions. His raw need matched hers and she clasped his shoulders, working to sit on his lap. His manhood jutted against her core. She undulated against him—teasing them until they were both gasping for breath.

He groaned, one hand gripping her bottom, grinding her against him. The feeling was exquisite, and she wanted more.

Cool air kissed the tops of her legs, and she didn't try to stop Albert when he fumbled with her dress, moving it out of the way. His strong, large hand slid up her leg, flexing against her muscle, tickling her inner thigh. She held her breath as his fingers came achingly close to her sex.

"Touch me," she pleaded, needing him there. Not just his hands, but all of him. "I want you, Albert." And she did want him, in her own strange way. She may not wish to marry, to have children, but she did want him. Who would not? He was everything a woman such as herself hoped for in a husband, a partner in life. He was nothing like Paul.

He grazed the curls at her apex before slipping deeper, teasing her aching flesh. She sucked in a hiss of breath, working herself against his hand. The feeling, too delicious to stop.

Victoria sat back, fumbling with the front falls of his breeches, needing him closer, wanting him inside her.

"Victoria," Albert gasped. He stilled her hand working him, he was harder than she'd ever felt him before. His penis jutted and thrust against her palm even as he tried to pull them back from the brink.

"We do not need to do this. There are risks. If you're so certain that you're not marrying me, you should not do this."

Victoria considered his words. Thoughts that had been racing around in her mind these past minutes. But she could no sooner hold back the sun on a new morning than stop what they were doing. "I want to give this to you. To us both."

His eyes flared at her words, but he reached up, clasping her hair at her nape, pulling her down for a kiss. "Just remember that I offered to stop."

She grinned, lifting herself a little and placing him at her core. "I'll remember everything," she said, coming down on him in one swift movement, taking his virginity. And if Victoria were honest with herself, her heart.

CHAPTER 35

Albert could not catch his breath. He held still, struck a little dumb as Victoria took him into her. He could do nothing but watch her. Her eyes closed, her long lashes fanning over her flushed cheeks. Her plump lips opened on a sigh of satisfaction that went directly to his soul. He shivered, fighting the urge to dominate, to take all that he could after the gift she had bestowed on him.

For so long, he had wanted her in this way, to do everything in the sketchbook they studied. The past weeks, the positions, the pleasure they had wrought on each other had led them here. To trust and give to each other fully. How was he ever to let her walk away now? The idea of years without the woman in his arms, of warming his bed, stretched endlessly and left him panicked.

How was it that she had remained immune to his love? He could not hate Armstrong more for the damage he wrought.

"Are you well?" he managed to ask.

She clasped his jaw and kissed him. "I am more than well." Their tongues entwined, teeth clunked, and all thoughts vanished when she started to move. With the patience he did not have himself, she rose and fell on him, torturous, slow strokes that drove him insane.

Her breathy sighs puffed against his lips through their kiss as she fell into an agonizing rhythm. Demanding more from him with every minute.

"Albert," she panted between kisses, working him with her body. It was too much. Too good, and he wanted more. He wrenched the bodice of her gown down, taking her breast into his mouth as she fucked him. Took her pleasure atop his cock.

Albert moaned, he was close, but he did not want this to end. He clasped her close, flipping her onto her back, and thrusting hard into her sweet body atop the settee.

"Take me." She bit her lip, her eyes hooded with desire, gazed up at him. "Harder," she urged him on. She clasped the end of the lounge, pushing against him as he thrust into her, working him to a fever pitch.

He could not breathe.

She felt too good. So damn tight and willing. A little wanton in his arms. He could not have asked for more the first time he gave himself up to pleasure.

"I need to taste you." She clasped his shoulders, mewling her acquiescence as he kissed his way down her chest, seizing his opportunity to lathe her wet, glistening cunny. She tasted just as he remembered, earthy and sweet. He suckled on her little pleasure bud, fucking her with his tongue. She clasped his hair, undulating against his face, gasping his name over and over.

He pushed her close to her edge, but he did not want the night to end. He never wanted them to cease. Albert sat back, watching as her vision cleared and a question entered her eyes.

"What are you doing?" she queried, a seductive smile on her lips.

"Tell me if you enjoy this, my darling." He ran one finger

over her mons, circling the little nubbin he had taunted relentlessly with his tongue. He pushed a finger into her heat, and pleasure flooded her features. Her body swaying to gain more satisfaction from his touch.

"I love that, Albert."

He teased her in that way for several minutes, sometimes dipping his head and lathing her flesh with his tongue. She slipped an arm over her mouth to stop her cries from becoming too loud.

Albert did not care who caught them at this stage. If her family discovered them, she would be his. Selfish as that may be, he wanted her above anything else. Even perhaps her own wishes.

"Albert, I'm going to come," she mewled, working herself against his hand.

He stopped, throwing her a devilish grin when she cursed him to Hades.

"What are you doing? Please, do not stop. Do not tease me so," she begged.

He came over her, kissing her neck, licking the delicate skin beneath her ear, electing a shiver through her. "Do you want to try another position in the book? I have one in mind if you're willing."

Her eyes met his, curious. "Which one?"

In a flash, he wrenched back, flipping her over onto her front. "Lift yourself up on your knees. Hold on to the chair and arch your back."

She did as he asked, no doubt remembering the position he mentioned. "Will this be enjoyable, do you think?"

He slipped her gown up over her ass, taking his time to admire her round bottom, her aching cunny that tempted him. "Oh, I think it will be," he said, coming up over her from behind, guiding himself into her wet heat.

Albert swallowed hard. Hell, this way was good, perhaps better than he expected. Certainly, he was deeper inside of her, and yet she still clasped him tight, milked him toward a climax.

She pushed back against him and took her pleasure as he gained his. He reached around, teasing her cunny, flicking the little bead between her legs, wanting her to shatter in his arms.

He thrusted hard, taking delight in watching his cock go in and out. He squeezed her ass, fighting the urge to spill his seed into her. She moaned into a cushion, his name a chant as they fucked. This was no lovemaking at all. They were taking what they wanted, giving each other what they both needed.

Victoria cried out his name. Her mewls of pleasure muffled in the cushions before her face. Her body convulsed, the muscles about his cock spasming and drawing him ever closer to join her in her release.

But he could not. He took her for as long as he could, pumping hard and continuous, giving her what she wanted, letting her ride out her climax on his cock. At the last minute, he pulled free, spilling his seed onto her back and ass. A messy business, but if Victoria did not want children, something she would need to accept should she ever lay with another again.

For a moment, they stayed as they were, both lost in their ecstasy, before Albert slumped back on the settee, helping Victoria right her dress and sit beside him.

Their breathing ragged, he could only imagine what he looked like. Victoria had lost several pins, her hair cascading about her shoulders. Her cheeks kissed with high color, and her lips swollen from his touch.

He met her gaze, the hunted look in her eyes robbing him of hope. He understood what it meant. A goodbye. A farewell between friends and lovers. Tears pooled in her eyes and he pulled her against him, holding her close. "I shall live in hope that one day your heart will heal, and you will come back to me, Victoria."

He felt her nod against his chest and the small sniffle of her upset. "I shall miss you, too," she said, and then she was gone, walking from the room and out of his life.

He could only hope that it was not for forever.

CHAPTER 36

They had been home at Dunsleigh for a week when her sister requested Victoria come and see her. Alice had been a little put out that Victoria had lied to return home, but the good sister she was had allowed her ruse to stand. Victoria had her horse saddled and started over to Kester House, trying to build up enough courage to speak to Alice over what had happened between her and Albert.

Since her return to Dunsleigh, her ideas on the future had been troubling and confusing, to say the least. One pertinent reason for her troubles was the vexing fact that she missed Albert terribly so and more than she thought she would.

The other evening while strolling the house late at night after not being able to sleep, she had walked to the library and cried into a tumbler of whiskey—the memories, the fun, and pleasure that she had found in Albert's arms too hard to bear.

If she did not get a hold of herself soon, she would start to think she had a drinking problem.

Lady Victoria Worthingham was no watering pot, so there was something seriously off in her life. She called after Pickle and Cabbage, her two wolfhounds accompanying her on her ride today. They trotted beside her, eager for their run and a friendly pat from Alice.

Kester House wasn't far from Dunsleigh, and the sight of the estate, nestled in a wooded valley, always brought a smile to her face. It was such a stunning home, and Callum had done a lot to make it perfect for her sister.

She found Alice on the settee in the downstairs parlor reading the latest *la belle assemblée*. "Picking out your gowns for next season already, I see," she teased, coming into the room and bussing her sister on both cheeks.

Alice chuckled, shuffling up a little on her chair. "Oh, I'm so glad you called. I thought that I had punished you enough over your little lie."

Victoria told her dogs to sit, and they slumped before the fire, content now that Alice had patted both their heads. "She is disappointed to have left Rosedale. She has visited here a great deal. I do apologize for that."

Alice waved her concerns away. "It is no mind. She is only here ensuring I am well, and I could use the company. It's terribly boring waiting for a baby to arrive and with you both away, I have missed you."

Victoria smiled, pulling the bellpull for tea, having not thought about the consequences of her excuse she had given their parent. Her only thought at the time had been running away from the trouble she'd caused. She was such a coward.

"I'm sorry for the difficulty. I shall talk to Mama today and tell her you're much improved and merely needed rest. I'm sure that will halt some of the visits." Victoria hoped. Alice loved her family, but being so close to Dunsleigh did sometimes mean they were rarely without them underfoot.

Alice watched her a moment, her eyes narrowing before she said, "Was Lord Melvin who you believed him to be? Is he the famous writer, Elbert Retsek?"

Victoria sat across from Alice and swung her legs up under

her gown on her chair, settling into a comfortable position. "I believe so, and I think he writes out at his hunting lodge. He snuck away there often, and when I saw him one day, he was scribbling away like a mad man. I do believe he is a writer, and I do think he's Elbert Retsek, but I never asked, and that is not why I'm home."

"How intriguing," Alice said, a mischievous light entering her eyes.

A footman came into the room and bowed. "Excuse me, my lady, the tea you ordered is ready."

"Thank you," Alice replied. "Bring it in, but we shall pour, and we're not to be disturbed." Alice waited for the footman to depart before she turned her attention back to Victoria. "Did you give him back the page from his book?"

"After what happened between us, I could not bring myself to ask him. I just wanted to flee. It all seemed so confusing, and I've acted atrocious, Alice. I was not thinking clearly or like myself at all."

Alice leaned forward in her chair. "I knew you had run away. I told Callum as much. What happened at Rosedale, Victoria? What did you do?"

What she did not do would be a more appropriate question. Victoria busied herself pouring the tea, taking up time setting out the almond tartlets before she admitted to her actions, her conduct that was reprehensible. She handed a cup to her sister, forcing the words out of her mouth that admitted her guilt. "You know how we have been friends with Lord Melvin for years. Well, due to that confidence, I offered to help him gain a wife by giving him lessons in etiquette, in conversation skills, on how to court a lady while I was a guest in his home."

"You did?" Alice's eyes went wide with surprise. "And how did that go, may I ask?"

Victoria sipped her tea, shaking her head as shame washed through her. "Terribly. Well," she corrected, "not terribly, he did learn and become more confident at balls and country dances. I taught him how to help a lady when she played the pianoforte on a musical night. On how to talk while walking or taking the air in the gardens. But that is not the worst of it."

"What is the worst of it?" Alice demanded, staring at her, leaning forward a little at her words.

"I gave myself to him," she admitted at last. "I do not know how it happened." Although she did know how exactly how it had happened and at her prodding. "I had told him I would not marry him, that I did not want a husband, not after the hell that Paul put me through. I want my freedom, to travel and not have children, as much as I adore all my nieces and nephews. But when I found him in the library on our final night, the pain in his eyes, the longing, well, I could not leave without being with him. I wanted him with such force that even now," she declared, standing and pacing before the fire.

"I want him still. I think of him day and night. Of his kisses, his smile, his silly little ways of making me laugh, and it cannot be. I do not want a husband. I made such an error of judgement with Paul, what if I do so again?" She sat back on the settee, taking her sister's hands. "You must help me. Tell me what I am to do."

Her sister's knowing grin did nothing to help in the slightest. "I will do no such thing, Victoria. The choice must be yours, but I do believe you are in love with him. Have you admitted that to yourself yet?"

"What?" she gasped. "Do not be absurd. Of course I'm not in love with him. In lust, yes. Infatuated, yes. But love? No. You are mistaken."

Alice raised one eyebrow. "Lust? You're a Worthingham. We do not lust after men unless we're in love with them. We marry for life and love only once. If you lust after him, you're emotionally tied to him, more than you ever were with Paul."

"I thought myself in love with Paul. I fear your beliefs about our family and love are unsound."

Alice shook her head. "Paul was not your soul mate." She clasped her hands in her lap. "Why did you leave Rosedale after giving yourself to him? How did his lordship take your leave?"

Victoria closed her eyes, leaning her head back on the chair. The image of Albert standing at his doors as the carriage rolled down the drive. The disappointment on his handsome face. The raw, unmasked pain. "I think I may have broken his heart."

"Hmm," Alice murmured, making her heart beat with renewed panic. "This is what I think you should do before any decisions are made. Our sister Elizabeth and Henry are preparing now to travel south and leave for Paris. They will be back before the next Season starts. I think you should go with them, see a little of the world as you wish. With the absence I think your decision on your future may become clearer than it is now."

Her sister's plan had merit and Elizabeth would never deny her company. Could a little distance and time help her know her own heart? What she truly wanted? "Even if I decided that I wish to marry Albert, what do I do about his desire for children? I have never had those motherly instincts that come so natural to you and our sisters. He will want an heir."

"Have you asked him?" Alice studied her a moment, her eyes narrowing. "You need to know if that is something he will live without to have your love."

To her shame, she had not given him the chance to decide if that was a future he could tolerate. She should have asked him instead of running off like she had. "I have not." She met Alice's eyes and saw only compassion and understanding there. Thank heavens, for she was not sure she could stomach shame.

"Do you not think you should have? Especially when there could be a chance that you are carrying his child."

Victoria shook her head, knowing at least with that predicament there was no problem at all." No, I started my courses the day we arrived home to Dunsleigh."

Alice breathed a sigh of relief. "Right then, this is what you shall do," she said, reinvigorated. "When Elizabeth arrives in the next few days, you shall go with them to Paris. I'm sure they will not mind. If you take your maid, you may do your own sightseeing to give them privacy, and I'm certain Josh will ensure you have your own private accommodations."

"I do not want to be a bother to them."

Alice waved her concerns away. "La. This is Elizabeth, the nice sister, remember? She will do this for you, but in return, you must do something for yourself."

"What is that?" she asked, unsure if she trusted the calculating light in Alice's eyes.

"That you will return to England and have your mind made up before next Season. I have little doubt Lord Melvin will be in attendance. After the lessons you were determined to help him with, he'll be ready to scuff the boards and choose a bride. But you need to see, really understand the choice you're making if you choose to let him go. If you see Lord Melvin and you feel nothing but friendship, then your choice is easy. It was only lust after all and no harm done."

"And if I do not feel only lust?"

"If you do not, then you need to find a way to win him back. Which if he's the sort of gentleman you believe him to be, honorable and kind, he will be waiting for you to come to your senses."

Hope rose up inside her. She could travel, see a little of Europe, and then decide her fate. Have a taste of freedom after knowing the delights of being in Albert's arms, and then she would choose which one she wanted forever.

She just hoped Albert would be there to enable her the

choice. No matter how difficult the outcome would be, she would have to take a risk, especially if he married before she returned and made the decision for her.

CHAPTER 37

The Season, 1812

Albert had not seen or heard from Victoria for several months, not since she had parted from him at Rosedale the morning after their night together.

Even now, after all this time, all he could think about was how to win her love. What he could have done to make her stay. To love him as he loved her. He was certain she cared for him. A woman such as Victoria, a Worthingham, did not give themselves to random people. It was simply not in their nature. Not any of the siblings.

No, Victoria cared for him, more than he believed she could admit to herself. To do so would mean she would have to choose between him and a life she dreamed of living. One where her heart was forever locked away from harm.

He spied her late husband's younger brother, noting the rogue caroused society without his wife on his arm. He narrowed his eyes, the family resemblance both in looks and character ran deep, it would seem.

The butler continued to call out the names of guests as they arrived. Albert stood to the side of the room, a glass of whiskey in hand, needing to calm his nerves. Although he was unsure if Victoria would attend this evening, he waited, hoping she would. He had missed her, and during the time apart he too had many days and nights to think of what he wanted in life. What he cherished more than anything, what he could live with and without to have the one person whom he loved.

He had done all that Victoria had asked of him after she left. He had attended numerous dances about Hampshire and attended every country house party where his presence had been requested. He went as far as spending Christmas with Lord and Lady Hammilyn. Although the memory of that Christmas party was one, he'd prefer to forget since Miss Eberhardt too had been invited.

She had been unabashedly forward during the week-long stay, rarely leaving his side. Certainly had he wanted to court any other young woman, which he did not, he could not have, for she had not left him alone.

His only escape was when he retired for the night, and even then, she had a habit of walking him to the stairs as if they were courting. He could not return to Rosedale quickly enough.

The names of the Duke of Penworth and his sister, Lady Victoria Worthingham, sounded out across the room, and several gasps and tittering of conversation turned toward the high society family who had arrived.

Albert looked up at the doors, his stomach clenching at the sight of Victoria paying her respect to the hosts. Her genuine smile, her generous laugh hitting him fairly in the chest.

A fist tightened about his heart. How had he allowed the months to pass them by without seeing her? He ought to have chased her across England and the seas to win her love. To show her she could have all that she dreamed, so long as she allowed him to be part of her adventures as well.

She was as beautiful as he remembered. Her long, flowing

locks tied up in a motif of curls, a strand of diamonds delicately threaded throughout her curls. Her long white silk gloves and silver embroidered gown made her look royal, untouchable, and lofty.

She was none of those things, he knew to his core, no matter how she may appear outwardly. When she greeted people as they made their way through the crowd, her smile and warmth were genuine, and he wondered what she thought of her trip to France. Had she enjoyed her time with her sister and husband?

Had she experienced so much freedom that his chances of winning her hand were impossible? He had pinned all his hopes on attending this Season and showing her that he would do anything that she wanted.

He could be the man whom she longed for if only she would give him another chance to prove his worth.

Fear had often clutched at his mind that her trip abroad may have solidified her decision to remain a widow, but damn and blast it, he hoped that was not the case.

He loved her. So very much.

The Duke of Penworth spied him and started his way, leading his sister in his direction, even though she was yet to notice him. When she did, it was like a physical blow to his gut.

She smiled, the little lines at the sides of her eyes crinkling. "Lord Melvin," she said, curtsying. "You do not know how wonderful it is to see you here this evening. I had heard you were in town, but I said I would not believe it until I laid eyes on you myself."

He bowed. "Your Grace, Lady Victoria, I am indeed here. Your lessons in comporting myself were successful, and I am in town seeking the woman I want to marry."

The duke cleared his throat, biting back a smile. "Melvin, I am glad I shall have at least you for company this evening. The Lettingham ball is never one known for excitement."

"Ah, but you forget." Albert lowered his voice so only Penworth could hear. "Lady Sophie is in attendance."

The duke's attention snapped to the crowd before them. "Is she? Do you know where? I have not seen her since the ball at her estate and I do not mind telling you, I would prefer it to remain that way."

Albert pointed toward the supper room doors. "I believe she is over there," he gestured. "Speaking to Miss Eberhardt." Albert moved a little, so the clingy Miss Eberhardt did not see him again and chase him about this ballroom all night.

The duke cringed. "I think I shall go speak with Lord Clifford. I see he is trying to gain my attention." The duke bowed. "If you'll excuse me a moment."

Albert bowed in return. "Of course," he said, wanting to be alone with Victoria in any case.

Victoria came to stand at his side, and pulled up one of her gloves that had slipped. He watched her, remembering her in his arms. Desire to have her so again licked at his every pore, and he took a calming breath, not wanting to scare her away.

Were they not in a ballroom full of guests, he would wrench her into his arms and kiss her until she realized he was perfect for her and she should marry him.

"I heard you attended Lord and Lady Hammilyn's Christmas house party. How did you find it? Did our lessons help you at all?"

His lips twitched into a bemused smile. "Which ones are you talking about, Lady Victoria?" he asked her without flinching. Two bright-red spots appeared on her cheeks, and he chuckled. "I see you understand my meaning, my lady."

She shushed him, biting back a grin. "Do not say such things, my lord." She thanked a passing footman who handed her a glass of champagne. "You are not supposed to remind a lady of her inappropriate behaviors."

He shrugged, sipping his whiskey. "They were not inappropriate to me. Far from it. In fact," he continued, "the memory of them has kept me company these many months you were away."

Victoria shook her head at his teasing. "But I am home now, and we're back in London. I do hope we can remain friends, Lord Melvin."

Frustration drove through him. Had Victoria made her choice? Was it to shun marriage, keep herself at arm's length to love? "We shall always be friends." The words were thick and all but choked him as he spoke them. He finished his whiskey, downing it in one swallow. "Tell me, how were your travels to France? I heard you left not long after returning from Hampshire."

"I did indeed travel abroad, and it was everything I had hoped. Paris was divine, and Elizabeth and Henry did everything to make my time there enjoyable. When we returned, Alice had birthed a daughter, so it was the perfect ending to a lovely year."

He had finished his book early and had locked himself away at Rosedale during the winter months, plotting his next release and hoping his publishers enjoyed his latest manuscript. He wanted to tell Victoria of his secret, but he did not know where to find the words.

If he thought that she would contact him, write to him, he had been mistaken. Not that he had not thought about writing to her, but then did not want to look as desperate as he was currently feeling.

"Congratulations on becoming an aunt once more. I hope Lady Arundel is well."

"She is very well, thank you." Victoria sidled closer. "I'm sorry that I did not write to you, Albert. I did think of you often and missed you a great deal. I know after all that I said, I should not be saying these things now, but they are the truth."

His gut clenched, and a small spark of hope caught alight. "I wanted to write to you too," he murmured, "but then did not send any of my letters. I did not think you would have time to miss me with all that you were experiencing."

"My sister charged me to travel abroad and to be in London this Season to determine my future."

"Are you certain of what you want?" he couldn't help but ask, even though the possibility of her reply could break him.

"Not anymore."

He turned to face her and stopped at the sight of Victoria's brother-in-law Gerald Armstrong making his drunken way over to them. The gleeful light in the man's eyes raising the hairs on the back of Albert's neck.

"Oh dear," he heard Victoria say, just as Gerald bowed, almost tumbling into them. The cur was due a comeuppance such as the one his late brother never received, and Albert was just in the mood to deliver one.

Victoria looked down her nose at Gerald as best she could, considering the man was several inches higher than she, it was no mean feat. Even so, Albert at her side, a pillar of strength, made her feel safe and above the nuisance of a man she used to call family. After Paul's betrayal, he had mocked her, taunted her that it was her fault his brother had fled to Europe. How she hated the man as much as the one she married.

Albert's dislike of Gerald radiated off of him and she was surprised the man did not flee.

"Mr. Armstrong," she said, giving him her hand. "Where is Bertha this evening? I do not see her with you."

"Gerald, my dear. We are family after all."

"We were family, sir. Not anymore," she returned, her tone bored. "You did not answer my question. Where is your wife? Are you so disillusioned at being married such as your brother that you have locked her away out in the country already?"

The man's cheeks turned a ruddy red, and she was glad of it. He had embarrassed her for months before Paul had been killed in a duel. She owed him no friendship or respect.

"She did not wish to attend the Season. She has little reason to be here."

"Really?" Victoria smirked. "Please pass my regards the next time you see her."

Mr. Armstrong's eyes narrowed. Albert chuckled and covered his laugh with a cough.

"Lord Melvin. I see you are now chasing my sister-in-law's skirts. Are you not an imbecile who cannot speak to a lady without, oh," he said, slapping his forehead, "I forget. You do not speak at all to begin with, to make a fool of yourself more." Gerald let out a bellowing, phony laugh, pulling the attention of other guests their way.

Victoria ground her teeth, not willing for the little weasel to get away with such rudeness.

"Your brother was a fool to let such a rare gem go, and I'm glad to see you here this evening to acknowledge your brother's folly to your face," Albert said, leaning close to Mr. Armstrong for only him to hear his last words. "Your presence here is not welcome," he added, his tone deadly.

Gerald looked between them, and Victoria could see his calculating gaze taking in everything he saw. So, like Paul, always wanting to cause trouble and strife. "You will not get too far with this one," Gerald said, gesturing to her. "She's a prickly, cold, miss and a bad lay, so my brother declared. You would have to grow fur, bark, and neigh for her to like you."

The crunch of bone hitting bone sounded before Victoria had any idea of what had occurred. She stared at the vacant location before her that was once occupied by Gerald.

She looked down, seeing him sprawled on the floor, a bloody nose for his troubles. He groaned but did little else. Victoria looked back to Albert, having not expected him to act so heroically.

Having not expected his act to make her pulse race.

"You hit him." She chuckled, covering her mouth with her hand. It was never polite to laugh at someone else's misfortune, but for Gerald, she'd make an exception.

"I would do more than that to him should he dare speak to you again," Albert said, turning to her. "I would slay anyone who mistreats or talks down to you."

Victoria stared at Albert, and the months slipped away, and they were once again alone at Rosedale. His sweetness touched a part of her that no one else ever had, and it was time she admitted to that emotion. For it did have a name. And once spoken, there was no tearing it back.

No ripping her from the man she spoke those words to.

Not ever.

CHAPTER 38

Victoria pulled Albert away from Gerald, who continued to lay about the parquetry ballroom floor, moaning about his bloody nose and his calling to face Lord Melvin at dawn.

"You will not be dueling with Mr. Armstrong, so do not even consider it," she said, leading them away from the kafuffle and out onto the terrace. The outdoor terrace area had not been utilized for the ball, and no lanterns hung from the wisteria growing over the paved space to light the guest's way should they wish to get some air.

Victoria pulled Albert about the side of the house, farther into darkness, needing to be alone with him, wanting him all to herself.

"I think we have gone far enough," he said, pulling her to a stop.

Victoria checked their surroundings, ensuring they were alone. She took a calming breath, hoping that what she had to say would be well-received.

That he would have forgiven her for crushing his wishes last year at Rosedale. That he wanted her still. "Albert, there is something that I must tell you."

He frowned, a muscle at his temple flexing as he stared at her. "You do not need to say anything. I know that you do not wish to marry again. You enjoyed your travels abroad and wish to continue them as you should. Seeing Gerald tonight reminded me of what a horrendous marriage you must have endured. I will not stand in your way of ever being another man's property."

She shook her head, knowing that he did not understand. Not at all. "No, Albert, you misunderstand me. I do wish to travel, that is true. I loved Paris and want to explore the world further, but that is not all. The entire time I was away, I did nothing but think of you. When boating down the Seine, I wondered what you would think of this and that, Notre Dame, the Lourve, the small, quaint restaurants, and the people. I walked the streets, and the entire time I wanted you beside me. Exploring the world with me."

He frowned down at her, confusion marring his brow. "What are you saying?"

"I'm saying," she said, stepping against him and wrapping her arms around his waist. "I made a mistake when I left Rosedale. I adore you, Albert. I missed you every moment of every day since the time I left Hampshire. I'm saying that although I do not want children, I do want you. I want a life with you, to explore the world with you by my side."

Victoria swallowed her fear. She was asking a lot for a man, for a lord with responsibilities, but she knew she had to be truthful with him. Allow him to make his own decision if a life with her was right for him.

"Would you marry me?" she asked him, holding his gaze and praying that he would say yes. That he would find her enough in the life that they would live and not require everything that normally came with a marriage.

. . .

Albert stared down at Victoria. Her strength, beauty, and vulnerability at asking him to be hers a strength not found in everyone. The words soothed his aching soul, and he wrapped her in his arms, holding her close.

He would never let her go again.

"I missed you, my darling Victoria. When you left, I thought we should see each other at balls and parties, two people who shared so much for a time, but a snippet only. As fleeting as a shooting star. I will marry you and love you until the day that I die." He paused, knowing there was one last thing to admit to her before the night was over. "There is something that I must tell you."

She stared up at him, her eyes bright and full of hope and happiness. "Are you going to tell me that you're the famous author, Elbert Retsek? I know you are already aware how much I love his books."

He chuckled. How lucky he was to have her. "How did you know? No one in England other than my publisher is aware."

"Well," she said, raising one brow, a mischievous tilt to her lips. "You did leave a page of your manuscript at Dunsleigh, which I found. I was certain that it was the same voice and tone as Retsek, but when Mama told me you had used the library to catch up on paperwork during your stay, I wondered if it was you. Lady Sophie and her teasing of you scribbling away at that hunting lodge day and night solidified my suspicions."

"Why did you never ask me?" he queried, curious.

"I knew you would tell me when you were ready. I'm a patient woman. I suppose I've had to be since I'm the youngest female in my family. I would wait forever for you too," she told him, running her hand across his cheek.

"All my heroines are mimicks of you. You are my muse, my reason and inspiration behind my words."

"Really?" Her smile brightened. "How lovely and happy that makes me." Victoria met his gaze, a pensive light entering her eyes. "Please assure me, Albert, that you do not mind that I'm asking for it only ever to be the two of us. I do not think I could survive the guilt should you ever resent me for not wanting children."

He shook his head, more than happy for the rest of their lives to be only them. If that is what Victoria wanted, he would not change her to suit his needs. "I have a cousin, a good man with a good heart who is married and can sire heirs well enough. We do not have to have children if you do not wish to."

"But I have wolfhounds and horses. You will not mind me bringing them to Rosedale?"

He chuckled, kissing her forehead, rocking her in his arms, hope and relief pouring through him like a balm. "No, I do not mind. You may bring whatever pleases you to Rosedale. A cat, birds, rabbits, whatever takes your fancy."

"Albert," she said, slipping her hands up about his neck. She played with the hair at his nape. He had missed having her in his arms, smelling the sweet scent of jasmine whenever she was around. "I'm sorry it took me so very long to understand what I wanted. You must know that had I not been so determined to have my way, I would have recognized what I felt for you months ago. I was scared to trust myself. To trust in what I felt for you after making such a momentous mistake with Paul."

"And what do you feel?" he asked her, hoping to hear the words she had yet to speak.

"That I love you, too. That I want you and no other in the world."

Albert leaned down, taking her lips in a slow dance of seduction. He'd dreamed for so long to have her beside him, warming his bed. Now she would be there for the rest of their lives. His wife. His heart.

"I love you, Victoria," he replied, holding her close. "I want to have adventures with you. Whatever makes you happy is agreeable to me."

She bit her lip, her eyes overly bright. "How have I come to deserve you? A man who is willing to forgo so much to love my quirks and ideals."

He shrugged, taking her lips in a short, soft embrace. "I've wanted you for so long. If that means to win your heart, I step away from what is expected of myself as well. I am willing to do that. With you as my wife, the sacrifice is no hardship."

"Thank you." She leaned up, kissing him again, and he deepened the embrace, needing her with a hunger starved these many months.

He walked her backward until her back came up against the ivy-clad wall of the house. She murmured acquiescence, and he kissed her deeply. The embrace turned lascivious, and they hurled caution and decency aside, dismissing their location or the ball that was in full swing nearby.

He shucked up her gown, lifting her to straddle his hips. Albert ripped at his front falls, needing to have her.

She helped him, guiding herself onto his cock with an assurance that left him breathless. He took her hard up against the ivy with little care. Victoria clutched at his neck, moving her hips to increase her pleasure.

Her breathless sighs and murmured words of praise pushed him on, continued them along the path to pleasure. It did not take long before the first contractions of her release pulled at his cock.

Albert did not draw out and find his release until she was spent. Soon she would be his, and they would not need to sneak about and grasp interludes such as the one they just had.

"I shall have the first banns called on Sunday, and four weeks from now, you shall be Marchioness Melvin."

He helped her regain her feet, ensuring her dress was back in place to return indoors. "Shall we go and speak to Josh now? He will be pleased I think that I'm to marry his friend."

Albert smiled. "I think the duke shall be pleased too." The sooner Victoria was declared his, the better he would sleep. The anxiety of losing her sometimes too hard to bear over the past months. "Let us go. A champagne toast to celebrate our forthcoming marriage is required before the night is over."

"Albert." She pulled him to a stop as he went to move away. "Thank you for being so modern in thinking. I do not think I could have married a man more suited to me."

He grinned down at her. "I'm an author of gothic romance, my dear. Are you sure you are not modern thinking toward me instead?"

Her smile warmed his soul. "We are a good pair then, are we not?"

Albert wrenched her back into his arms, kissing her soundly. "We are the very best, and I will spend every day for the remainder of our lives proving it to you. You have no fear of ever having your heart broken again. I shall guard it with mine."

"I cannot wait." She laughed as he took her hand and pulled her back toward the ball. An announcement was needed to declare his intent. Lady Victoria Worthingham, sister to the Duke of Penworth, was no longer a coveted widow in town for she had said yes.

The future Marchioness Melvin.

How well that sounded.

EPILOGUE

The Grand Canal, Venice 1817

Victoria leaned out over the balcony on the house Albert had leased for them during the summer months in Venice. She breathed in the salty, fresh air of the Adriatic Sea. Still unable to quite comprehend that this would be her home for the time being or how very beautiful the city was—one of the finest she'd seen during their many years of travel.

She looked up and down the canal, observing tourists and locals alike on gondolas, hanging out their washing or shopping for their night's dinner at local food stalls.

They were to stay here for several weeks before returning to England to review Albert's estates, having traveled from Rome. Another city that she could not wait to return to and explore more.

Victoria let out a contented sigh. How very fortunate she was. Not just in her situation in life, but how blessed she had been to marry Albert. To have found her greatest love within her second marriage.

As promised, he had showered her with love and devotion and never asked for her to change her mind and give him children.

She often worried that she was selfish. Fortunately, Albert's cousin had a male child, and so should the worst happen, the lineage was secure first through Albert's cousin and then his son.

"What are you doing out here, my love?" he said, coming up behind her and wrapping his arms around her waist. He leaned his chin on her shoulder, rocking her slightly.

Victoria clasped his arms to her stomach. "Watching people and remembering how wonderful our time has been abroad. Not just here in Venice, but each year since our marriage. I do not think I tell you often enough how much I adore and love you," she said, glancing over her shoulder at him.

She could feel the smile on his face. "It is no hardship to be married to you, my darling. There are no thanks necessary."

Victoria turned in his arms. They had spent the afternoon in bed, making delicious love. Albert had joined her wearing only his breeches, his toned abdomen tanned and muscular after years of traveling abroad hers to enjoy.

She ran her hand over his chiseled stomach, hers fluttering with desire. "But it is true. I never wish for our charmed life to end."

He kissed her softly, and her breath caught. She loved him more today than the day she had asked him to be her husband. The idea of losing him often made her panicked, so much as she adored him.

"It shall not, my darling. There are many more adventures yet to be had." His eyes darkened, wickedness lighting his blue orbs. "More adventures inside our bedroom," he said, pulling her slowly from the balcony.

Victoria allowed him to persuade her, laughing at his words.

"Should we not venture outdoors and see some of this great city?"

He continued walking her toward the bed. "The city has been here for hundreds of years. It can wait another day."

And it did wait, for two days in fact. But the wait was worth it, as were all their adventures together.

Always.

I hope you enjoyed, *Only a Marquess Will Do,* book four in my To Marry a Rogue series!

I'm so thrilled you chose my book to read, and if you're able, I would appreciate an honest review of *Only a Marquess Will Do*. As they say, feed an author, leave a review!

If you'd like to learn about book five in my To Marry a Rogue series, *Only a Lady Will Do,* please read on. I have included chapter one for your reading pleasure.

Alternatively, you can keep in contact with me by visiting my website or following me online. You can contact me at www.tamaragill.com or email me at tamaragillauthor@gmail.com.

Tamara Gill

ONLY A LADY WILL DO

TO MARRY A ROGUE, BOOK 5

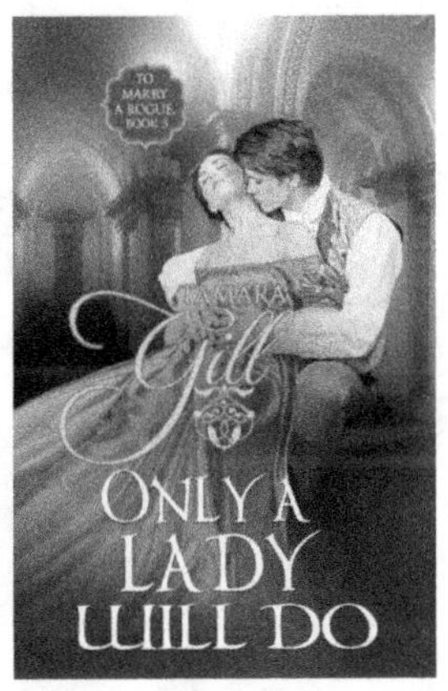

She's exactly what he isn't looking for...and everything he never knew needed...

Josh Worthingham, Duke of Penworth, must marry—and not just any bride will do. He needs a true lady to be his duchess. It's what's expected of him, and he can accept no less. So, why is it that the only woman who snags his full attention is the entirely inappropriate Miss Iris Cooper?

Iris may be the granddaughter of an Earl, but that's where her lofty connections to the ton end. She knows securing a good match won't be easy—especially not when she still carries the scars of her failed first union. There's no way the Duke of Penworth can ever be hers. But a girl can dream, can't she?

Can a stolen kiss in a drawing room turn Iris's dreams into reality? Or will their differences—and the dark secret Josh is harboring—destroy their one chance at happily ever after?

CHAPTER 1

London 1812

How had he managed to get himself into this mess? Josh Worthingham, Duke Penworth, lowered his head and tried to use the ferns and abundant greenery to shield his location that his mother had placed around their London home for the ball. She had been adamant that she wanted the room to represent the delightful outdoors, the trees, moss, grasses, and flowers that grew in the parklands about their estate, Dunsleigh.

His mother had pulled off the effect, and it was stunning. If not a little over the top for Josh's liking, but the foliage did at least enable him to hide.

The guests too gasped and smiled, looked about with awe, just what his mother would adore being this was her final year the duchess Penworth, a celebration for her time as one of the pillars of society. One must go out with a bang if one was to be remembered.

Not that his mother was going too far, but it was due to his declaration that this Season he would marry. Find a wife suitable for the role of a duchess and let his mother hand over the busy reins of her position in society.

He could only hope that the colossal mistake he'd made last year in Hampshire did not follow him to town. He caught sight of Lady Sophie and cringed. Being respectable and kind did not mean he would offer the hand of marriage. He had shown such respect to many ladies over the years and had not proposed. Why the rumor he would ask Lady Sophie had arisen, he could not fathom, nor would he allow it to continue.

When had the rules changed? He had danced and had discourse with many ladies during his years scuffing the boards in London. When had talking and dancing morphed into his choice of bride?

An absurd notion.

He caught sight of Lady Sophie, surrounded by her many beaus, but he did not wish to be one of them. At one time, she may have piqued his interest, but that had long passed. Nor had he ever shown more interest than a gentleman should. His mother had raised him right, and he was one duke who did not bend the rules.

There was something about the lady that he did not like, a littleness to her that was ugly no matter how beautiful she was. No amount of rouge or diamonds could alter one's personality if it were rotten at its core.

A finger flicked his ear, and he started. His older sister Elizabeth laughed, coming to stand at his side. "Still hiding, I see. We have been in London for a month, Josh darling. I think it is time you came out of the shadows and faced the lady that seems to be telling all of London how enamored you are with her. Of course, she's only telling a select few of her friends so the rumor does not spread too far and wide, but it would seem it has scattered to mama's ears at least."

Josh groaned, hating that he would have to flee the Season if he could not find a way out of this mess. Maybe Elizabeth would like him to travel north to Scotland and check on their estate while they were in London this year.

"It is a mess that I cannot escape. I danced with her in Hampshire and conversed as one would since they were hosing the ball. How can a lady from that form the opinion that a proposal is imminent." He met his sister's amused gaze and frowned. Was no man safe from such women? Was this how the ladies thought to trap men into their marriage nets.

Well, he would not succumb to such antics. He would choose his lady when he found the suitable one as position as Duchess.

Not just any lady would do.

Oh no, his lady needed to be witty, intelligent, and beautiful if he could be so vain to desire such a thing. But most of all, she needed to be from an upstanding family, without reproach, without a blemish to her name, and a sizable dowry. Not that he needed such funds, but he did not want to be one of those fathers who left everything to his eldest son and had nothing for his other children. His parents had bestowed fortunes on all their children, and he wanted to be the same.

"You must have made an impression in Hampshire." Elizabeth sipped her negus, watching the throng of guests behind the green foilage with him. "You must also stop hiding, return to the ball and speak with all manner of ladies and gentlemen too to quell the rumors. While I would not suggest avoiding Lady Sophie at all costs, I think asking another of her friends to dance, not paying too much attention to the lady, would be wise. I'm certain by acting so, all this nonsense will soon pass, and there will be another bet at Whites that does not include you."

He groaned. "You know of the bet?" How he loathed that book and the trouble it wrought. Not just this Season but in the past. And at his own doing.

Fool.

Elizabeth raised a dubious brow. "Of course, does not everyone."

That was probably also true. His good friend Anthony, Earl Thetford had thought it a lark in making a bet at his expense. Who would be the lady that the Duke of Penworth marries? Several names were listed, Lady Sophie's with the best odds. None of them would be the women he married. He had not found her as yet. His sisters had married for love. He knew that to his very core. The way they looked at their spouses reminded him of how his mama once looked at his father before he passed.

He wanted that for himself. To marry was for life, and he did not want to regret his choice should it be wrong, for there would be no changing it after the fact.

"That book ought to be burnt for all the trouble it's caused many families in London."

Elizabeth threw him a curious look but did not pry into his thoughts. "Did you hear," she said, changing the subject, "that mama is going to be sponsoring her closest friend's daughter this Season. She could not make it tonight but will be here tomorrow."

Josh inwardly groaned, having heard already. A Miss Iris Cooper from Cornwall. A vicar's daughter whose mother had been born a daughter of an Earl but married beneath her station and reportedly was shunned by her family for her efforts in love.

He knew his mama had debuted with Miss Cooper's mother the same year, and their friendship had remained one of the pen since the family never came to town.

"I did hear she was to arrive tomorrow. I will relocate to my bachelor lodgings for the duration of her stay, which I hope will not be long. The sooner she is married, the better."

"Be kind to her, Josh. You have always been a loving brother. I hope you will assist in finding a suitable match for Miss

Cooper and not scuttle away at your club and gambling dens while she's here in town. She has not had an easy life, from what I have heard. You need to be kind."

He could no sooner be cruel to his sisters or his mama's sponsor, even if he wished to. It was not in his nature to be an ass. "I promised mama I would escort them several times a week to any balls or musical events, operas, and such. I shall do the pretty and vet any suitors that step forward for her hand. I will ensure she marries well."

Elizabeth threw him a shrewd glance. "You will need all our assistance if she's to wed well. She will have nothing but her wits, charm, and looks to win her a match with no dowry or title. Let us hope she has all three in abundance."

"The Countess Buttersworth, her grandmother, will not wish to guide her? Surely, after all these years, she could not still be angry at her only daughter marrying a vicar?"

Elizabeth finished her drink and handed it off to a passing footman. "Mama heard the Countess is quite put out that her granddaughter will be back in town. She had a Season several years ago, but it was not successful. I do not know all the particulars, but mama said the Countess is set to give her the cut direct."

Lady Buttersworth was an old, cranky witch. Who could treat family with such cruelness? "I trust in mothers choice of friends. If she is fond of Miss Cooper and her mother, I'm certain Miss Cooper will make a match. With or without her grandmother's help."

"And what of your life, dear brother? When shall I be able to welcome a Duchess as my new sister? Will it be this year, you think? Another rumor surrounding you says that it will be."

Josh rubbed his jaw, thinking over his sister's words. No doubt his mother had told his siblings of his statement. "I am set on finding a suitable bride for the position of Duchess this Season. I have decided she must be a lady of the finest breeding, well-spoken and educated, and above all else, take London by storm with her beauty and grace."

Elizabeth snorted, covering her lapse in manners with a cough that Josh did not buy for one second. "How lovely. I wish you all the very best in finding this gem." She started off toward where their mama stood but turned before gaining too much distance. "Perhaps you ought to go fishing and catch a mermaid, dear brother. I'm certain you shall have more luck in finding one of those mystical creatures than the one you just mentioned."

Josh gaped before shutting his mouth with a snap. His idea for a bride was no mystical being. Why, his perfect lady could be here tonight, hiding in the greenery like him.

He stepped out of his hiding place, determined to find his jewel and crown her with a ducal coronet. The Season was young, and so was he, and he would prove his sister wrong and enjoy throwing his perfect bride before her when he found his match.

Cornwall

"Come here, you little," Iris reached for the piglet but missed the little mite. It scuttled away into the pen just as her foot caught on the trough. With a splat and a yelp, she landed face down in pig shit.

"Damn you. I'm so going to so enjoy eating you this evening," she mumbled, lifting herself. The stench of pig excrement, of rotten scraps from their home, made her eyes water. She kneeled, using the fence to pull herself upright, and tried again. The pig was fast, and with her limp, she was slower than the little animal but more determined than ever to catch him.

"Have you caught the piglet yet, darling? Cook wants to put

it in the oven in the next hour, or it'll not be ready for your going away dinner this evening."

Iris groaned, staring heavenward. London. She shuddered at the thought of traveling there, being courted by those money-hungry swains that she had not the ounce of interest. Nor did she have the money to tempt them into marrying a cripple.

Not after what had happed the first time she had traveled to town. Seven years ago now, full of hope and dreams. How they had come crashing down, along with herself, leaving her lame and with a hideous scar along her temple to her eyebrow.

Dudley, Baronet Redgrove her late betrothed.

Iris pushed the painful memory aside, looking for the piglet and finding it staring at her. Its little chest rose and fell rapidly, and its frightened eyes gave her pause.

She turned about, opening the gate to the pen and leaving the little animal alone. They could have something else for dinner this evening. She could not bring herself to kill the poor little mite, no matter what her mother said about the fact.

She kicked off the mud and shit from her boots and dress as she started for the well at the back of the vicarage.

She would also probably have to strip down to her shift before her mama let her indoors too.

"Where is the piglet?" her mama asked, hands-on-hips an apron wrapped about her waist with all sorts of grime and food wiped onto it. Iris's lips lifted at the sight of her mama and Earls daughter and heiress, once upon a time. Should her grandmother, the Countess Buttersworth, see her only daughter now, she would drop dead at the sight of her, Iris was sure.

Her mama seemed to think it was her place to bother their cook in the kitchen, even though she was a terrible cook herself. The daughter of an Earl had never stepped foot in the kitchens back at their estate in Derbyshire and had to learn how to boil water. Her mama had married for love and had adjusted her life to suit her heart and her husband's career in the church. She was a good woman, and Iris was determined to be just like her if she could.

"In the pen. I cannot catch it. We shall have to eat the chicken the Smiths's brought around yesterday for us."

Her mama came out to the well, helping her haul up a pale of water. "What are we going to do with you, Iris. You cannot travel to London smelling like manure. We will have to bathe you overnight in vinegar to get the stench out," she said, undoing her buttons on the back of her gown.

When they had the bucket atop the stone well wall, Iris washed off as much grime and pig pen as possible. "You could always allow me to stay here. I am more than willing to find a quiet country squire to marry. I do not have to travel all those miles to find a suitable gentleman. And do not forget, my lame hip will thank you for it if I do not."

Her mama reached out, washing a little spot of god knows what from her cheek, a sadness in her clear blue eyes. "You deserve so much, my darling—more than a country squire. You deserve to have the Season that was stolen from you. Now that you are well enough, the time has come to have you married, settled and happy. Let me do this for you."

"But does it have to be with the Duchess of Penworth that I have my Season? I do not want to be a burden to them."

"You will not be a burden. The duchess is so excited to have you this year. She is a lovely woman and friend. You will not be disappointed. I wish I could be with you, but our position here in the parish, the people need us more than you. You, my dear, do not. You are an intelligent, beautiful woman who has the world at her feet. I think you shall take London by storm."

Or she wouldn't, and merely hobble through the streets like an old cripple she felt she was at times. "I have never met the duchess. What if she does not like me. Or I'm a burden?"

"She will love you, for she loves me. Our friendship is strong, and she does not have an unkind bone in her body. All her daughters are married now, and she welcomes having company in her townhouse this Season. Now, come, my dear. You shall need to bathe before dinner, and we cannot keep you up too late. You have a long journey before you."

Iris decided not to debate the subject any further to stay here in Cornwall, which wasn't something she should pursue. Her mama was determined, and an Earls daughter to her very core, she usually gained her way.

But something told Iris that when it came to her taking London by storm, of being a success that they believed she would be, that her parents were seeing her through rose-colored glasses. She was no gem. She was a scarred cripple, no doubt one who would be mocked over the next several months by those without empathy. Her time for a future had passed. She had buried all her hopes seven years ago with Dudley.

Want to read more? Get Only a Lady Will Do today!

LORDS OF LONDON SERIES AVAILABLE NOW!

Dive into these charming historical romances! In this six-book series, Darcy seduces a virginal duke, Cecilia's world collides with a roguish marquess, Katherine strikes a deal with an unlucky earl and Lizzy sets out to conquer a very wicked Viscount. These stories plus more adventures in the Lords of London series! Available now through Amazon or read free with KindleUnlimited.

Lords of London

KISS THE WALLFLOWER SERIES AVAILABLE NOW!

If the roguish Lords of London are not for you and wallflowers are more your cup of tea, this is the series for you. My Kiss the Wallflower series, are linked through friendship and family in this four-book series. You can grab a copy on Amazon or read free through KindleUnlimited.

LEAGUE OF UNWEDDABLE GENTLEMEN SERIES AVAILABLE NOW!

Fall into my latest series, where the heroines have to fight for what they want, both regarding their life and love. And where the heroes may be unweddable to begin with, that is until they meet the women who'll change their fate. The League of Unweddable Gentlemen series is available now!

League of Unweddable Gentlemen

ALSO BY TAMARA GILL

The Royal House of Atharia Series

TO DREAM OF YOU

A ROYAL PROPOSITION

FOREVER MY PRINCESS

ROYAL ATHARIA - BOOKS 1-3 BUNDLE

League of Unweddable Gentlemen Series

TEMPT ME, YOUR GRACE

HELLION AT HEART

DARE TO BE SCANDALOUS

TO BE WICKED WITH YOU

KISS ME DUKE

THE MARQUESS IS MINE

LEAGUE - BOOKS 1-3 BUNDLE

LEAGUE - BOOKS 4-6 BUNDLE

Kiss the Wallflower series

A MIDSUMMER KISS

A KISS AT MISTLETOE

A KISS IN SPRING

TO FALL FOR A KISS

A DUKE'S WILD KISS

TO KISS A HIGHLAND ROSE

KISS THE WALLFLOWER - BOOKS 1-3 BUNDLE

KISS THE WALLFLOWER - BOOKS 4-6 BUNDLE

Lords of London Series

TO BEDEVIL A DUKE

TO MADDEN A MARQUESS

TO TEMPT AN EARL

TO VEX A VISCOUNT

TO DARE A DUCHESS

TO MARRY A MARCHIONESS

LORDS OF LONDON - BOOKS 1-3 BUNDLE

LORDS OF LONDON - BOOKS 4-6 BUNDLE

To Marry a Rogue Series

ONLY AN EARL WILL DO

ONLY A DUKE WILL DO

ONLY A VISCOUNT WILL DO

ONLY A MARQUESS WILL DO

ONLY A LADY WILL DO

TO MARRY A ROGUE - BOOKS 1-5 BUNDLE

A Time Traveler's Highland Love Series

TO CONQUER A SCOT

TO SAVE A SAVAGE SCOT

TO WIN A HIGHLAND SCOT

HIGHLAND LOVE - BOOKS 1-3 BUNDLE

A Stolen Season Series

A STOLEN SEASON

A STOLEN SEASON: BATH

A STOLEN SEASON: LONDON

Time Travel Romance

DEFIANT SURRENDER

Scandalous London Series

A GENTLEMAN'S PROMISE

A CAPTAIN'S ORDER

A MARRIAGE MADE IN MAYFAIR

SCANDALOUS LONDON - BOOKS 1-3 BUNDLE

High Seas & High Stakes Series

HIS LADY SMUGGLER

HER GENTLEMAN PIRATE

HIGH SEAS & HIGH STAKES - BOOKS 1-2 BUNDLE

Daughters Of The Gods Series

BANISHED-GUARDIAN-FALLEN

DAUGHTERS OF THE GODS - BOOKS 1-3 BUNDLE

Stand Alone Books

TO SIN WITH SCANDAL

OUTLAWS

ABOUT THE AUTHOR

Tamara is an Australian author who grew up in an old mining town in country South Australia, where her love of history was founded. So much so, she made her darling husband travel to the UK for their honeymoon, where she dragged him from one historical monument and castle to another.

A mother of three, her two little gentlemen in the making, a future lady (she hopes) keep her busy in the real world, but whenever she gets a moment's peace she loves to write romance novels in an array of genres, including regency, medieval and time travel.

www.ingramcontent.com/pod-product-compliance
Lightning Source LLC
Chambersburg PA
CBHW060550310726
48982CB00008B/1069/J

* 9 7 8 0 6 4 5 2 0 4 7 3 5 *